FLESH
like
SMOKE

edited by
Brian M. Sammons

illustrations by
Neil Baker

An April Moon Books Publication
Published in arrangement with the authors
Edited by Neil Baker

First Edition 2015
Published in Canada.

www.AprilMoonBooks.com

ISBN: 978–0–9937180–4–5 (softcover)

Dedication

This one is for my mom, who always allowed me to be as weird as I wanted.

Brian

This book is dedicated to the visionaries who spawned my love of shapeshifting horror - and who continue to do so today.

George Waggner, John Landis, Joe Dante, John Carpenter and Joe Johnston. Jack Pierce, Rick Baker, Rob Bottin and Dave and Lou Elsey.

Neil

Contents

Malleable Forms
by
Brian M. Sammons

When Neil Baker told me he was going to start up his own publishing house called April Moon Books, the first thing that popped into my mind was that he had to publish a werewolf anthology. I mean, come on, with a name like that, it's mandatory. So of course I immediately did a Lovecraftian black magic book called *Dark Rites of Cthulhu* for him. But the idea of a collection of lycanthrope stories had infected (cursed?) me, and it was something I kept coming back to over and over again.

Once I had completed my *Dark Rites* for April Moon Books, I knew the next thing I did for them had to be about werewolves. I had put off scratching that itch for too long and could not resist anymore. The pull of the moon was just too great, and I knew I had to let loose and howl at it. Thankfully Neil seemed to have the same full moon fever that I did, so in record time the book was a go, but then something odd happened. While I love werewolves with a wild passion, I didn't want to limit all the stories in this book to just those iconic man-beasts. I truly believe that variety is the spice of life, and so the thought of an entire book about people shifting into only one kind of animal seemed somewhat limiting. Well thankfully, there are countless other were-creatures in myth and folklore that get nowhere near the press that werewolves get, so the answer seemed simple: open the book up to any sort of were-beast imaginable.

After that was sorted out, next we had to come up with a title for the anthology. Originally I was going to work 'moon' into it somehow, as it not only made sense considering the publisher doing the book, but the focus on werewolves. However, once werewolves were not the sole focus of the book, that title seemed less solid. There are plenty of were-beasts from all over the world that have no connection to the moon at all. So

1

after a short brainstorming session, the title of *Flesh Like Smoke* came into being, and what a title it is. After a few days of thinking about how mysterious it sounded to me, I knew that just having were-creatures wasn't going to be enough anymore. I wanted horror stories about every kind of shape changer imaginable, and so that's what you now have in your hands, dear reader.

Now don't you worry, all you lovers of lethal lycanthropes, for the iconic werewolf is still the pack leader here. But you will also find tales of other well-known were-beasts, not to mention many shape-shifters of far less definable nature. These sixteen tales span from the time before history was recorded, to the far-flung future that holds little in common with the world as it is today, to every era in between. Cursed souls and those that willingly become bestial to exploit the raw, animalistic fury that comes with the change, people who shape-shift for fun, and those that never knew any other way of life are all found here. This is a book about changes, some for the better, most for the worst, where nothing is as it seems, and flesh is like smoke.

Brian M. Sammons - Jan. 24th, 2015

Philopatry

Philopatry
by
Edward M. Erdelac

NOBODY AT O'MALLEY'S BAR took much notice of the old priest who came in from the stone cold November night, brushing the rain from his black hat and his dripping beige topcoat. It was a Tuesday, so there weren't too many people there *to* take notice. The men were in their drink. The local stylenes, cackling their lipstick stained cigarette laughs crossed and uncrossed their cheetah print legs and paid him no more than a glance. Priests were like a fourth class of male, more unavailable than a married man or a queer even. O'Malley himself would only raise his eyebrows at the entrance of some colored guy from Roxbury. As long as this baby sprinkler paid for his drinks, he didn't care.

Terry Dunne knew priests drank. He had carried 30-racks of PBR over to the rectory at St. Brigid's on Broadway as an altar boy that one of the packies down the block donated every other week. His whole life he had thanked God he'd been born a Catholic in a two toilet Irish battleship on the corner of Dorchester and East 9th and not some dry mouthed, button down, door to door bible thumper from a dirt farm in Alabama dancing with snakes instead of girls.

Of course, in recent years the Church had had that whole goddamned pervert priest thing they had tried to cover up. Now he was thankful he had never heard the call to wear the turned around collar. He wouldn't have been able to hold his head up let alone dish out a communion wafer with that shit going on around him.

He was now what his mother had called 'a lazy Cat'lick,' only going to church on Christmas and Easter, maybe eating scrod on Fridays during Lent instead of a cheeseburger, if he remembered.

So when the white-haired priest sat down next to him at the bar and

4

said, 'Hello, Terry,' in a tired, rattling voice, he sighed inwardly and feared he was in for it from one of these old schoolers who still thought calling a man out on his shit was the way to bring him to God.

This one looked like somebody had put him through the ringer. He was shivering, the white around his dim blue eyes shot through with blood like broken windshields in a bad car accident, his spotted skin as pale as something fished out of the Chuck River.

"You remember me?" he asked.

And just like that, dawn broke on Marblehead. Like an old toy you found covered in dust and cobwebs in the attic, Terry realized he did remember this old priest, and the memory of it brought a smile to his face. Damn, if it wasn't the very same father who used to take the beer cases from him at the back door of the rectory.

"I'll be goddamned! Hey, Fadder Mike. Yeah, sure I remember you."

He reached over and pumped Father Mike's hand. It was like a fish with fingers.

The old man's face cracked into a thin smile.

O'Malley glanced over at the ruckus they were making and Terry held up his hand for him to come over.

"Hey whatta you haven', Fadder?" To O'Malley he said, "This is my ma's favorite priest from back in the day at St. Brig's."

O'Malley nodded, disinterested, and looked at the priest expectantly.

"Nothing for me," said the old man.

O'Malley's eyebrows registered disapproval.

"Ah, gimme two shots of Jameson," said Terry. When the priest opened his mouth to protest, he slapped him on the shoulder. "Not to worry, Fadder. I'll drink yours."

While O'Malley fished out the glasses, Terry turned on his stool and leaned on the bar.

"When'd you get back to Southie, Fadder? Last I heard you left for what, Ireland somewheres in like '98."

"I've been back three weeks," said Father Mike, watching the caramel colored liquor trickle from the silver pour spout into the glass.

Terry took the glass and downed it almost before O'Malley had moved to the other. They used to have Father Mike over to the house for coffee once a week. His ma had always put out the doilies and the blue willow cups for him.

5

"How is your dear ma, Terry?"

Terry slapped the glass on the bar and gasped back the hot aftertaste.

"Up Mt. Auburn, under the tree."

"I'm sorry. I hadn't heard."

"Eh, how could you? Happened 'tree years ago. I was doin' a stretch in South Bay."

"That I had heard. Was it as rough as they say?"

Terry chuckled and took the priest's drink. He paused as the glass touched his lips.

"It was no picnic. They got all these cameras all over the place, s'posed to make it a model facility, all the guards on their best behavior; but there ain't any in the elevators. The bulls'd pull you in there and play knick knack paddy whack on your friggin' skull up and down for six or seven floors. You'd be lucky if your brains weren't runnin' out your ears time the doors opened again."

Father Mike stared at him as he threw back the shot and put the glass next to the first. The ringed wood bar was slashed and chipped away, like generations had cut meat on it. Terry picked at one of the slivers with his thumbnail.

"I'm sorry, Terry."

"Ah, I been doin' better since. The fuck you doin' back in Boston?"

"Philopatry."

"Huh?"

He shrugged. "I go where the Church tells me."

"Figure'd the next time I saw you, it'd be on TV, you standin' in the background, wearin' a little red hat, hangin' with the Pope."

The priest smiled thinly, his throat working behind his collar.

Truth be told though, the old man looked like hell. Didn't they put priests out to pasture? Terry expected Father Mike ought to be kicking back on some farm watching the cows and dozing with a Bible open in his lap. Whatever retired priests did.

"Terry....," said the old priest, leaning in. "I've got somethin' I want to discuss with you. But not here."

Terry looked at the old man and idly fished a couple salty peanuts out of the bowl by his hand.

"I was thinkin' about walkin' down to Dunkie's, gettin' a regular an' a honey dip to settle my guts. You wanna come?"

"Yeah, that'd be fine, Terry. Let me buy, huh?"

He reached in his coat pocket. Terry noticed the old ring on his finger. Terry remembered it because Father Mike was the only priest he'd ever seen wearing one. It was a pewter or silver medal on a silver band, a picture of a saint holding two swords over his head, a pair of dogs at his feet.

An inscription read; *'Deum memento, regressus victor.'*

Terry slapped down money for the drinks. "Nah, I got it, Fadder."

Outside it was still cold but the rain was dying off. The cars swished through the leavings and the gutters gurgled as they sucked the streets down to a tolerable level. Their breath puffed out like fog as they talked.

"What do you know about the murders at Gate of Heaven last week?" Father Mike asked.

Terry had seen it on the news. A pair of teenaged girls had been found in the alley behind the church on East Fourth Street. The dee-techs were out all over asking questions. You could tell them from the real people by their cheap shoes and neat hair. They looked like wannabe FBI. A little too eager, or a little too old. Kid table feds. Anyway, nobody knew enough to tell them.

"Couple of hoodies out after dark," said Terry. "News said they got done same as that gook kid over on Washington two weeks ago."

"Do you know what happened to that boy?"

"Somethin' bad, I heard. O'Malley says some sicko cut him up. I don't know the particulars."

They stopped at the traffic light, watching a Honda full of drunk townies swerve into the turn. A beer can rattled and spun in the gutter.

"He was torn to pieces, Terry," said Father Mike, his lips trembling, and not just with the cold. "Like a piece of tissue paper somebody wiped their ass with. His liver and his heart were torn out. They were *eaten.*"

"Fuck," said Terry, appreciatively.

Father Mike turned to him as the light changed, splashing his skin red as the Devil's. "And I know who the skid is that's doin' it, Terry. I *know!*"

Father Mike looked ready to blow his top. His fists came out of his pockets shaking. One gripped a little brown pill bottle, which he rattled and wrestled with for a minute before Terry reached over.

"Here, lemme get that, Fadder." He twisted the child proof cap. It was a bitch, even for him, let alone an old guy with failing bones in the cold and a weight like he had bearing down on him. He handed it back.

Father Mike turned the bottle over and shook a pill into his quivering palm. He slapped his hand to his mouth.

"What's that, for your blood pressure, or something?"

"Yeah," said Father Mike. "I gotta get out of this cold."

They double timed it up the block to Dunkie's. Terry sprang for a pair of regulars and skipped the honey dip, but got a box of munchkins for home. He didn't think he'd have the appetite for it, but who knew what he'd feel like tomorrow.

They took a quiet corner booth and sat holding the coffees between their hands, feeling the warmth radiate. It was bright white in there, like a hospital.

"You zooin' on me about this, Fadder?"

"God's honest truth," Father Mike replied, staring into his coffee but not drinking.

"How you figure you know who the nutjob is doin' this?"

The old man's eyes flitted up, the steam ascending from the bottom of his face, dissipating in his white hair, a wispy mask of fog.

"The bastard told me as much in the confessional this past Saturday. He told me everything. How he follows them, stalks them, like an animal. What he... does to them." He made a rapid sign of the cross, put the hot coffee to his lips. He winced, but kept drinking.

Terry leaned back in his chair. "Ain't it a sin for you to be tellin' me this? I mean, ain't you got some kinda confidentiality rule about the booth? Like a lawyer?"

"Don't you think it's a sin to just let it to go on?" he said, putting the half empty cup down.

"So don't I," Terry said, nodding, rubbing his eyes. "So don't I."

"Terry," whispered Father Mike, leaning across the table. "I was told... I asked around. And I was told that you... that you're..."

Terry gave him a stony look and held up his hand.

Everybody knew Terry Dunne around the parish.

They knew about the shootout in Mattapan back in the 90's, where four trigger happy micks who'd robbed an armored car and killed the guards under the nose of the Winter Hill outfit had been left bleeding in the gutters and how Terry Dunne started driving a Lincoln after that. Everybody knew who put the body of the wiseguy in the shipping container at Conley's yard, the one that rotted in there all summer, froze, and blew up in the spring, so the cops had to pour what was left through a colander to find the bullet.

They knew how Pat Lonnigan, who'd stuck up a Cumbie's just to get pinched so he wouldn't have to pay all the horse money he owed Mickey O'Callahan, had somehow rolled out of the top bunk in the cell he shared with Terry at South Bay and busted his head wide open on the floor in the middle of the night. Everybody knew about the Jamaican nurse that had moved into Terry's ma's place that week and took care of her till they carried her out.

"If you're gonna preach to me now..."

"I wouldn't, Terry," Father Mike said. "Bless you, I wouldn't. But somebody's got to put a stop to this."

Terry shifted in his seat. "So call the cops."

"You know it's not enough, Terry. If you'd... heard the things I heard in that confessional. He's a miserable excuse for a human being."

"How come you didn't give him three Hail Marys and tell him go jump in the Mystic?"

"He won't end it himself, Terry. Even after all he's done... the bastard's afraid of Hell." Father Mike shook his head. He wheezed and had to cough it down. "He knows what he is. But he can't stop himself. He won't."

The priest clenched his fists and slammed one on the table, making the coffee splash on the white. The jerk at the counter looked over.

"What do you do with scum like that?"

"Alright, Fadder. So this guy's a mad dog. He oughta be put down, I agree. But..."

"I know where he'll be," the priest said excitedly. "Tomorrow night. You know Castle Island, the fort?"

Terry scratched his neck. He needed a shave.

"Yeah, sure," he said.

His ma had took him there every summer when he was a kid. The old fort had been there since forever, but the island had stopped being an island when the reclamation project had connected it to the mainland with a big concrete causeway. He used to ride his bike there, all the way around Pleasure Bay and back to Sullivan's, where his ma would have a hot dog and crinkle fries waiting for him.

"What is he, a park ranger?" Terry said.

"He's a transient," said Father Mike. "I've seen him around the parish. Heard him lots of times, panhandlin' in the foyer. That was how I recognized his voice. He sneaks in and hides till the park closes, sleeps in the fort."

"How do you know that?"

"I followed him. He's gone back there two nights in a row. He'll be there tomorrow night. I can point him out."

But not to the cops, Terry thought bitterly. *And you can't do it yourself.* Priests could tell you everything you ought to do till it came time to do a man's actual work, be it killing or fucking. Then the hand washing started.

Terry wanted to go back to O'Malley's suddenly.

"If it's money you want..."

"I wouldn't do somethin' like this for money," Terry said sharply.

Money *had* been on his mind though, until Father Mike had come out and said it. Had he really been thinking of a way to make money out of this? What a no good son of a bitch he had become.

Father Mike nodded. A slight smile played across his face. "I didn't think you would, Terry. You were always a good boy."

"I was a piece of shit. I still am."

Father Mike shrugged. "You live with wolves, you learn to howl. But there was always a good kid in there. Maybe God's put this before you. Before us both."

Terry was shaking his head. "You ain't pullin' the trigger, Fadder."

"For a priest, breaking the vows of the confessional, it's like pulling a trigger."

"Don't say that," Terry snapped. "It ain't nothin' like that. You ain't never... you don't know nothin' about that, Fadder."

Why had this old bastard come and dropped this in his lap? His stomach was roiling. He'd thought he'd put all this behind him. Had he become the kind of guy people came to with shit like this now? Well, hadn't he always been that guy? Maybe. But the last time had been for Ma.

But what would Ma say if he knew about something like this and just let it go? What would Ma say if he turned on the TV in a couple days and some other kid had got chewed up and spat out on account of this crazy asshole?

Why did this have to fall to him? He didn't like murder. Back in the day he'd been a nut, drunk most of the time. Pulling a trigger on somebody had been like milking a teat that dripped money. Easier than working a real job, too.

But Pat Lonnigan, Jesus, that had been bad. The sound his head had made on that floor, like a pumpkin busting wide on Cabbage Night.

And when they'd put the light on and come in, Christ. All that blood, and the sight of Pat just staring with the top of his head popped open like a can of stewed tomatoes, like something out a horror movie. One minute snoring in the dark, the next bleeding in the white light, all the inner workings laid bare.

He closed his eyes. The white of the Dunkie's reminded him of the brightness of the cell. He got a flash of all kinds of bad things. Spilled brains. Little girls and boys with skinny legs and arms and all that red...

"Awright, Fadder. Awright, I'll handle it."

"You're still a good boy, Terry. A good man."

"Awright."

"You want to meet me outside O'Malley's tomorrow night?"

Terry nodded quietly, standing.

"You got a car?"

Terry nodded again.

The priest told him a time.

Terry left him sitting there with his munchkins.

He was numb the walk back to the T. He rode home with his head between his hands, listening to the clacking of the rails beneath the floor. The liquor worked its way up from his guts. He puked just before the doors slid open. He stumbled out onto the platform and up the stairs and home to his ma's house.

He passed out on the couch in the front room, and woke up before dawn shivering because he'd left the front door wide open.

He was nauseated. His head ached. He went to the toilet and jabbed his finger down his throat to get the rest of the sour taste from his mouth.

He shuffled into the kitchen and put on a pot and some toast and went down into the cellar to get his piece out of its hiding place, an Adidas box taped up under the stair.

It was a .45 SIG. The same type he'd carried in the 90's, though not the same one. He'd dropped three or four pistols in the bay over the years, but he always went out and bought a replacement since they shot pretty clean right out of the box.

The action was a little stiff. He'd got this one before he'd gone into South Bay. Never had a chance to break it in. He jacked seven rounds through the gun to test it. No jams.

He picked up the shells and pushed them back into the clip.

He took the pistol upstairs with him. He set it on the fridge and hung his jacket on Ma's chair. He poured himself a cup of coffee and stood chewing the toast, listening to the empty house settle.

It was paid for, but too big for him. He figured he ought to rent it out, but he didn't want the headache of checking in on strangers. He also didn't know a thing about selling a house, and he didn't want some realtor ripping him off, so here he sat, watching the dust and trash collect, the pile of dishes growing in the sink.

Ma would've boxed his ears to see her kitchen like this.

He put his coffee down. He took his jacket off the back of his ma's chair and draped it over his own.

He walked around the house with the pistol, waiting for nightfall.

It started raining again around noon and was still raining when he woke up from a nap to find the house dark.

He had a crap and put on his coat and went out to the garage to start his car. It was bitter cold and the rain was pattering, but when he pulled out of the driveway it stopped like the world was passing through a long tunnel.

He stopped for a six pack of roadies and pulled up to the curb in front of O'Malley's, two cans rolling on the backseat.

"You're late, Terry," Father Mike said when he got in.

"You want a beer, Fadder?" Terry asked, as they started east.

He could feel the priest looking at him across the car in the dark, even make out his blue face in the intermittent passing of light from the streetlamps.

"How's your head, Terry? Are you going to be able to do this?"

"Clear as my conscience. How's yours?"

"Jesus, are you drunk?"

12

"Relax, Fadder. I do my best work with a sixer in me."

They headed down Broadway toward Pleasure Bay, the dark sky above them fuming but restrained compared to the downpour of the previous night.

Stopped at a light, Terry looked over and saw Father Mike's hand on the dash, gripping it. The ring caught the red light. He was biting his knuckle, eyes closed. "You OK, Fadder?"

The priest nodded quietly. When the light turned green, whatever had affected him subsided.

"You got your pills?"

"I'm out."

"Want me to take you to the hospital?"

"No, no," said Father Mike. "No hospital. I'll be fine."

He wanted to see this through. Terry gave him props for that at least. He wasn't going to finger a guy and send Terry in to whack him while he bailed. Still, the man was a priest. He felt like he ought to give him an out.

"It's awright, Fadder. If you can't go through with this. Just. . . "

"I'm fine!" Father Mike snapped, turning to look at him, his eyes glaring.

"OK," said Terry.

They hit William J. Day Blvd, the big Farragut statue standing out in the rotary against the dark bay.

Terry banged a left and the trees of Marine Park were a blur on the driver's side, the waters of the bay churning, the narrow strip of land and the fort just visible across it on the right. Father Mike looked out across the bay, his hand splayed on the dashboard.

"Somethin' I always wanted to ask you, Fadder. From when I was a kid."

"What's that, Terry?" Father Mike answered, not turning around, his voice calm, no trace of his earlier outburst.

"What's with that ring you wear?"

Father Mike turned away from the window and held his hand and the ring out like a new bride. "It's for an Order I belong to, Terry."

"Order?"

"You know, like the hibos or the Knights of Columbus. That's St. Philopater Mercurius."

13

"Never heard of him."

"He was a Roman soldier, in the time of the pagan Emperor Decius. He was Saint George's cousin."

"No shit?"

They were passing the Conley Container Terminal on the left now. The lights of the forklifts and the cranes blinked at Terry, the trees finally giving away, affording a view of the great stacks of shipping containers, carriage-less boxcars packed with seafood and liquor and cars. That was where he'd stuffed that wop they'd sent down from New Jersey to kill Peachy Muldoon.

His thoughts went to that night, running through the maze of containers, his heart thudding in his ears, expecting at every corner to kill or be killed. Father Mike kept talking.

"When the Berbers invaded Rome, Decius led his troops against them. The Emperor was afraid, but Mercurius counseled him to hold fast. The hagiography says the archangel Michael appeared to Mercurius and gave him a sword with which he conquered the enemy. In reality, the 'sword' St. Michael presented to him was a unit of mercenaries, the Cynocephalae. The Dogs' Heads. Greek mountain warriors. God sent them to reinforce Mercurius. They fought like devils, and killed so many Berbers, the enemy broke off their attack and fled." He tapped the ring. "The inscription reads, *'Deum memento, regressus victor.'* 'Remember God when you return victorious.'"

It was well past closing but the parking lot lights were on.

"Pull over here," Father Mike advised, "and cut your lamps."

Terry did as he was told.

They got out of the car, the cold bay wind whipping their coats, the roar of an Iberia Airlines jet passing overhead, a great dark shape festooned with blinking lights, diving for Logan airport. Terry took his scally cap from his pocket and jammed it on his head.

Father Mike gestured for him to follow and went off up the road. Terry paused. He saw the priest's pill bottle on the ground. He picked it up and squinted at the torn label. The only word he could make out was 'colloidal.'

"How about security?" Terry asked when they had walked up the road a ways. The noise of the jet engine faded to a dull roar.

"It's the off season. Only one man on duty this time of night," Father

14

Mike said.

There was only one car in the parking lot. They skirted the lot lamps. Terry saw a single light twinkling far down the bike trail to Head Island. The night watchman, probably in one of those ATV's, making the rounds.

"I went wade fishing under the pier here as a boy. It's one of my earliest memories," Father Mike remarked.

They walked across the lawn through the swaying trees to the fort. Fort Independence had been built sometime in the 1800's, if Terry remembered the signs he'd read in his boyhood. It was a pentagon, five high granite walls capped by five high bastions, surrounding a grassy parade ground, some of the ramparts still lined with deactivated old fifteen inch iron cannons aimed impotently out at the harbor. The double studded wood doors were ajar, probably for the night watchman.

Their footsteps echoed through the stone corridor of the sallyport, which led to a second set of doors that opened onto the interior lawn.

Terry stepped out onto the parade ground. The stone corridors ringing the lawn with their empty barracks and silent magazine chambers were dark, medieval. He had never been here at night. The nostalgic feeling was gone. They said a guy had gotten walled up in here and died. Supposedly Edgar Allen Poe, a soldier here at the time, had written a story about it. Terry could almost believe this place had ghosts.

But he couldn't believe a homeless guy could get away with sleeping here and not get rousted by the night watchman.

"I don't see nobody," Terry said, turning about, peering at the shadowy alcoves. A guy could hide anywhere, sure, but he wouldn't get a good night's sleep. His eyes rested on Father Mike, reaching between the half open inner doors to click the padlock shut and quietly pull them closed.

He looked at Terry, hands in his pockets, dim, wrinkled face pulled down in a tight frown, the breeze stirring his white hair.

"What gives?" Terry asked.

Father Mike walked slowly across the grass.

"It's me, Terry. I'm the job you're here to do. I'm the one that killed that Vietnamese kid on Washington, and the two girls behind the church."

"What?"

"I can't control it anymore, Terry. I'm like an incontinent old fart, but I shit slaughter and bloodshed wherever I go. I did it in Cork and they transferred me to Dublin. After Dublin they sent me back to America.

I was in Phoenix for a month before it happened again. So I ran. The Church just keeps moving me."

Terry took out his pistol and pointed it at the advancing priest. "That's close enough, Fadder."

Father Mike stopped a few feet away. He looked up at the dark sky, at the shrouded moon high overhead.

"It's the Dog Heads. The church promised to always take care of them and their descendants. As reward."

"Reward for what?"

"For loyalty. We swore an oath. Well, my ancestors did. They always came when the Church called. The bloodhounds of the Inquisition. They hunted down all the enemies of the Church. The Order of St. Mercurius, Terry."

"What're you talkin' about?"

Father Mike shrugged. "I was just an orphan, a sailor's bastard from Southie. But the Church knew what I was. They took me in, taught me ways to control it. Gave me medicine to suppress the symptoms."

"What symptoms?"

"Lycanthropy, Terry. Conriachtna. Werewolves."

"Werewolves."

"Yes."

"You're outta your gourd. Aw, this is a goddamn shame," Terry spat on the grass. "Just like the goddamn baby rapers. Fuckin' church takin' care of their own."

"Yeah," sighed Father Mike. "But their cures don't work on me anymore. I'm too old, I guess. I don't know why the Church doesn't end it, Terry. I just know the moon comes up," and he looked up at the whirling clouds again, at the silver behind them, "like it's gonna come up tonight, and I wake up with the blood under my fingernails and flesh stuck in my teeth."

"You fuckin' freak..."

"More than you know." He looked at Terry again. "Now do it, Terry. Before it starts. I don't wanna hurt you."

"Nut job."

"Terry... please. I can't help what happens. If I bite you..."

"What, then I join the club? Like in the movies?"

"It doesn't always happen, but it could, Terry. If your blood takes to it. Let's don't find out, huh?"

The door to the sallyport rattled.

"Hey!"

Father Mike whirled.

The night watchman was at the doors. Finding them locked, he was cussing, keys jangling.

The steel roar of a 747 boomed in the night. It seemed to dissipate the clouds. The moon broke through, the silver light dappling the grass and Father Mike's white hair.

Terry hesitated.

Father Mike turned back to him.

Right there in the moonlight, the plane engines deafening in his ears, Terry saw the dark part of Father Mike's eyes spread like ink in water. It took almost no time at all. The hair burst across his cheeks and neck, sprouting in thick tufts of white like some kind of night blooming foliage. His blackening lips drew back, the gums popping and streaming blood as the teeth elongated and tapered into dog-like fangs, a too-wide grin, a satanic leer.

Terry had never been so totally afraid that he had thought with his legs first, but he was halfway to one of the rampart stairs before he dared to look back.

The huge, shaggy white creature burst from the priest's clothes and bounded not after him, but towards the sallyport doors. It moved so fast it seemed to race the jet that swiftly crossed the sky over the fort, a silver streak.

It loped on long gorilla-like arms, pulling the distance beneath it, kicking it away with a pair of scrawny, inhuman haunches. Its misshapen head was lowered like a prow on its thick neck, the long, upswept ears flat against the heaving shoulders. Its pure hide was scintillant. Mercurial.

The watchman pulled open the doors.

He was a big bellied man in a green jacket, a radio squelching on his sagging belt. There was a look of surprise on his pale face as the huge white wolf thing barreled into him.

The jet went over the water and was gone. Terry heard the watchman screaming, gurgling as his mouth filled with blood. The thing had him flat on his back. As it dipped its sharp head between his double chins, its muscled arms tore rapidly into him, ripping out chunks of his flesh, flinging it in all directions.

Terry turned away and huffed up the stone steps.

Nothing up here but the wind. He looked around for somewhere to go, but it was just a sheer leg breaking drop, about thirty feet. Across the water the lights of downtown glowed peacefully, unaware of the absolute insanity down on the parade ground.

How could that thing be real? How could Father Mike be it? Could he kill it? Didn't he need silver bullets or something? Father Mike hadn't given him silver bullets, but he had brought Terry here to kill him, hadn't he? Maybe silver was bullshit. Or maybe Father Mike had meant to kill him all along… but why, when he could have his pick of meals on the streets?

A gust of wind whipped at him, urging him to move, to do something. He ran along the top of the wall past the useless iron guns toward the sallyport. Maybe he could drop down somewhere there, get across the park, to the parking lot, bust into the watchman's car before Father Mike was… finished.

He ran as fast as he could for as long as he could, which wasn't long thanks to the beers and the smokes. He stopped after only a short sprint and had to put his hands on his knees and retch.

When he was done heaving, he snatched a look down at the parade ground.

The thing was staring at him, a nightmare face of white hair and red blood, barely man, only a little animal, mainly monster, a string of shimmering guts hanging from its maw like links of hot dogs in an old cartoon.

The body of the watchman lay beneath it, entirely hollowed out, the bones of the broken ribcage pale as ivory in the night. The corpse looked as if something inside it had exploded for a good five feet in every direction. Even the arch of the sallyport was dripping with blood. The thing had consumed him in a shark-like frenzy.

It barked. The noise was strange, high pitched and yet throaty, the unholy mix of the bay of a wolf and a man.

It sniffed the air, growled, and began to run.

It darted across the parade ground toward the stair.

Terry ran again, his heart threatening to explode out the back of his torso, his wretched belly twisting in knots as his numbing legs pounded old stone. He stumbled and threw himself against the wrought iron railing over the sallyport. Down below he saw the watchman's red and black ATV with its tool bed and hard top. How fast could the thing go? It was more than a golf cart, but it wasn't a GTO.

He looked back.

The thing took the stairs four at a time and skidded into a turn when it reached the top. He heard its nails scratching on the stone and gravel as it swung around and started running towards him.

He lifted the gun and popped off four shots to dissuade it. It flinched and began to slalom. He didn't think he'd hit it, but it knew what a gun was. It wasn't scared enough to stop coming, but it slowed and dodged.

Maybe he had a chance after all, but not with his back to space.

He clambered over the railing, took an eighth of a second to try and gauge the distance, then pushed off. He fell through space, his stomach slipping somewhere up behind his lungs, and landed on the roof of the ATV. His left leg gave away underneath him. He bounced and tumbled onto the pile of tools in the back. He groaned, but managed to hold onto his pistol, even though something sharp tore his left pant leg open and sliced the calf beneath.

He scrambled on his knees and crawled into the cab, praying the guy hadn't had his keys with him. He was rewarded with the feel of the cold bit of metal between his fingers as he groped the starter.

It started up immediately, the engine whining. He kicked the pedal to the floor. The thing lurched off down the walkway.

He thought he hit a rock in the dark for a moment because the entire body of the ATV shuddered and slammed him back and forth. The hard top bent inward and smashed him in the top of the head, opening a gash that quickly poured a cascade of blood in his left eye.

The thing had leapt off the wall and landed squarely on the roof. He could hear its claws scrabbling against the metal. He pressed the muzzle of the pistol against the roof and fired twice, deafening himself, but hearing a doggish whine above. He jerked the wheel left so hard the ATV almost tipped. He saw the pale furry shape smash through a wooden picnic table and rise shaking its head in the rearview mirror.

He made for the concrete path down the causeway to Head Island.

The creature flung the broken table away and came snarling in pursuit.

The speedometer displayed an optimistic fifty on the far right. He stood on the accelerator and willed the orange needle there. How fast could that goddamn thing run? He squeezed the wheel and rocked in his seat, as if he could, by momentum, increase its acceleration. A furtive glance showed the great blood flecked white wolf-thing swelling in the rearview. The creature was foaming from exertion. The machine was likewise thrumming beneath his feet. Maybe they were both giving all they could give. Maybe the old age of the monster would make the difference.

Then it sprang forward with one last supreme effort and grabbed onto the tailgate. It dragged behind for an instant. Terry felt the pull. Then it was heaving itself into the bed and lunging for the cab. Its wild head came through and snapped at him, lips curling back from vicious fangs, its breath hot in his ear and reeking of blood. He felt its teeth clamp down hard on his right shoulder, passing through leather and muscle and grinding his joint like a soup bone.

He screamed as one great shaggy arm slipped in and raked its yellowish claws up his trunk, trying to scoop his guts out. He was spared a disemboweling only by a momentary jump of the ATV as it left the pavement. He reached up and jammed the .45 into the werewolf's face and got off the last bullet, blowing out his own eardrum to no apparent effect.

He jerked the wheel hard right. The ATV spun in the gravel and flipped.

He didn't count how many times it turned over because after the first revolution he was flung ass over end into the wet sand, his shoulder torn violently free of the monster's bite. The sound was like a go-cart with a string of metal garbage cans behind rolling down that stairwell from *The Exorcist*.

Terry lay flat on his back, bleeding and spitting salty sand. He might have blacked out. The wind had been knocked from him. He wasn't sure, but thought he might have broken a rib or two. His chest felt warm and yet the chill wind penetrated. He glanced down at the dark wound there, a mass of oily blood, the shirt and jacket shredded to tatters. He couldn't feel his shoulder, couldn't move his arm, but he did wiggle his fingers in the gritty sand. He watched another plane streak low across the night sky. He waited for his ears to stop ringing, decided they wouldn't, and strained to roll on his side.

A few feet away the wheels of the ATV were spinning in the air, half in the surf, broken against one of the pier pylons. All the tools and equipment in the bed were strewn about the sandy beach beneath the causeway. His pistol was gone.

There was a thrashing sound in the water, and a wounded dog whine from the pylon.

Terry pushed himself slowly up, falling twice back into the wet sand before getting to his feet. There was no strength in his right arm. It was as if it wasn't there. But he could move his fingers. He would be alright. He squinted about for his pistol, but the only gleam he found was a steel hacksaw, handle in the sand, where it had been thrown from the open toolbox. He squatted down and got it in his left hand, then slowly waded out to the pylon. The water there was only knee deep.

He could hear the thing panting heavily. He should turn and run, but he knew if he did, if the thing was able, it would just chase him down. He passed warily around the end of the overturned ATV. The vehicle was right against the pylon, the metal of the front left quarter bent around it. Wedged between steel and wood was the creature, one white shoulder and arm protruding from the twisted metal, thrashing pitifully, straining to keep its head above the lapping seawater.

Terry's last bullet had ploughed a furrow in its cheek and torn away much of the lower half of its right ear. Its grin had widened to horrendous proportions, the row of teeth along the long jaw totally exposed.

It whined like a puppy.

Terry stared at it for a minute before its black nostrils caught his scent above the intrusive fish smell of the waves. It growled low in its throat and redoubled its useless efforts. It was possible its back was broken. It definitely wasn't going anywhere. Its face was wholly animal, but its feral black eyes retained some kind of mad humanity, like the eyes of a mental deficient.

Terry backed off and waded around the far side, where the arm couldn't possibly reach him. He got within inches of the ferocious face, which now twisted to snap at him.

At least three kids had passed over this thing's tongue. He wondered now about the half remembered children in his own class who had gone missing in his youth. Kids who he had written off as having moved out of

Southie during the summer, or bused off to the colored schools because their parents couldn't pay tuition. Father Mike had said he used to be able to control it. But had he? Had he let loose on those kids during his monthlies? Something like this, how much could you really control it? How much did you really want to?

He leaned against the ATV and lifted his booted foot up, pressing it to the side of the thing's muzzle. It struggled anew, but it was thoroughly pinned, and probably partly paralyzed. He found he could force its head against the pylon with ease. He watched it under his heel, the tongue lolling out, the jaw feebly working, the teeth grinding against his sole now and then, the big black eyes rolling in their sockets to try and see him.

The throat beneath the jaw pulsed.

He put the hacksaw to its neck, pressing the serrated edge into the furry, yielding flesh.

The creature seemed to understand and let out a pitiful howl that raised the hairs on the back of Terry's neck. He gave it a rip like he was starting a lawnmower. Blood bubbled up and gushed from the ragged wound, but every slap of the swelling and retreating tide bathed it and washed it clean. He didn't stop, but stooped and straightened, sawing the throat vigorously. He found he could put his right arm to work after a bit.

The noise it made as it kicked and splashed in the surf became less like an animal howl and more like a man's shrill shrieking.

"You thought I'd make it quick, you son of a bitch?" Terry snarled, mainly to shut out its horrible screams in his ringing ears. "Fuck you! Fuck you, Fadder!"

He gripped it by the scalp and sawed until the edge ground against the vertebrae. The noise stopped, the wicked jaw hung slack. And in his very hands, the long white fur began to come away, shedding so fast into the surrounding water it was like somebody had taken a leaf blower and just scattered it.

For a moment it was a bare wolfish face with a ridiculous head of well-groomed white hair. Then it seemed to melt. The ears retracted and reformed, all the sharp angles softened, the teeth retreated, the bones ground together as they moved in the face and the skull altered until the slack, mask-like face of Father Mike hung from his fist. He dropped it in revulsion. Half severed, it fell cheek to shoulder, the exposed partially broken vertebrae and connective tissue crackling wetly.

Terry threw down the hacksaw and retched violently into the water.

The water washed everything away.

The tinsel and wreaths were up at O'Malley's. One of the whores had put Elvis' rendition of O Little Town of Bethlehem on the jukebox. She swayed with the fat john in the Santa hat who'd given her the dollar.

A tall young red headed priest stepped in the door and slapped the snow from his coat.

At the bar, Terry slammed back his Jameson and gestured to O'Malley to come over.

The bartender had the bottle ready. "'Nother, one, Terry?"

"Nah," said Terry, shaking his head and planting his money on the bar. "Be seein' you."

He dropped something into the glass that clinked.

O'Malley watched him duck out the back exit and peered at the thing left in the shot glass.

Terry had been in here before his stay in South Bay. He'd come in maybe twice a week, tops. He was a guy that preferred to drink alone and at home. But for the past three weeks, he had been in every night. O'Malley remembered him coming in looking like hell, all bandaged up, limping, with his arm in a sling. It was the night after the cops found two more of that whackjob slasher's victims out on Castle Island. A night watchman and a priest, cut all to hell, the priest's head sawed off.

O'Malley had recognized the priest as the same old guy that had come in and talked to Terry that night. At first O'Malley had wondered if it had been Terry that had done it, but nah, that wasn't Terry's thing, to do a guy up like that. He was a murderer sure, but he was no psychopath.

Anyway, that was the first time the sicko had done his business twice in one month. Everybody was still waiting to see if he'd do it again in December or take a break for the holidays.

O'Malley had tried to mark Terry's visits by the healing of his cuts and bruises, though that had proved untrustworthy. Whatever Terry had gotten into, it hadn't been as bad as it first looked. His arm was out of the sling in two days. The nasty cuts on his face were gone before that.

O'Malley picked up the shot glass for a closer look, then turned it over and let its contents drop into his open palm. It was a ring with a saint on it and some Latin. When he looked up, the redheaded priest was standing there looking at it, too. Their eyes met, and O'Malley's hackles rose just a bit. The priest had weird eyes. Probably it was the light and the eggnog, but they seemed too big, too dark.

"Where did you get that?" the priest demanded. He was FBI by his brogue - full blooded Irish.

O'Malley's eyes went to the back door. He opened his mouth to answer, but the priest reached out and snatched the ring from his hand.

It was then that O'Malley noticed the same design on the priest's finger.

Terry Dunne did a lot of things, but it was low to steal from a priest. "He take that from one of yours, Fadder?"

The priest was watching the door. He turned back and looked surprised at him, like he had forgotten he was there.

"You want I should call a cop?"

"No, that's alright," said the priest, moving for the door. "We take care of our own."

Her Father's Skin

Her Father's Skin
by
Christine Morgan

SHE GIVES CHASE through the snow, through the night, through the wind. Darkness howls and sleet stings. Shadows loom and reach, bare branches raking like claws. Ice cracks underfoot as she crosses a stream, and the water, not frozen, feels even colder in its sudden splash.

Somewhere ahead, her quarry stumbles and blunders, too old for this exertion, too weak and too frail. Only a mad desperation drives him onward, drives him deeper into the forest. Where he thinks he is bound, she knows not, only that she must catch him.

Her legs are stronger. Her breath gusts in clouds of frost-steam. Twigs that, to him, snag and catch and hinder, snap in brittle splinters of dead winter wood as her larger body bursts through the brush without slowing.

He falters. He falls. He flails and wails in a snow-drift. Blood shed from cuts, scrapes and scratches makes a scatter of stains on the unblemished white. His thin form quakes and trembles. He is stick-thin and scrawny, scarred, skin and bones and scant meat.

Cautious now, she approaches, wary of what he might do in his final, cornered extremity. He struggles to rise, fails, and falls again. His head turns. He sees her with eyes gone wide and wild.

She sinks to a knee and rests a hand on his shoulder.

"Father," she says.

In the great hall at Bjornsberg, many fires blazed their heat from earth-sunken rings of hearth-stones. Folk filled the mead-benches, feasting and drinking, voices raised in hearty laughter. There were warriors and farmers, fishermen, women, children, and thralls. All the household had gathered, and guests come besides.

26

At the high table sat Ullar Bjornsson, earl in all but name. The men looked to him as their lord and war-leader. He was not yet thirty, fit of arm for the sword and the shield, fair-haired and handsome, his chest broad, his gaze as steady as stone. His reputation was known to be proud but just; what he may have lacked in wisdom, he made up for in generosity.

His wife and young sons sat to his right, his brother and his sister to his left.

His mother, the true lady of the hall, had long since - if not quite ungrudgingly - deferred both her place and her duties to her daughter-in-law. When the day did come when her son was earl in name as well, no one doubted but that Ulla would remarry; in the mid-forties of her years, she had kept a fine figure and was muchly admired by widowed suitors. Meanwhile, however, she bided her time in a dim corner, tending to her ancient and ailing husband.

Earl Bjorn, or the white-bearded husk of the man he'd once been, slumped with head lolling. Straps of leather held him to his chair, preventing him from falling to the floor-rushes. He muttered and mumbled, half his face twitching. Spoon-fed broth and grain-mash dribbled from the corners of his toothless mouth.

Few at the feast remembered him any other way. Even were he not stricken by illness and infirmity, he would have been the eldest among them by far. His age-mates and battle-companions had all long since died. His marriage to Ulla was his second, done less for love than for politics, and he had been an old man already when their children were born.

It was said that, in his youth, Bjorn fought alongside the famed king Hrolf-Kraki, but many made similar claims about their ancestors. They likewise made claims of dragon-slayers, giants and trolls, sorceresses, monsters, dwarfs and dark-elfs. Myth and legend, god-talk... such was the stuff stories and sagas were made of, the embellished telling of tales to enliven cold northern nights.

The mead-bowls passed hand to hand. Thralls brought in more platters of roasted fish and stewed pork. To prove to their guests the wealth of the hall, Ullar distributed gifts of fleeces and furs, combs carved from ivory, cloak-clasps and belt-buckles, and other small treasures. In return, their guests uttered loud and effusive praises of Bjornberg's hospitality, stating that never yet in their journey had they until now received so welcoming a reception.

27

They had arrived on horseback soon before dusk, six men under the peace-banner of the new young boy king. Who was, it was said, a great-grandson of Hrolf-Kraki, very enamored of the old sagas and tales. Farulf, who led them, wore two arm-rings of silver and another of gold. His woolen tunic was dyed deepest green, trimmed at cuffs and collar and hem with wolf's fur. His grey-streaked black beard was trimmed neatly short, and he spoke with the honey-dipped tongue of a poet.

Whatever their message or business, of course, Ullar had bidden it wait until later. They had traveled far and must be weary; let them rest and refresh, let their horses be seen to, let them bathe in the hot-springs if it was their desire. After they had done so, and been properly sated on food and drink, he would be only too glad to hear them.

And so, it was done as Ullar instructed.

Now, Farulf stepped forth and again gave great flattery and thanks. "It is not much to offer to repay such generosity," he said, "but my nephew rides with us, Rannulf, son of my sister, and he is reputed to be of reasonable skill at the harp. Would you permit him to play and sing, before we must talk of more serious matters?"

Ullar could hardly, and would hardly, refuse. An eager hush spread through the hall, until all was silent but for the crackle of flames, the hoot of wind in the chimney-holes, and the ceaseless vague mutterings from old Bjorn's dim corner.

Rannulf stood and bowed, then took his harp from its case. It was a well-wrought instrument, the wood polished to a shine, the strings bright as stars. When he struck it, the notes rippled water-pure in the smoky air. He took a place before the high table, nodded his respects to Ullar and his family, and then - in a gesture that did cause Ullar's lips to tighten - turned to nod to Bjorn and Ulla as well.

The ancient earl took no notice, drooling and mumbling into his beard. But, as Rannulf's clear voice rose in song, even Bjorn quieted, seeming to listen.

"Father," she says, her hand on his shoulder. Her voice is a sob, thick in her throat as she speaks. "Father, what's happened to you?"

He stares with a blank fright, as if he does not know her. Snow powders his white hair and beard even whiter. It cakes the thin linen long-shirt in which he'd been sleeping. Below its tattered hem, his bare legs poke crooked like gnarled branches. His feet look frost-grey and bloodless. His body shivers violently.

How he has done this, she cannot imagine. How he has come so far from the hall, so far into the forest, when most days he can hardly cross from his chair to his bed without help.

Yet, here he is, he has come so far, and so fast she was hard-pressed to follow.

"Where are you going?" she asks as she lifts him. "There's nothing out here but the old charcoaler's hut."

And, possibly, she thinks - although the thought is unwelcome - dangers beyond that of the winter night's cold. The woods are a feared place, feared with good reason. The woods are home to bears and wolves. They might be the refuge of murderers, outlaws, escaped slaves and thieves.

She braces him against a tree while she reaches for her cloak-clasp, intending to wrap him in the garment to carry him home. The moment she lets go of him, he does not fall again but darts away like a hare, ducking and springing, evading her grasp.

Then he is running again, running despite the numb and frozen state of his feet.

"Father!"

He does not stop. She gives chase once more, at first calling after him and then sparing her breath for pursuit. The land slopes upward in rugged tangles of stumps and undergrowth, blackly treacherous. A root, rock or hole might end this race without warning.

Ahead, the woods open to a hillside clearing, the pale-blanketed expanse offering welcome visibility. She glimpses at the edge of it the old charcoaler's hut, years abandoned, its roof half-collapsed.

Her father pauses midway in the clearing. He turns this way and that as if searching for something. She gains several strides on him before he utters a strange cry of mingled despair and relief, and sets off at a rapid stagger.

A stark ridge of granite juts up at an angle. The wind has scoured the snow from its barren back, but rows of ice-fangs and ice-fingers cover its lee-side. It seems this is what he's been seeking; he makes for it and begins scrabbling along the ground at its base.

This time, she does not bother approaching with caution. She removes her cloak and swing-tosses it like a fisherman casting a net. The heavy fleece-lined wool drops over him. He grunts in surprise, knocked flat, but she is already on him. She wraps him the way she might swaddle an infant, though he struggles. He works one arm free to claw and scrape at the snow.

As she hauls him up, she sees the pile of mossy stones his scrabblings and scrapings have exposed. It is no natural arrangement, she realizes, but something deliberately made. Those stones have been placed there, stacked there, as a marker.

Or as a cairn.

The thought sends a worse chill through her than does the sleet-laden night air.

She has seen cairns before, of course, burial mounds with stones piled atop them to prevent animal scavengers from unearthing and eating the dead, or deter robbers from stealing grave-goods.

But this cairn, so far from anything, out here in the woods...

This cairn, so small, much too small for a proper grave... made long enough ago to now be moss-encrusted...

She looks at her father, mind clamoring questions. She finds, to her astonishment, that he meets her gaze with one of plaintive urgency. His bunched, tremulous hand wavers as it indicates the cairn. His eyes brim. A terrible effort tries and fails to bring words to his lips.

"I'll dig," she tells him. "If that's what you want, what you must have, then I'll dig."

Hear me! For so it was in the days of the heroes
　　Powerful war-lords and warriors, the best of men
　　That King Hrolf-Kraki, born of love and deceit
　　Assembled an army to avenge his father's death
　　Among them were twelve surpassing all others
　　The king's close companions, brothers-at-arms
　　God-granted by Odin the gift of shape-changing
　　When the battle-lust seized them, the wild war-fury
　　The violent kill-hunger, the wrath and the rage
　　A red mist descended on them, a frenzy for blood
　　They would cast aside their mail-coats and leather
　　Throw down their weapons, their helms and shields

The clothes from their bodies would be ripped asunder
Fierce beasts becoming, unleashing savage slaughter
The *Ulfhednar*, wolf-pelted with fast, flashing fangs
And the *Berserker*, strongest of all in their bear-skins
Unstoppable in combat, life-takers, slayers of foes
Howls, roars and bellows their dreaded war-cries
A raging of claws, teeth and sinew, a bestial thunder
Unhurt by iron spear-points, by axe-blades and swords
Fearing neither fire nor steel, fearing not even death
But striking terror to the marrow of all in their path
So that brave men pissed and cowered, fainted and fled
Across the field where the rats and ravens harvest
A great crop of death grew, a gluttonous bounty
Flesh torn and bones broken, an agony of screams
Limbs ham-strung at knee-back or ankle-tendon
The thigh's thick crimson river overflooded its banks
Skulls cracked like eggshells in the crush of bear-jaws
Breastbones smashed and shattered, ribs sprung agape
Guts glistened in glaring war-light, organs exposed
As bloodied wolf-muzzles burrowed deep, snarling
Seeking soft throats and pulsating, still-beating hearts
Carnage strewn over the churned earth, the battle done
The enemy's shield-walls dashed, their army in ruins
The dying-song and war-cries, the wailing of wives
Glorious to the ears of Hrolf-Kraki, declaring victory
That night in the mead-hall the warriors gathered
Ulfhednar and *Berserker* most honored among them
Removed now of their wolf-pelts and bear-skins
Men once more, the king's guard, his war-brothers
The harps silver-stringed, the drinking horns flowing
Skalds and poets recounted the day's great deeds
Names ever-remembered, long-lasting reputations
Hrolf-Kraki bestowed upon them generous gifts
Arm-rings and neck-torcs and brooches of gold
Jeweled bowls and goblets, a rich treasure-hoard
And prized above all their lord's love and acclaim
Hear me! For so it was in the days of the heroes

31

The ground under the cairn-stones is cold and hard, but she digs.

The sleet turns to a rain that soaks her clothes from the outside even as sweat soaks them from within, but she digs.

She has only her hands, and a stick, and her trusty belt-knife, but she digs.

Her digging calms him, the old man, her father. He sits huddled on a log, wrapped in her cloak, and watches. He seems heedless of his bare feet, and by now the frost-grey is darkening to black blotches; he will be lucky not to lose toes, though she supposes that such a loss would hardly much hinder him, all considered.

What she finds is not a grave, but a small wooden chest. It is weathered but well-made, the fitted lid carved with intricate, beautiful workmanship. The style reminds her of the designs decorating the door-posts of the hall; they could have been made by the same hand. If so, it would have been well before her time. Those posts had been set when the hall was first built.

Her father groans when she lifts the chest from the earth. His expression is equal parts longing and loathing. He shudders, groans again, and averts his face.

The wood proves damp-warped, the lid swelled shut. Opening it will, she decides, have to come later. The weight is not such that suggests hoarded silver or gold. She can carry it as well as her father, if she needs to. She is strong-built, stout-limbed and sturdy.

As she starts to rise, her gaze catches a faint glint at the bottom of the hole... not the hole she dug, but a smaller hole yet deeper beneath it.

She reaches down. Her fingers, stiff and numb though they are, find a piece of metal, an amulet of silver in the shape of the world-tree. A silver chain trails from it, snagged on something below.

In the smaller hole is a blanket-wrapped bundle, and she understands now that the cairn did mark a grave after all. A child's grave. The rotted cloth crumbles wetly away at her touch, revealing pale, delicate bones.

When she looks at her father, his face is no longer averted. His eyes are fixed on the sad and fragile remains. Tears trickle over his wrinkled cheeks to his beard. He weeps, and in that moment she both understands... and does not.

That she and her brothers are the products of his second marriage, she has always known. Just as she has always known his second marriage was rather less than a love-match. His first wife, the wife of his youth and his heart, had given him one son who died in infancy. The soft-sleep, the cradle-death, claimed him after less than a year, to their great devastation.

Her mother maintains this is why he never warmed to her brothers. Why he had not wished them named for himself, and kept them at more of an arm's length indifference. A girl-child, however, held no threat to those cherished memories. He could have affection for a daughter without feeling it a betrayal of his firstborn.

But how can this be that same poor, dead babe? Buried out here in the woods, marked by a plain cairn of stones, instead of at the barrow-hill mound with its mother and kin?

How can this be that same poor, dead babe, when its bones show a far grimmer fate than the silent cradle-death? The fine, fragile dome of skull alone says enough, punctured through as it is in several places.

She, having seen her share of slain lambs and animal-bites, would all but swear these marks had been made by the jaws of a beast.

The harp-strains and words faded, Rannulf finishing his song-saga to great loud acclaim from the folk of the hall. Even the old earl, in his dim corner, thumped approbation on his chair's armrests.

At the high table, Ullar's wife and his mother wore disapproving looks, not caring for such tales of battlefield carnage. As for Ullar himself, his eyes somewhat narrowed, but he praised his guest's performance and tossed him a ring set with amber as reward.

The mead-bowls were refilled and passed around again, and with them went plates heaped with cakes slathered in boiled bilberries and cream. Farulf then once more stepped forward, for the time had come to address the business of his visit.

He reminded them that, as of course they all knew, Helgi, their wise and noble king had died the previous year, leaving the care of the land to a half-grown son. This son, Hrugr by name, had been raised by his uncles on stories of Hrolf-Kraki, and now wished to make for himself a similar court. To this end, the boy-king had sent out emissaries, including Farulf's very company, to seek them among the earls and the lords.

"Why?" asked Ullar, his scowl returning. "Does he not have brave men enough at his hall already?"

These words caused a few of his visitors some hesitation, as they

33

wondered if the meaning of them was flattery or insult. Farulf merely smiled... or at least showed the white flash of teeth through his beard in a wolf's grin.

"He does, and many," he said, "but he wishes more, an honor guard of bold champions, famed warriors as in the legends. As in the days of magic and heroes."

"Days of superstition," said Ullar, "which have long passed. You cannot mean to tell me that our king would surround himself with men claiming to be *Ulfhednar* and *Berserker*. What next? Giants and trolls? We have laws now, and peace."

"We have also our history. Men of Bjornsberg were among King Hrolf-Kraki's armies, were they not?" Farulf inclined his head in a respectful nod toward the old earl, who had begun to become agitated. "Indeed, just as my own grandfather was, was not your father –?"

A wordless cry burst from Bjorn's throat. He struggled against the straps of his chair. His gnarled fists thumped the armrests with increased vigor. Ulla rushed to him, hissing at him to be calm and behave, that he was making a spectacle before the whole hall and their guests. If he heard her, he ignored her, struggling all the harder and voicing louder, though still inarticulate, cries.

Ullar, face reddening, gestured to some thralls. They hastened to lift the chair entire, Bjorn still in it, and bore it swiftly into the smaller private family chambers beyond. Ulla followed, so embarrassed she could not meet the eyes of even her own children.

As the sounds of his distress continued unabated, an awkwardness overtook everyone upon the mead-benches. Gazes shifted in search of any distraction, then found it as Ullar turned back to Farulf with thunder upon his brow.

"If the kingdom has need of armies," he said, "I can bring five hundred men with mail-coats, horses, swords and shields. If raiding is wanted, I command four dragon-ships. But I will not caper in a bear-skin at the whim of a child."

When he does not object, she gently enfolds the bones in the cloth and replaces the tiny bundle into its lonesome grave. She is shivering by then from the cold but covers it with earth and piles over it the mossy stones.

The carved wooden chest, she does not leave behind. She tucks it under one arm, bracing its weight on her hip. In the other arm, she hefts her father, wrapped in her cloak. Though the combined burden is not too heavy for her strength, the weariness of her exertions makes her consider the journey to the hall with despair.

Better the old charcoaler's shed, she decides. It is not far. They will be less than comfortable, but should safely pass the rest of the night.

It proves better shelter than she had surmised. The roof may be half-collapsed but the walls are intact, and the wood left in the woodbin is dry. There is a cot upon which she settles her father. He sinks down into either unconsciousness or sleep.

Soon, she has a small fire kindled. She strips off her wet shoes and leggings, her dress and her shift. Naked, she crouches by the flames, rubbing her limbs, wringing the rain from her hair. The shivers ebb. Her teeth cease their chattering.

She checks her father and finds him breathing in slow, deep dream-mumbles. It will be a gods'-mercy if he does not catch the damp lung, and she is certain he'll see the loss of some toes. If, that is, he lives long enough for it to matter.

Her heart wrenches with sorrow. How she wishes she could have known the man that he was, the man who had gone into battle alongside Hrolf-Kraki. Not this frail shell, this husk impaired of both body and mind. This is no way to be, not for a warrior, not for anyone.

Sighing, she tucks the cloak more snugly around him. She takes the wooden chest to the fire and examines it more closely. This is what brought her father raving out into the forest, and she must have answers. Using her knife-blade with care, she pries at the lid until the warped wood squeals open.

Inside, she finds three items, the first two smaller and atop the third. One is a length of cord, twisted from sinews. The other is a pot of salve, somehow still supple, not solidified into a crust. She sniffs it. The scent is strange, a mix of tallow and bonemeal and blood and ash. The pot itself is painted with faded, flaking runes.

The third and largest item, at the bottom, is a folded fur. A thick pelt, a bear-skin, and when she lifts it out she sees that it is cut in the crude shape of an over-tunic with sides unstitched. It is also rent and torn in many places, as if pierced by arrows or spear-points, hewn by axe-blades and swords.

The thoughts in her mind cannot possibly be true.

Can they?

The stories... the sagas... the song Rannulf sang... Hrolf-Kraki's champions, the *Ulfhednar* and *Berserker*... her father's agitation, driving him on this mad errand...

She looks at the ragged pelt. She looks at the sinew and salve. She looks at the sleeping old man, drooling into his beard.

Her fingers scoop into the greasy substance. It melts oily and pungent as she smears it onto her arm. She feels a faint tingling, not at all unpleasant. The more she scoops from the pot, the level of the salve does not seem to change.

When her entire body is covered, glistening in the firelight, she draws the bear-skin over her head and belts it with the cord of twisted sinews.

Nothing happens, and she nearly laughs aloud at her own foolishness. Ullar must never hear of this, she tells herself.

Then the tingling of the salve becomes a spreading rush of heat that sinks into her flesh. The bear-skin adheres to hers like something alive. Her joints burn. Her bones seem to pop, her gristle to grind and her tendons to stretch.

The sensation is that of a cracked stubborn knuckle or a cricked stiff neck, a mix of brief agony and satisfying relief, and it wracks her from head to foot. She drops to her knees, then to all fours. Fur bristles, rippling, along her limbs and torso. Dark thick claws sprout from her fingers and toes.

She is the bear.

Ullar's declaration brought the evening to an abrupt, uncomfortable end. Farulf laughed it off, but it was clear the time for feasting and drinking was over. Not long thereafter, the tables were put aside. On the sleeping-platforms, furs and blankets were spread. Sounds of slumber soon arose.

The earl's family retired to their rooms at the rear of the hall. It was there, some hours later, Bjorndis Bjornsdottir woke to find her mother torn between anger and tears.

"That old madman, your father, has run away!" Ulla said.

"Run?" she asked, fully astounded. "Father? How?"

"The gods alone can say." Ulla flung exasperated hands in the air. "It took us ages to quiet him after his outburst earlier, but then he somehow got from his bed, out the side door, and escaped."

"He'll freeze to death!"

"Dolt of a girl, do you think I don't know that? Now I must wake your brothers, and when Ullar hears, how furious he'll be! He'll have to rouse the household, and our guests, and send out searchers –"

"Let me go after him," Bjorndis said as she pulled on her dress and her shoes. "He can't have gone far, not in his state. I'll find him and bring him back. No one need be the wiser."

Ulla contemplated briefly, then nodded. "Wear your cloak, girl, and don't forget your belt-knife. There might be beasts in the woods."

The bear's shoulder easily pushes open the shed door. The bear's paws crunch in the snow. The bear's moist black nose tests the air, detecting the tang of winterberries, the sting of evermint.

The bear's ears follow a swift gurgle of white-water to a creek tumbling over rocks between icy banks. Fish flick and dart silver in the deeper pools. A swipe of claws snags one, slaps it ashore where it flips its fins and thrashes its tail.

The bear's teeth rip through fine scales to the fresh, pale, cold meat. Thin blood flows and thin fish-bones splinter. The fish is half-devoured before it fully dies.

It is delicious. Bjorndis has never tasted anything so succulent and sweet. Her every sense seems more keen. Her pelt is warm, her body powerful, her spirit racing with exhilaration.

This, she realizes, is what her father lost. What her father gave up.

Her previous understanding is at last clear. Perhaps the echoes of memories linger in the bear-skin, the way strong scents or flavors linger long after the source is gone. Perhaps some pains are too great to be let go.

He had so loved the child, his little son. The moon could have risen and set for the child's delight. A bold boy, curious, sturdy, cheerful, and fearless. Bright laughter like golden bells… tiny trusting hands that clutched with equal affection at a father's beard or a bear's shaggy fur…

Until the day, that most terrible day, when those tiny hands tugged too hard, yanking out tufts.

The sudden rage overtook the bear for a moment, only a moment.

But, a moment was enough.

Some pains are too great to let go. Some griefs are too great to be borne.

As are some shames.

They told no one the truth. Cradle-death, they said, and buried their son in secret, while a wrapped stone took his place on the barrow-hill.

His dear wife forgave him. In a way, that was worst of all. Her forgiveness cut sharper than would have her hatred. Her forgiveness, and then her gradual, despairing decline.

Bjorndis, in bear-shape, returns to the charcoaler's shed. The door still hangs open, askew on one hinge. Inside, the fire has burned low but not extinguished. Much the same can be said of her father.

As she comes in, a draft of fresh air makes the flames briefly leap to new life. And, again, much the same can be said of her father. He sits up, her cloak falling from him.

She tries to speak, but of course she cannot. A guttural growl is the closest she comes.

He springs from the cot, again with startling spryness for a man of his age and ill health. He snatches up from the cold dirt floor the stick she'd used to unearth the chest and the grave. He brandishes it at her. A sour stink of sick-sweat surrounds him, sick-sweat and madness. His shout is as unintelligible as her bear's-growl, his face hectic and wild. He swings the stick.

It glances from her thick fur-covered skull. Bjorndis recoils. He swings it again and the stick strikes the bear's tender black snout a hard, smarting blow.

Before she knows what is happening to her, the red mist roils over her. She roars full-throated, shaking the shed's flimsy walls. A lunge, and a swipe of her huge paw, knocks the old man sprawling. He lands with a brittle snap of bones. His hip breaks with a pop like a pine-knot in the fire.

He screams, but he continues swinging and jabbing with the stick, battering at her face, gouging its end into her shaggy neck and chest.

Her forelegs pin him, frail ribs giving way beneath the bear's immense crushing weight. Her jaws gape in another bellowing roar.

In the instant before she rips the life from him, Bjorndis returns to herself in a clarity of horror.

But she sees, in her father's eyes, a different kind of clarity.

She sees that he knows her, that he has known all along. That this is what he wanted and craved. To see his long-dead son's murder avenged, and to be released from his own wretched torment.

To be granted a warrior's violent end.

And she, loving her father, wearing his skin, cannot refuse.

Chaney Jr. Overdrive

Chaney Jr. Overdrive
by
Glynn Owen Barrass

A T 2:00 AM THE HIGHWAY stood empty, empty and desolate but for
him, a passenger in his black Chevrolet driving of its own volition
on autodrive. The twinkling stars and the moon, oh glorious moon! bore
mute witness to his predations. While the car took care of the road, he
performed the important work, scanning both sides of the highway for
hitchhikers.

The highway was his trail. He knew it well, having made this journey
three times already tonight. So he knew that he would reach the outskirts
of Central City in just under ten minutes. The skyline of towering, angular
buildings, above which hovered a perpetual brown smog, was growing
closer. Almost time to make a return trip.

The beast was hungry, he could feel it clawing at the insides of his
chest, trying to wriggle up through his throat and release an almighty,
bestial howl of hunger. It was an itch that needed a victim, and tonight,
tonight was proving devoid of prey. He was about to give up and turn
around when something moved in the corner of his eye, five lanes to his
left.

I got one! He smiled and said, "Car, driver control."

"Returning in five, four..." The onboard computer's female voice
counted down as he cricked his neck, clenched his hands on the steering
wheel. Even from this distance, the figure across the highway was un-
doubtedly a woman. This gladdened him further. Males were too difficult,
and the beast wasn't interested in their pain. A warning 'beep' informed
him the controls were his and he slowed the speed before turning the
wheel, driving across the lanes towards his intended victim.

The beast calmed a little and issued a low growl, almost a purr, as he absorbed the sight of the woman. She had a big red sack on her shoulders, blonde hair in dreadlocks tied up on her head. Pale, skinny legs in dungaree shorts. She looked like a festival-goer, going to... perhaps the one in Grantville?

The woman smiled, the victim waved and removed the sack from her shoulders.

His headlights struck her and she blinked, a little startled, and raised a hand to shield her eyes.

The beast growled. His flesh tingled with goosebumps.

Selina ordered the taxi to stop the moment she saw the flashing blue lights. It was the place, she knew this without checking with the driver. She removed her Police ID from her pocket and flashed it before the scanner on the rear of the driver's seat. The door unlocked.

"Have a good one," the bearded, bald Armenian driver said, and she left the car with a '*Thank you*', stepping onto the sidewalk.

Three white and black prowl cars flanked her destination, pumping exhaust into the already smoggy air. The vehicles were lined across the sidewalk with two pairs of uniformed officers at either end. Past the uniforms she saw four drones at the entrance to an alley, a holographic red and white striped barrier flashing between their tall angular frames.

Selina paused on the sidewalk before the humans, showed her ID, then passed them to walk across concrete awash with the drones' illumination.

The drone took longer to register her ID. Its yellow, bowling ball shaped head turned an array of black sensors to her badge, scanning it before the barrier switched off. A few short steps later and she was past the drones and inside a slaughterhouse.

Wide but narrow, the alley terminated at a dead end. Blood was everywhere. It was black in the shadows, bright red in the drones' newly illuminated barrier. The stuff was spattered across the concrete walls, pooled on the cobbled floor. Shreds of clothing littered the floor like bloody rags, alongside red clumps of body tissue and the jagged white of smashed bone. The smell of death was thick, cloying, coppery but also sugar sweet.

Selina wasn't alone in the alley. Near its termination stood a tall, anthropomorphic fox dressed in a red velvet suit. Truly dapper, it had a purple kerchief in its pocket and held a slim wooden cane within its white, furry paws.

The fox turned, smiled a wide, toothy grin, and tapped the mono-grammed pocket near its left lapel.

The fox form flickered and disappeared, leaving a grey haired, middle-aged man in its place. The wrinkled grey suit he wore was quite a contrast. Detective Combs, she guessed, had been on educational duty when the call came in.

"A fox in a chicken coop comes to mind," she said, and gingerly stepped into the alley.

"Huh," Combs gave her a smile that resembled a grimace. "I was at a nearby Rec Centre ending up a presentation when this came in. You know, that damned initiative between the Mayor and the Captain. You?"

Selina sighed. "Out on a date. This is the same MO, I take it?" It was a silly question, the wall-to-wall blood made it obvious this was the third of what the media had dubbed the 'slaughterhouse murders.'

"Yeah absolutely positively." Combs waved his arms expansively. "This vic must be in a hundred different pieces."

The sound of footsteps made Selina turn and she saw two people dressed from head to toe in white approaching past the drones. Even their faces were concealed, except for the eyeholes.

They paused and the one to the left, a woman by her stature and build, said in an electronically enhanced voice. "Great, just great. You fuckers have contaminated this area all to hell, you know."

Her companion sniggered.

Selina's friend said, "Doubt it. And anyway, it's all yours now."

The CSIs' gazes followed them as they passed the barriers and the uniformed police. She felt like giving them the finger, but didn't.

Combs said, "My car is just over here if you need a ride."

"Sure thing," Selina answered and sighed. "But I should come back to the precinct and write this up with you."

"Leave that to me, really," her partner said and patted her shoulder. Combs was a good man, a thirty year Homicide veteran. She couldn't wish for a better partner.

They reached the sidewalk opposite the alley and encountered a crowd of look-e-loos gawking at the scene.

"God damned parasites," Combs exclaimed and shoved a path through them.

Selina followed his route, ignoring the disgruntled voices of the crowd. Beyond them, parked on a street corner, was Combs's metallic red Mustang, a big, garish, immaculate car that was her partner's pride and joy.

She thought of home, and bed, and smiled.

He still had blood under his fingernails, even after licking them clean. The last prey, oh she'd been a riot, and he'd left her a bloody mess.

The beginnings of an erection formed just imagining her screams.

And here he was again on Highway 72, his current hunting ground at least until the police announced the latest victim's name and he was forced to relocate.

The beast usually left him alone for a month or so after a kill, yet tonight he had felt the urge again, too strong to resist. Howling, scratching at his insides, wild, feral. Why was the beast so hungry? Not that he minded, because he'd found her straight away. The perfect victim. Thin, short, dark hair, backpacks at her feet as she held up her thumb enthusiastically.

Oh god baby I'm gonna eat you alive. His mouth salivated. He pulled up beside her and climbed from the car, all smiles, just a normal Good Samaritan.

"Hey man, thanks," she said. Her voice held a slight accent, one he didn't recognize. As he walked around the car he saw that she was possibly half Mexican or something.

She was pretty, small and delicate. He imagined snapping her bones as he paused before his trunk.

"You can put your things in here," he said. "Oh, and where are you heading?"

"As north as you'll take me," she said with a smile. "I was wondering though, could you take us both?"

A man appeared, formerly concealed behind the bushes to her right. He had a big grin on his face. Chunky build, long red hair, freckled, he walked to his companion and began picking up her, their bags.

The trunk was halfway open and his hands shook as he slammed it down. No, not this way, it doesn't work this way.

"Hey hold up," the redhead said, his accent was British.

By the time he reached the car door the shaking in his hands had filled the rest of his body. The beast was filling him out, replacing his anger with raw, bestial strength.

Not here, not now.

"Hey mate, what the hell's your problem?" The redhead rushed round the front of the car, put his hand on the bonnet. With the other hand he pointed. "Look you've got a big enough motor, haven't you? You can take my girlfriend and me. Hey, can't he, Sally?"

"Don't point at me," he said quietly, teeth gritted.

"Yeah, well, fuck you. God damned pervert!"

All he could see was the finger, pointing, accusing. It filled his vision. He saw red.

The redhead was no longer pointing, for the offending finger had been snapped backwards, sending the big man to the ground, whining like a child.

The man's companion screamed, began running towards her downed companion when one look at him froze her in her tracks. He licked his lips and thought of all the terrible things he could inflict upon her delicate frame. Before getting in the car, he kicked the redhead in the face, bursting his nose on his boot.

She awoke just after 7:00 AM, showered, dressed for work, and less than an hour later was on her way to the precinct. At 8:15 AM she arrived at the squad room, the open plan area already a hive of noise and activity. Her fellow Homicide detectives were sat talking into their computers or earpieces as uniforms walked around them. Combs's desk, facing hers, was empty, and it wasn't like him to be late. She made herself a coffee, greeted some colleagues, and sat down to deal with her accumulated paperwork.

Selina's department earpiece trilled; she retrieved it from under some files and fitted it into her ear. "Hello?"

"Heya girl, it's Müller!"

Müller, the Assistant Coroner, Selina cringed. "Yeah, what can I do to help you?"

"You sound frowny, can I turn that frown upside down?"

Selina looked around in embarrassment. Of course, no one else could hear them.

"Müller, it's early. What-"

"Oops sorry, is your partner with you?" Müller asked.

"No, not yet," Selina replied, her mood growing worse due to the interruption.

"I'd like to talk to both of you, set up a VR meeting, if possible. This is rather important."

Selina sighed. "Okay, give me a minute." She tapped her wristwatch and a small floating screen appeared above its face. A couple of taps brought a virtual keypad up and she dialled Combs's number. A few seconds later, he replied.

"Selina, I'm sorry. Traffic is deadlocked and I'm trapped right in the middle of it."

Her partner sounded harried. "That's alright, Combs. But I have Müller on my earpiece and she wants to talk. Can you access the VR interface through your car?"

"Uh, hold on. I got the lead here somewhere."

There was quiet, then the sound of fumbling, Combs searching through a glove compartment Selina knew from experience was filled to capacity. She took the opportunity to swallow some coffee, and he returned.

"Ready, I'm plugging myself in now," he said.

"You hear that, Müller?" Selina asked. "I'll just interface while you create an environment."

"Ready," Müller said.

Selina opened a desk drawer and removed and untangled a slim white lead. She proceeded to plug one end into the port behind her ear and the other into her department computer. "Ready," she said.

"Bump," Combs added from her wristwatch.

Selina's view of the squad room pixelated, turned white, and she was in Müller's VR office. The virtual room was large, square, and lined with wall-to-wall metallic freezer drawers, the ceiling and floor plain white. Müller stood at the room's centre, smiling and arms folded. She'd given herself the avatar of a petite, Japanese Goth girl, her thick black hair in huge pigtails. Beneath her white lab coat, Selina saw striped black and purple tights and transparent nine-inch heels.

Her own avatar, she knew without looking down, was nothing extravagant, just her in a nondescript black suit.

"No Combs?" Müller asked and put a black lace glove to her chin, tilting her head. "Just us girls, eh?" She winked an eye heavy with mascara.

To Selina's relief, Combs materialized to her right, wearing his fox avatar. He grinned toothily and greeted them both.

"We succeeded in IDing the girl," Müller said, looking a little disgruntled, "She's called Veronica Flint." She raised a hand and tapped thin air, which brought up a 3D head and shoulder image of a pale woman with blonde hair styled into dreadlocks. "Aged twenty-four, unemployed, but that's not all. I put her image in the Citycam program and found her hitchhiking along Highway 72 two nights ago. She was picked up by a car."

Selina stared at the victim's face and thought, What a terrible waste. The poor girl.

"This could be the break we're looking for!" Fox Combs said with enthusiasm. "Got the driver's ID?"

Müller grinned widely, revealing teeth braces lined with little jewelled skulls. "I got the ID, I got his name and his address."

"Well give us them, already," Combs asked.

"No 'good job,' 'nice work,' or anything?" Müller stamped her foot crossly.

Selina broke in with, "I'll give you a pat on the back when we return to the precinct, I swear."

"DEAL!" Müller cried. "The possible perp's name is Randal Harsh. He lives at 872 Belvedere Square."

"Thanks Müller, and good job," Combs said.

Müller squealed excitedly then signed off. The room disappeared and Selina found herself back at her desk.

"That woman is nuts," Combs said from her watch. "But the traffic's clearing up so I'll be at the precinct in ten."

"How about we just meet at the potential perp's?"

"That'll work. Car, directions to Belvedere Square," he said, then, "You know Müller has a crush on you."

She pictured his grin and snapped, "Just don't go there, alright,"

Laughter issued from her watch followed with, "Sorry. I just won't go there."

A few words were needed with the Captain before she left, and Selina told her what had transpired with Müller. Captain Quartaroli, a tall Hispanic woman with half her face heavily scarred from an incident no-one liked to talk about, told Selina to run with it. Like Combs, she used her car's GPS to direct her to Belvedere Square, the windscreen on her Honda 'Hifit' acting as a screen, providing overlaid dots to follow on the streets of downtown Central City. Belvedere Square was located in Upper Westside, so when she reached Little China she knew she didn't have far to go.

"Potential for medium to heavy traffic, diverting your route," the GPS said in its generic, well spoken female voice, and the overlay changed from a left turn to straight ahead. Curious as to what had changed the GPS's mind Selina examined the street as she passed. Traffic was building up along the street of Chinese pagoda style stores, and at its end she saw a dragon avatar, gaudy pink and hissing smoke as Chinese girls danced around it.

Selina wondered if the parade had hindered Combs earlier, and continued following her route.

Ten minutes later she arrived at Belvedere Square. It was an area that had probably been well to do in earlier years, but now looked a little too lived in, the park at its centre not much more than wasteland. She spotted Combs across the street from the park, sat slouched against his car. Finding a parking spot opposite him, she pulled in, locked the car and approached. Combs had his watch raised and was tapping away on the virtual screen. He switched it off as she stopped before him.

"This guy has no priors," he said, "And that's his car parked up over there."

"What floor is he on?" Selina asked.

"Fifth," Combs replied. "I hope they have a working elevator, my knees are playing up today."

Selina recalled the time Combs had fallen while chasing a perp. He'd limped for a week after that incident.

They left the street and followed the sidewalk to 872. The building was a tall, narrow apartment block, blue like those surrounding it and covered in satellite dishes with a few solar panels dotted here and there.

"Have you thought about getting surgery on your knees?" she said.

"Heh no, I pride myself in having nothing artificial but my teeth," he replied, taking the stairs to the building. "Plus I don't really know if my insurance would cover it."

Rather than try and buzz them in, Combs used his portable scanner to bypass the security. Seconds later they were in the building and stepping down a musty smelling, cream-walled corridor lined with doors and tacky art. The blue tiled carpet felt sticky underfoot, the fluorescent light fittings providing coffins for dead bugs.

The seediness of the place weighed on Selina, made her think they might have found their man. An elevator stood at the corridor's termination, to the right of a stairwell. It proved not only functional, but fast, and quickly brought the pair to the fifth floor.

"Well here goes," Combs said and stepped out first. The fifth floor looked as squalid as the first, Harsh's apartment door the first one to their right. Combs stood before it and knocked while Selina stood hidden to his left.

A minute of waiting brought no reply. Combs went to knock again and the noise of bolts being pulled stopped him.

The door opened and a voice said, "Who are you?"

Selina leant over and saw a man in striped blue boxers and a stained white vest. His face chubby and his head balding, his pale body was so hairy she experienced momentary disgust.

"Detective Combs and Alonzo," Combs replied. "Are you Randal Harsh? We'd like to ask you a few questions."

"Uh... yeah, but cops? Listen, right now isn't too convenient."

Selina moved in beside Combs and Harsh backed off a step. "This won't take long, sir. It's about the hitchhiker you picked up the night of the twelfth."

Harsh's face sank. If he was going to bolt, now would be the time. Instead, he said, "Oh, you better come in then."

They followed him inside and, despite the man's slovenly appearance, his apartment looked clean. It had a pair of black leather couches, various tall, metal lamps, and a black-carpeted floor. The yellow walls were covered in holographic images of recent sports stars, one wall holding a huge floor to ceiling TV screen. The screen depicted a baseball match frozen mid-action, and by the VR hardware on the floor beneath it, it appeared they'd interrupted him while playing.

"I can't believe this, you know," Harsh said, "I mean, I hardly touched her."

Selina shared a look with Combs and said, "Maybe you should start at the beginning?"

Harsh slumped onto one of the couches. He was visibly sweating.

"Okay, now this is how it went down. I picked the chick up, yeah? Drove for a bit, then, uh... you know, put my hand on her leg and asked her for a bit of fun while I drove."

Selina approached the couch and stood over him. "That was it? Then what happened?"

Harsh looked about ready to cry. "She gave me hell, got out and walked on."

Another look to Combs told her he believed the man; she did too, he was just that pitiful.

"Look I have an ex-wife and a kid I hardly see as it is. Am I gonna be charged?" Harsh put his head in his hands.

"No, not if you help us," Selina answered and smiled at Combs.

"Yes, sir," Combs added. "Did you see any other cars out there, anything that might have looked suspicious?"

Harsh looked up with eyes wet with tears. "There was something, yeah. A black convertible. I passed it twice. Once on my way to Los Indios, where my brother works, and once on the way back."

Combs approached the couch. "The same car. Are you sure?"

"Without a doubt," Harsh replied, "He was driving really slow."

They returned to the precinct with Combs trailing Selina's car, kept in touch along the way through their watches. Their talk was solemn, for the result from Harsh wasn't the one they'd hoped for, but the lead regarding the black car had Selina in contact with Traffic Control to check highway recordings from around that time. Traffic Control told her two hours, and she cursed them when she disconnected. She cursed some more until they reached the precinct, the pair heading up to Quartaroli's office with a request Selina thought the woman would refuse.

Their boss's office was spacious, bright, the back wall behind the blonde captain's cluttered steel desk bearing a floor to ceiling screen that currently displayed a fish tank screensaver.

They sat down, and Combs started talking.

"The lead was a bit of a bust, boss, but we have an idea about getting the bastard that did the deeds. We think this predator's using Highway 72 to catch his victims, and we want to set up a sting to catch him."

Quartaroli raised an eyebrow, an ugly look, coming from the side of her face melted like wax. The silver cybernetic eye didn't help. "It sounds dangerous. Selina?"

Selina was half looking at Quartaroli, half at the luminous jellyfish hunting across the screen behind her. She gave the Captain her full attention, and mused how beautiful the woman would look without the scar.

"It could be a viable lead, boss," she said, "And we're not looking for any extra manpower."

"Hmmm, but that's the thing isn't it, Selina? You're putting yourself on the line so extra manpower would be a boon. But just you and the old man..." she waved dismissively at Combs. "I dunno."

Seeing that they were losing the Captain, Selina said, "I've been on to Traffic Control to try and identify the car. That's another way we could get hold of him."

"Traffic Control, huh?" Quartaroli touched her wristwatch, a screen animated, and she tapped a number. "Captain Quartaroli of Homicide. One of my detectives contacted you about IDing a car?"

Quartaroli had security settings on her call, so what followed, only the Captain could hear.

"No, not good enough. I want it now."

Quartaroli smiled at Selina and Combs, then, "Oh right. No way. Okay then thank you."

She cut the connection and leaned back, placing her hands behind her head. "God give me strength! They found a black car driving that night, and last night. The driver has false plates, and some kind of scrambler fitted in his windows so his face was blurred. It's a black Chevy, as if that's any use."

Combs cleared his throat and said, "Boss, let us do this."

She turned to him and pursed her lips. "Okay, but you watch out for her, okay?"

Selina looked to Combs, then the Captain. "Boss, I trust him to look out for me."

Quartaroli turned a silver eye on her. "Okay but you keep in full contact with him, and the precinct, at all times. I'll also authorize a special prowl car and drones for the old man here." Her words about

Combs's age were said in jest, they had been married once, after all. "And happy hunting. I want that scumbag booked or cooked."

They thanked Quartaroli and left the office, Selina noticing that Combs bore a little more of a spring in his step than earlier.

"You're still into her aren't you?"

Combs grimaced and replied, "Just don't go there, Alonzo."

In a past life, he'd worked as a cyber warfare specialist, spying on battle plans, hacking into the brains of insurgent leaders in Uzbekistan. At some point, someone in that war-torn hellhole had infected him, passed on the beast, the need.

Trapped between sleep and waking, he fought bed sheets sodden with sweat. A clump of sheet was stuck in his mouth, and he gagged and worried at it alternately. He dreamt of tearing flesh asunder, feeling hot blood spray his mouth and body. He was also struggling, struggling to break free from his frail human body, but his flesh kept him trapped. With an effort, he pulled himself from the dream, spat out the saliva soaked sheet, and tossed the rest of the bedding aside to lay panting on his bed.

It was dark outside, so he'd slept all day, again. This wasn't a problem. The dream had enticed him, teased him, showing him the beast's freedom. The last time he'd hunted had ended in abject failure. He couldn't go through that again.

"I'll set you free tonight I swear," he said, his voice hoarse and his mouth so dry he felt swallowing would make him scream. The shadows on the ceiling teased him as much as the dream had, the nebulous shapes forming the faces of victims past and future.

"It's time," he said, and swallowed, relishing the lump of pain falling down his throat.

Nervous wasn't the word for it. It was more like... anticipation mingled with a little fear. Combs had dropped her off fifteen minutes earlier, and two cars, neither black, had already passed her. Selina was expecting, at any time, that certain car to pull up and invite her inside.

It was late, just after 12.30 am. She'd been home already, slept a few hours, then Combs had picked her up in the prowl car. They'd shared a flask of strong black coffee on their way to the highway while he poked fun at her appearance. She'd given herself a teenaged girl's avatar, projected by the button-sized devices attached to her real clothes. Pink hair in bunches, her fake form was dressed in a purple leather jacket and tight black spandex pants. The jacket had a hologram on its rear displaying an animated sailing ship on rough waters. She would stand out, which was the plan.

It had taken the highway's cold night air to finally push the cobwebs from her mind; whereas her partner had been bright eyed and jolly from the get go. Combs was happy just to be out on the field in a prowl car with optical camouflage. He was out there now, somewhere to her right, watching.

They had to find him. If they didn't catch the perp tonight they'd have to share their information with the press and he'd find somewhere else to hunt.

She walked for another five minutes across the bare earth flanking the highway, then turned to start heading in the other direction. Then, she saw the car, a large black Chevy, heading her way from the city.

"Combs," she whispered into her ear mike, "I have something. It's got to be him."

"I see it. Now play it cool Selina, the drones are a few metres from you and I'm ready to go at your word."

Selina looked right, saw nothing on the shadowy embankment, but trusted the camouflaged drones were somewhere nearby. She began walking left across the highway with her arm and thumb raised.

She had his attention, for right away the driver increased his speed to reach her, then pulled up in the middle of the highway.

"Damn, he's keen," she said.

The driver unwound his window as she approached. He was muscular, with a nondescript face and short brown hair. Wearing a black shirt with the sleeves rolled up, he had a military tattoo on his visible arm - a digitised skull and crossbones with the words 'Cybernet Glory' set in a scroll beneath.

He gave her a smile that didn't reach his eyes and said, "You need a lift?"

"No doubt," she replied in a voice she hoped made her sound like a teenager, then walked around the car to climb in the side door. "My boyfriend and I had a row and he just dumped me here. Can you believe it? I just wanna get back to Los Indios and give him hell."

She felt sure this was the one, and not just because of the car or the darkness in his eyes that lingered too long on her before he started down the highway.

"So, late to be out, huh?" she asked.

"Huh," he said in reply.

Not a talker, I get it. "Wouldn't it be easier for you to put the car on auto drive?" she asked, hoping for more of a response. *Combs, I hope you're nearby.*

The driver closer his eyes for a few moments, swallowed loudly, then replied, "Wouldn't it be easier for a little slut like you to just SHUT THE FUCK UP?"

Selina flinched at his rage. She squirmed towards her door, reaching for the handle.

"Oh no you don't," the man said and she heard the door lock click.

"Listen you're-" she'd been about to say 'under arrest,' but his fist, slamming into her face, put paid to that and knocked her unconscious.

Selina awoke laid on a hard, lumpy surface with the taste of blood in her mouth. She opened her eyes, saw a cloudy sky spotted with stars, lifted her head a little and found herself surrounded by trees. Her attacker was nowhere to be seen. The side of her face throbbed where she'd been punched, and raising her hand, she touched it gingerly. The inside of her mouth was lacerated, but slivering her tongue around proved that no teeth were broken.

Where the hell am I, though? She sat up, climbed to her knees and looked around. There was no visibility beyond the trees, Selina guessing her attacker had driven somewhere and dumped her.

So he's not here, and my backup isn't here... thanks Combs.

Her earpiece was gone, and lifting her left arm, she went to check her watch and stared in confusion.

The watch face was smashed, but what worried her more was that instead of her leather jacket, she wore a grey sleeve. The material was rough wool, and further examination connected it to a long dress, her legs bare beneath with red velvet slipper shoes on her feet.

The crazy bastard removed my avatar, undressed me and put me in this? The thought increased her worry as she rose unsteadily to her feet. She also found that atop the dress, she was wearing a long, red, hooded cloak.

My gun's gone, too. Damn... I have no weapon to speak of.

A quick search of the clearing presented no scattered branches large enough to use as a club, and feeling confused, and vulnerable, she entered the woods hoping she'd find some sign of civilisation. Her feet clumped through thick undergrowth, crunchy in some places and wet in others. The air was warm, clammy, stinking of soil and rot, the looming tree branches blocking out the sky except for the odd glimpse of tiny, distant stars.

Combs? Damn where are you? I'm alone here and I need you.

A sound of crunching, louder than her own footsteps, made Selina freeze mid-step.

Behind me, there it is again: slow, stealthy movements.

She turned, slowly, her breath held in her throat as she prepared to face...

One glimpse of the hulking shadow sent her running, trying her hardest not to trip as the shadow pounded through the woods like some huge jungle behemoth.

Its monstrous breathing was so loud it drowned her own panicked breaths, but not the sound of its stamping feet. Unused to such exertion, her legs started to weaken. The breathing got louder and she smelled the fetid, meaty breath of the thing pursuing her. She was doomed; it was going to catch her.

Then the trees cleared and she encountered a house, stood alone in a clearing like the one she had so recently departed. The building looked ancient, its pointed, black tiled roof bearing a smoking chimney and white plaster walls framed in zigzags of wood. Two windows smothered in pink flowers flanked a large wooden door, above which stood a circular window between the roof's inverted 'v.' Selina didn't stop to question this archaic vision, but instead used her last reserves of energy to charge towards the door, praying it was unlocked. It was, and when she got inside she slammed the door and found bolts to push that felt slippery beneath her sweaty grip.

"What the hell is out there?" She leaned against the door, her body perspiring from the exertion. Her shoes were gone, lost in the escape, and she stared down at mucky, numb feet atop varnished wooden boards. The shadowy room around her was like something from a kid's fairytale, the walls and ceiling formed from thick-varnished wooden beams. There was a roaring fireplace against the right wall, the fireplace and chimney hewn from chalky blue stone. The room's heat was oppressive, and all she wanted was to cool down. An oil painting hung from the chimney wall, depicting a young boy with long blonde hair, dressed in a yellow and blue outfit from an era she didn't recognize. In his hands he held a rifle or shotgun with a huge metal barrel.

A weapon! She headed towards the fireplace and braced herself against the heat. A sheen of sweat formed on her arm as she removed the dark metal poker suspended beside the painting. She hefted it in her hand. Not bad, for a start but...

Selina looked to the door and windows. The thing wasn't pursuing her, for now.

Searching the shadows, she found a cupboard in a corner near the door. Inside it were plates, some cutlery, and knives too blunt and small to be of any use.

The wall opposite the front door held another door, and to its right Selina encountered a device on a low table, something she recognized as a media player from the previous century. A wooden box with a piece of circular black plastic atop it, it had a metal trumpet for sound amplification. Interesting, but no use against whatever lurked outside. She tried the new door and found it locked.

Damn!

Selina gave the door handle another shake, then flinched as a massive vibration rocked the room. She turned, brandishing the poker. The room, no the house, shook again as something huge bounced against the front door, warping the wood with its force. A third jolt shook the house and the media player came to life.

Who's afraid of the big bad wolf?
The big bad wolf, the big bad wolf,
Who's afraid of the big bad wolf?
Tra la la la la

The sound was scratchy, the female voice melodic. A second chorus started and Selina hissed, whacking the player with the poker to kill the sound.

She turned from the trashed machine to the door, spread her legs and braced herself for the attack. Whatever was waiting outside for her, she wasn't going out without a fight.

Silence followed. Selina looked from the door to the tiny windows flanking it. Her hand grew slick holding the poker. She was on the cusp of breathing easier when a sudden explosion of sound and violence threw her across the room.

"Ow!" She landed face down on the floor. Bruised and riddled in splinters, she moaned and rolled over to face whatever had burst through the door behind her.

No...

The gasp of horror remained trapped in her throat as the massive hulk of black fur squeezed through the remnants of a thick wooden door smashed to kindling.

The beast bore a wolf form turned biped. Huge and muscular, its fur-smothered arms ended in taloned paws. It smelled of raw meat and damp fur. That brutally canine face, those huge yellow eyes... the beast's mouth was crammed with fangs like ivory knives. The mouth grinned and a growl vibrated through the room.

Selina was frozen to the spot. The unnatural creature filled her vision. Its eyes filled with bloodlust, the beast's mouth salivated. The growl ceased, and the horror attacked.

Lacerations tore through her chest, her shocked scream transforming into a pitiful wail that was snuffed as something hard smashed against her face.

I'm going to die here.

"Selina!"

As if from a great distance, she heard Combs's voice. All she could do, however, was struggle and cry as the black beast overwhelmed her, and suddenly, reality shifted.

The house pixelated, wavered, then disappeared, and Selina found herself curled up in the open boot of a car. Her chest was on fire, and touching it she found it wet with blood. A shape loomed over her, and the man from the car blotted out the night sky. Then he crumpled, and Combs replaced him, white-faced and clutching his own lacerated, bloody chest.

Her partner stumbled, almost fell forward, then stopped himself. Selina couldn't move to help him for her pain.

Combs groaned through gritted teeth and said, "He gave me a merry chase... his car has some kind of dampener that interfered with the drones. I found him plugged into you Selina. Stood there with knives ready to tear you up."

"Uh... ow." She bit her lip and swallowed the pain. "It was all VR?"

"Right till the end. He hacked your vision and inserted an environment. Listen, the drones tasered him, but he got me good."

Despite the hellish agony in her gut, Selina raised herself, holding her stomach. The blood poured as she moved.

"Stay still," Combs said, "An ambulance is coming."

"It's okay... I just... Just want to see the asshole."

Combs's chest dripped crimson, but he was still standing, which was more than could be said for the perp at his feet.

The man lay motionless, his hands at his sides. He had makeshift claws attached to his fingers, big surgical blades red with blood. A yellow lead lay beside his unconscious face, Selina guessing it had only recently been interfaced with her.

Combs looked up, "I see flashing lights. Here comes the cavalry."

"Promise me Combs, uh..." Selina climbed to her knees with difficulty. By the way the wetness pooled around her legs, she guessed her blood loss was massive. "Promise me this pain is only fake, that it's all just virtual."

"Heh." Combs leaned over and touched her shoulder. "We'll leave that for the robot medics to decide."

Selina reached up, clasped his hand.

Combs gripped back tightly. "You did good, partner," he said. "Now let's put this bastard away."

Blood and Bone

Blood and Bone
by
Tim Waggoner

KATY HOFFMAN glanced at the dashboard clock, saw that it was 8:52, and then smacked a hand on the steering wheel.

"Damn it!"

She wasn't normally an aggressive driver. She never drove faster than five miles above the limit, and then only when she felt she needed to match the speed of traffic. She always came to a full and complete stop at intersections, and she always signaled before turning or changing lanes. She never cut people off, and she never rode anyone's bumper. She didn't blow her horn at slow drivers ahead of her, and she didn't give the middle finger to those drivers who irritated her.

But this wasn't an ordinary morning. Today was her annual performance review with her supervisor, that all-time, grade-A, number-one bitch, Shannon Fuentes. She'd been up most of the night worrying about it before finally falling asleep close to dawn. She'd been so exhausted that when her alarm went off, she hit snooze and fell back to sleep. Now she was going to be late - big-time.

She was driving behind a Ford pickup with a bumper sticker for a Presidential candidate from two elections ago, and while the vehicle wasn't going all *that* slow, she pushed down hard on the gas pedal and yanked her steering wheel to the left. She pulled into the lane for on-coming traffic - which at that precise moment was empty of cars - and surged forward. Despite herself, she felt a heady rush of excitement as she drew even with the other driver, and she couldn't help taking a quick glance to see what his or her reaction would be. A bald, middle-aged man with glasses and a neat soul patch turned to look at her, his features twisting into a savage mask of hatred. He bared teeth that were yellowed, overlarge, and very, very sharp.

Her excitement gave way to fear, and without realizing that she was doing so, she eased her foot off the gas. Instead of passing the pickup, she remained alongside it, unable to take her eyes off the man's bestial teeth. Stubble erupted on his bald head, as well as his cheeks and chin. As she watched, grayish-black hair sprouted in thick tufts from his flesh. No, not hair. *Fur.* His neck thickened and his shoulders broadened, straining the fabric of his shirt. The hands on the steering wheel became larger and thick-fingered, and black claws extended from the fingertips. His features became animalistic - eyes feral-yellow, nose black and squarish, ears pointed and set farther back on the head - but rather than favoring one animal in particular, they were a blend of several. Canine, feline, ursine, porcine, anthropoid... She saw all of these and more in the creature's furred-and-fanged countenance. There was only one word which could describe what he had become: *Beast.*

He snarled and snapped at her, foam flecking his lips and splattering the inside of his driver's side window.

Ignore him, she told herself. *You're late. Pass him!*

Her own teeth began to ache at the roots, and her hands tightened on the steering wheel. Her skin tingled and itched.

Go, go, go!

She felt her teeth begin to sharpen and ran her tongue across their developing points. The tingling sensation on her skin intensified until it felt as if she were burning. Her fingers felt as if hot needles had been slid into the soft flesh beneath the nails, and she felt her claws begin to emerge. She was almost there. All she had to do was let go...

A loud horn blast startled her, and she whipped her head around to face forward. Framed in the windshield, an SUV flicked its lights and honked its horn as the two vehicles drew rapidly toward collision.

She had only a split second left to make a decision. She could slam the gas pedal to the floor and attempt to cut in front of the pickup before the SUV smashed into her or she could remove her foot from the gas, press down on the brake, and pull in behind the pickup. She could feel the Wild inside her, roiling with turbulent force, urging her on, shrieking at her to jam the gas pedal to the floor.

But she lifted her foot and pulled the steering wheel hard to the right. Her Acura slipped in behind the pickup as the SUV roared by, its driver holding a fur-covered hand out the open window, clawed middle finger raised skyward.

Heart pounding and cold sweat on her smooth, hairless skin, she looked forward and saw the driver of the pickup looking at her in his rearview mirror. His eyes blazed with triumph and his lips were stretched back, revealing his sharp teeth in a cruel grin.

Katy ground the flat surfaces of her teeth in frustration and self-loathing. She reminded herself that drivers were supposed to leave one car space between their vehicle and the one in front for every ten miles an hour they were traveling. Hating herself, she eased off the gas and dropped back.

"What is *this?*"

Katy was four, and her father held a square piece of white cardboard that she had drawn on in crayon. In the center were simple renditions of an anatomically correct naked man and woman surrounded by a menagerie: exotic animals like lions, tigers, elephants, giraffes, zebras, and penguins, mostly, but there were several puppies and kittens thrown in for good measure, along with a single lopsided bird that was supposed to be a duck but which looked more like a seagull with a severe thyroid disorder.

"Nothing," she said. She tried to look innocent, but she could feel her cheeks burn with shame. Before her father had entered her bedroom, she'd pulled one of her dresser drawers partway open and used it to prop up the picture, creating a simple makeshift shrine. Then she'd paced in a circle on front of the dresser, whispering, "Please, please, please," over and over, as she prayed to God to turn back time so that she - and everyone she loved, like her mother and father, her Gram-Gram, and Jenny across the street - could live naked and free in a beautiful garden paradise with all sorts of animals as friends.

Her father - a skinny bespectacled man in a light blue shirt and dark blue slacks - pointed to the picture of Eve, specifically to her breasts, which Katy had drawn with prominent brown nipples. He pointed to them.

"And what are these?" he demanded.

She gave the first answer that popped into her head.

"Buttons."

Father frowned. His eyes edged toward yellow, and the stubble on his face grew darker.

He pointed to the woman's vagina, his fingernail growing larger, sharper.

"And this?"

"Another button."

He stared at her for several moments, and she met his gaze for as long as she could, lower lip quivering, but in the end she lowered her head.

"Why did you do this?"

Father's voice was stern, but there was an underlying softness to it that indicated a certain amount of understanding, even pity.

She gazed at the floor as she answered.

"I wanted everything to go back to the way it was. When we were free and happy."

Father looked at her a moment longer before sighing and putting the drawing back on the dresser.

"There's a reason we left the Wild," he said. "It wasn't Paradise. Life was hard, cruel, and all too often short. Things are better now, sweetie. Try to remember that."

He bent down and kissed her on the top of her head, and then he gently touched his claws to her cheek before turning and leaving the room.

Katy looked at the picture she'd drawn. The man and woman were now covered with fur, and their teeth and claws dripped red. The animals around them had been slaughtered, torn to bloody pieces.

She wept.

By the time she reached the office, it was 9:17. Her meeting with Shannon had been scheduled for 9:00 sharp. She parked a little too close to an Accord, the driver still behind the wheel, talking on her phone. She snarled at Katy as she got out of her car, and Katy lowered her head and hurried across the parking lot toward the building. She kept her gaze focused on her feet as she went inside and stood in front of the elevator. She pressed the UP button, finger hairless, nail short and neatly trimmed. She stood quietly while she waited for the elevator to arrive, doing her best to contain her anxiety. Shannon already had it in for her, and the last thing she wanted to do was compound her lateness by showing weakness in front of the woman. So she concentrated on keeping her body still, her expression calm. But she couldn't keep her right foot from tap-tap-tapping impatiently on the tiled floor as she waited.

"Nervous?"

She turned, startled. Rick Hoskins stood next to her, smiling, although his eyes were cold and glittering. Rick worked for the same company she did but in another department. A better department. He wasn't particularly impressive-looking - a pudgy man with ruddy features and thinning black hair, dressed in an ill-fitting gray suit - but he exuded an aura of strength and confidence. Katy figured he could probably give Shannon some competition if he wanted.

She became aware of her tapping foot then, and she stopped it.

"A little," she admitted, not quite meeting his eyes. "I have my performance review this morning."

"With Shannon, right? She's a real ball-buster. Or in your case, an ovary-buster." He let out a bark of a laugh, revealing canine teeth that were a bit too long and too sharp. A sly look came into his eyes then. "Shannon and I have always gotten along pretty well. We have... history."

A musky scent filled the air then, a mingled odor of heat, sweat, and lust. Rick continued talking, his teeth a little sharper, face and hands a little hairier.

"I'd be happy to put in a good word for you with her." His eyes glinted and a thin line of drool ran from the corner of his mouth. "That is, if you're willing to do a little something for me."

She saw the erection straining against his pants, and she knew exactly what he wanted.

Before she could answer, the elevator dinged as it arrived. Relieved, she turned away from Rick and got on before the doors had finished sliding all the way apart. She pressed the button for the third floor, and then stepped back until she was pressed against the rear of the elevator, as if she wanted to put as much distance as possible between herself and Rick. She thought he might step onto the elevator, too, but although he walked up to the edge of it, he didn't get on. His lips stretched into a mocking sharp-toothed smile. It was the way a shark might smile, she thought.

"Think it over," he said. "You and I could do a lot of good for each other."

The musk-stink increased and drifted into the elevator car until it seemed to fill the enclosed space. She felt stifled, and she took shallow breaths to avoid breathing in any more of the rank odor than she had to.

The elevator doors hadn't closed yet, and she pushed the third-floor button several more times, each jab faster and stronger than the last.

Rick's smile stretched into a wide grin that held no mirth, only hunger. More than that, there was a certainty to that grin, one that said he was confident she would accept what he no doubt viewed as a more-than-generous offer. And why not? He considered her beneath him, in so many ways. Why wouldn't she leap at the chance to have someone of his status and influence as her benefactor?

The doors finally began to close, but obeying a sudden impulse, Katy lunged forward and put out clawed hands to stop them. She glared at Rick with yellow-tinted eyes, and her lips curled back from predator's teeth.

"Fuck off," she said in a low, rough voice, her words more growled than spoken.

His grin didn't falter, but his eyes became ice shards.

"You're going to regret this," he said, low and dangerous.

She let go of the doors and they finished closing, shutting out the sight of Rick's toothy grin and cold, furious gaze.

There was a jarring jolt, and the elevator finally began to rise. Katy let out a relieved gust of breath, but she followed this with a loud cry - no, a *roar* - of frustration. The hair on her hands grew thicker, her claws more pronounced, and she slashed out at the elevator wall. She struck the wall again and again, and then moved on to raking her claws on the other walls as well. If anyone had been monitoring the security feed from the elevator camera, they would've seen a beast spitting and snarling as she whirled around, arms swinging wildly, claws cutting criss-crossing furrows into the elevator's walls. But when the elevator juddered to a halt and the doors slid open, Katy stood there, face and hands normal once more, hair mussed, clothes disheveled and soaked with sweat. Trembling, she stepped off the elevator and did not look behind her at the damage she had done.

Katy, fifteen, ran into the house, dropped her backpack to the floor, and pounded up the stairs. Tears streamed down her face, making her vision a watery blur. She threw open her bedroom door, slammed it closed behind her, and then ran to the bed and collapsed on it. She buried her face in her pillow and sobbed.

A few moments later there was a soft knocking and then the door opened.

"Katy? What's wrong?"

She didn't take her face out of her pillow, and her voice was muffled as she answered her mother.

"Nothing."

It was a stupid answer, one she knew would do nothing to deter Mother. She was sobbing too loudly to hear her mother cross the room, but she felt her sit down beside her. An instant later, she felt gentle fingers begin to stroke her hair.

Shame burned in Katy, and she wanted to do nothing more than lie there and cry. But slowly, haltingly - with numerous pauses to break into sobs - she spoke.

At first Mother continued to stroke her hair, but somewhere along the line she withdrew her hand. Katy sensed her mother's body tense, and she heard a low, almost inaudible growling that came from deep in her throat. Katy wasn't able to face her mother while she told her story, but when she finished, she rolled onto her side. She looked at Mother, trying to gauge her reaction. She hoped to see sympathy, kindness, understanding, and they were all there in her mother's expression. But she also saw shock, sadness, disappointment, and maybe disgust as well.

Mother was a lean, tall woman - taller than Katy's father - with dark red hair and a light, almost ivory complexion. She wore a white blouse and jeans, and while Katy wished she would hold her tight, she knew Mother could be a fastidious woman, and Katy figured she didn't want to get blood on that white blouse of hers. It was, after all, one of her favorites.

"Show me." Mother's voice was toneless, but it was clear that she wasn't asking.

Katy moved into a kneeling position on the mattress. She was wearing shorts, flip-flops, and a T-shirt with a picture of a boy band on the front. One of the boy's faces was obscured by a bloodstain. She took hold of her T-shirt's hem and pulled it up to expose an abdomen covered in deep scratches and ragged bite marks. She had similar marks on her back, legs, arms, breasts, and butt. She hoped Mother wasn't going to make her display those as well. She was embarrassed enough as it was.

Mother leaned closer to examine Katy's wounds, then she leaned back and gestured for her to lower her shirt.

Katy did so with a certain amount of relief, but then she saw that she'd gotten blood on her comforter where she'd been lying on it, and her shame deepened. A few bloodstains were nothing compared to what she'd been through, but the sight of them made her feel like breaking into a fresh round of sobbing. She managed to restrain herself, though, if only just.

She waited for her mother to speak again, but all she did was look at her, her expression unreadable. The silence was too much for Katy, and she started talking.

"I wanted to at first. I liked him. He was nice to me." She gingerly touched a dark wet spot on her T-shirt. "But he didn't stay that way."

"Did you try to stop him?"

Mother's question hit Katy like a punch to the stomach. She shouldn't have *had* to try to stop him.

Mother must've realized how her question sounds, for she added, "I mean, did you tell him that you were... uncomfortable with what was happening?"

"I..." She tried to come up with an excuse of some kind, too ashamed of the truth. But in the end, it was all she had. "No. I was scared."

Mother lunged toward her, her face a mask of fury. Amber eyes blazed from her fur-covered face, and white fangs gleamed in the light filtering in from Katy's bedroom window.

Katy let out a strangled cry and pulled back until she was pressed against the wall and could go no farther. Her pulse thrummed in her ears as her mother leaned her face closer, closer, until her black snout-like nose touched Katy's small, perfectly human one.

"Thought you'd like to take a walk on the wild side, eh?"

Mother's voice was guttural, bestial, and despite Katy's determination not to cry again, fresh tears began rolling down her face.

"Let me clue you in on something, my girl. There's only one God in this world, and that's Hunger. It's ever-ravenous and its belly can never be filled, no matter how much it eats. If you don't want to be food, you've got to get tough. You've got to *fight*. Do you understand?"

She didn't, not entirely, but she nodded anyway.

She could feel Mother's hot breath on her face, and she looked into those yellow eyes, and even though she was afraid right then, downright terrified, in fact, she thought she'd never seen a more magnificent Beast.

Fierce amber gave way to bright green, and Mother pulled back a couple inches - face hairless, teeth flat - and gently kissed Katy on the tip of her nose.

"Come on, let's get you cleaned up." Mother eyed Katy's shirt and then her comforter. "And then we'll do a load of laundry."

Despite being late, Katy ducked into the restroom to adjust her hair and clothes and splash cold water on her face. The latter didn't do much for her make-up, but she couldn't go into Shannon's office with sweat-slick skin. When she felt as composed as she was going to get, she left the restroom and headed down the hall toward Shannon's office. She avoided looking into any of the other offices as she passed. Her co-workers were doubtless aware that it was her time on the chopping block, and she didn't want to see their smirking faces. She felt their gazes upon her, though, and she imagined she heard them inhale deeply, as if they were scenting fresh meat.

Shannon's office door was closed, as usual. No open-door policy for her. There was nothing on the door's wooden surface to personalize it, either. No comic strip cut out of the newspaper, no amusing workplace-related meme printed out from the Internet... The only way to tell this office belonged to her was the small plastic sign on the wall next to the door which said, SHANNON FUENTES in white capital letters.

Katy hesitated in front of the door. She checked the hall clock. 9:28.

She took a deep breath, let it out slowly, then knocked.

Shannon didn't answer right away. She never did. Katy knew that she hated it when someone knocked twice, saw it as a sign of impatience bordering on rudeness. Still, there was a chance that she hadn't heard. After all, Katy hadn't knocked that loud. She raised her hand to knock again, and that's when Shannon opened the door.

"Good morning, Katy. Ready to sit down and chat?"

Shannon was a slender woman of medium height, but she possessed a striking, almost unearthly beauty coupled with a nearly overwhelming presence which made her seem much taller. She wore her glossy black hair long, and her makeup was minimal and applied with a steady, precise hand. Today she wore an expensive-looking crème-colored sweater pullover with a high collar that reached almost to her chin, and the hem stretched down to mid-thigh. Black tight-fitting slacks showed off her toned legs, and her brown leather boots were polished and free of any scuff marks. Katy wondered if she ever actually walked around in the things or if she wore them only in the office to preserve that purchased-just-this-morning look. She kept her accessories to a minimum. Katy supposed when you were that beautiful you didn't need to accessorize much. Today she wore pearl earrings, a gold necklace, and a copper bracelet around one wrist. No rings, as if she wanted to project an image that she was a woman who worked with her hands, though typing on a computer keyboard was as manual as her labor ever got.

"I guess so," Katy said.

She hated how unsure she sounded, but she always felt intimidated by Shannon.

Shannon smiled, her full lips parting slightly to reveal a white slash of teeth.

"Great! Come on in."

Shannon turned and walked to her desk, leaving Katy to close the door. Shannon sat and folded her hands on the desk's surface and - still smiling - waited for Katy to take the simple chair in front of her desk.

Shannon's office was large, one of the biggest in the building, with a window that provided a view of a green field and copse of trees beyond. Katy imagined being out there right now, running through the grass with bare feet, the wind in her face, the sky overhead, the trees calling to her, inviting her to come explore the mysteries concealed beneath their branches.

"Something on your mind?" Shannon asked.

Katy faced her and put on a smile that she hoped looked more sincere than it felt.

"Just admiring the view."

"It *is* lovely, isn't it? Does me more good than a dozen therapists." She paused and gave Katy a small smile. "I thought maybe you were thinking about Rick. His stink is all over you."

Katy tensed but didn't reply.

A manila folder containing a dozen or so papers sat on Shannon's desk. The woman opened it, took a pen from her middle desk drawer, and jotted something down on the top page of the file. *Katy's* file.

Katy tried to read what she'd written without being obvious about it, but Shannon's handwriting consisted of small cursive letters set close together, and Katy couldn't make it out. Probably something along the lines of *Katy is easily distracted at meetings - and she's a huge whore, too.*

Bitch.

Shannon's office was primarily utilitarian in design and décor. Desk, chairs, office phone, PC, printer, file cabinets... But there were a couple personal touches. A framed photo of her husband and three kids - all of whom were equally as gorgeous as she - hung on the wall, alongside a framed motivational poster that depicted a tiger shouldering its way through green jungle plants toward the viewer. Its eyes were a startling green - *Like Mother's*, Katy thought - and the caption below it was a single word: DETERMINATION.

Shannon finished writing and put the pen down beside the folder. She did not close it, though.

"Shall we begin?"

Katy inhaled deeply, and as she did so, she drew in the office's scents. Shannon's was predominant, of course. A raw, faintly vaginal tang that made Katy wrinkle her nose in disgust. But there were more: sour desperation, acrid resentment, burning rage... the residue of yesterday's performance reviews, Katy knew. She wondered what scents she'd be adding to the collection today.

"First off, let me remind you that this is a *review* process, not an evaluation. We're here to acknowledge your strengths as an integral member of our team and identify opportunities for performance enhancement. This is supposed to be a *positive* experience, so let's both do our best to make it one, all right?"

She fixed Katy with her overlarge eyes and widened her smile. Her teeth were sharper than they had been before, and tiny flecks of yellow tinted the chocolate brown of her eyes. Katy glanced at the woman's nails and saw they were growing longer and more pointed with each passing second.

She felt a growl building deep within her, but all that came out was a mumbled, "Sure."

"Great! So let's hit the positives first."

Shannon continued talking, but Katy paid less attention to her words than to her tone and body language. They revealed what Shannon truly thought about her.

You're pathetic. Weak. A waste of the company's time and resources.

She thought of the man in the pickup snarling at her as she'd attempted to pass him. She thought of Rick glaring at her as she got into the elevator. *You're going to regret this.*

She thought of her father's words. *There's a reason we left the Wild.*

Her mother's words. *If you don't want to be food, you've got to get tough. You've got to fight.*

"I think that about covers it," Shannon said. "Do you have any questions or anything that you'd like to add?"

"No, thank you."

Shannon nodded. Her eyes were almost completely yellow now, her ears tapered to points, and her cheeks and chin were covered with downy black hair.

"Good. Then let's move on to opportunities for performance enhancement. I think we should begin with your punctuality." Her smile widened. "Or rather, your lack thereof."

Shannon ran her tongue across her sharp teeth and her nostrils flared. Her eyes gleamed, and they spoke to Katy, their message clear.

I own you, bitch.

"No," Katy said softly. "You don't."

Shannon frowned. "What... "

With inhuman grace, Katy leaped out of her chair and landed in a crouching position on the desk in front of Shannon, She swiped her claws across the other woman's throat, and blood sprayed the air, splattering onto Katy's face and clothes. It was glorious.

Shannon attempted to fight back, but Katy lunged toward her. The two women fell to the floor and Katy straddled Shannon, pinning her down. She went to work in earnest then, employing her claws and teeth - *especially* her teeth - to maximum effect. When she was finished, the walls, floor, and ceiling dripped red, and what little of Shannon remained intact was unrecognizable as something that had once been a woman.

Katy looked down at Shannon's remains and licked a glob of blood from her lower lip.

"Good talk," she said.

She rose to her feet, bathed in crimson and feeling truly alive for the first time since she'd been born.

Father had been wrong. Maybe they had left the Wild, but it had never left them. There was no sign of the Beast on her at that moment, no outward one at any rate. But she knew from that point forward it would never be far from the surface.

She sat in Shannon's - no, *her* - seat. It felt good, but it needed to be cleaned, as did the rest of the office. She'd get someone in here to take care of it soon. She also needed to call HR and let them know she'd given herself a promotion. But first she needed to take a meeting.

She picked up the phone and entered the number for Rick's extension.

"Hey, Rick. This is Katy. Shannon would like you to stop by her office for a few minutes. She thinks you can provide some valuable perspective for my performance review." She paused, listening. "No, I don't know why she didn't call you herself. Now get your ass over here."

She hung up, sat back, and waited.

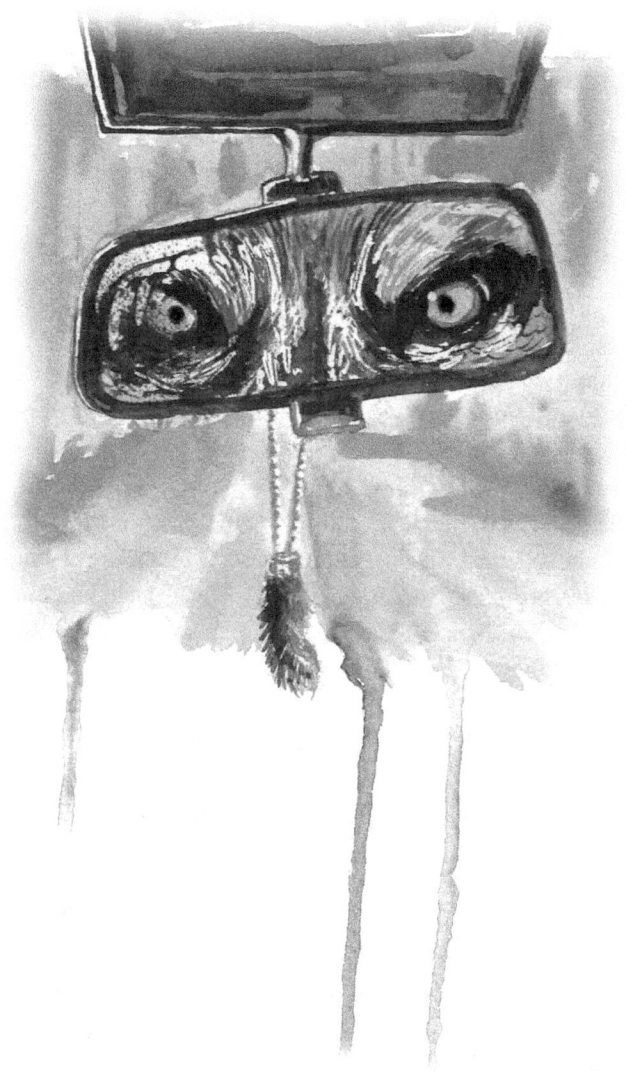

Bruce, Waking Up

Bruce, Waking Up
by
Paul McMahon

B RUCE SLID HIS FINGERS into the waistband of his briefs, trying to decide if he should strip completely. Dedrick hummed in the bathroom, the tune familiar, but Bruce was too preoccupied to place it. It reminded him of childhood, and that brought home just where he was and what he was about to do.

His face prickled, his heart pumped cold air against the inside of his skin. Tonight was the culmination of years of feeling broken and alone while his friends bragged about which girls they'd dated and how close to naked they'd been. Bruce always sat quietly, smiling when they smiled, laughing when they laughed, all the while feeling jealous of the girls they talked about.

He'd never told Mother any of this. She would be heartbroken, he was sure. Their relationship had been forged at Father's bedside, watching as he lost his long fight with stomach cancer. Since the funeral, Bruce had left Mother's side only to attend school and for the very occasional night out with his friends, and never, ever for a date.

Until tonight.

He'd tried so many times since graduation to talk with Mother about his orientation, but he hadn't been able to say the words. Finally, he decided to make absolutely sure. He told Mother he was going away with friends, then boarded a bus for New York City by himself. He got off in Castleton, Vermont to stretch his legs and search for a vending machine snack, met Dedrick, and never re-boarded.

Dedrick stopped humming for a second, then started up again. With a quick, decisive movement, Bruce stripped off his briefs.

Losing his virginity wouldn't be anything like he'd hoped it would be, nor likely anything he would want to remember come tomorrow, but it was too late now.

Dedrick, still humming, stepped into the room wearing a string bikini and a smile. An older man, gray hairs crouched amid the whiskers on his cheeks and lurked amid the thatch across his chest. His body was terrific, though, his stomach irresistibly flat and his legs perfectly defined. He tossed Bruce a bottle of baby oil. "Rub that on your hands."

Bruce snapped the cap and poured a generous puddle into his cupped palm. His dry skin slicked down immediately. He couldn't help but think about how the oil would feel being rubbed onto the rest of his body. His back, his chest... his penis. He imagined the hands doing the rubbing belonging to someone else, someone whose movements he wouldn't expect. Someone who could surprise him with a sudden erotic flick of the wrist.

He was getting hard. If felt wonderful, liberating. For the first time in his life he was naked with another man, and he knew he would be touched, caressed... loved.

"You are a thing of beauty," Dedrick said.

"Thank you. So are you."

He winced. Bad enough that Dedrick had picked him up at the bus station like a common hustler, now he sounded like a bashful virgin.

"Have you ever done this before?" Dedrick asked.

Bruce shook his head, feeling foolish.

Dedrick approached, stopped two feet away. His eyes seemed pale blue at the bus station, but here, close up, they were the color of steel. Bruce felt Dedrick's gaze glide over his body, head to foot and back again, lingering on his penis each way. "You almost make me sorry I didn't get my handcuffs."

Fear, like a shard of ice, pierced his heart. Suddenly Castleton, Vermont seemed like the farthest, darkest corner of the planet–

–and then Dedrick's hands touched his waist, warm, hot, Bruce never knew a person's hands could be so hot, and Bruce saw his own hands, slick with oil, sliding over Dedrick's shoulders as the man's body pressed against him, and it wasn't just his hands that were hot it was everything, all of him, even the lips pressing against his mouth, forcing it open, and he could feel, actually feel Dedrick's erection pressing against his own as Dedrick's kisses crept beneath his jaw, hot, hot kisses running down his neck to the crook of his shoulder, hot tongue licking his flesh–

–and then *pain!*

Biting!

Bruce screamed, tried to shove Dedrick away, but his hands were slick with oil and had no grip and the teeth were still there, grinding, sinking into him as blood ran down his arm, and he could smell it, fresh, acrid, his. He slammed his knee into Dedrick's balls. Dedrick screamed, doubled over. Bruce flung himself forward, knocked Dedrick aside, ran for the bathroom. He slammed and locked the door behind him.

Never should have, never should have, his mind taunted, but he had, and now it was too late to undo. He would "Make Things Right," as Mother would say. Get dressed, get away, talk with Mother and accept who he was. He'd undressed in this bathroom to begin with, so he would put his clothes back on, commando, and be gone before Dedrick could stand.

From beyond the door, footsteps.

Bruce grabbed a washcloth, ran it under the tap without waiting for it to warm up.

The doorknob rattled. "Brucie, honey? Open the door."

Dedrick sounded pained. Good. He washed the lines of blood from his arm and inspected the wound. It looked bad. Deep. Probably needed medical attention.

He scanned the floor for his clothes.

"Brucie? I'm sorry."

His clothes were gone.

Dedrick had been in here last. He must have hidden them. Bruce opened the closet, saw nothing, rifled through towels and medicine on the shelves.

"Don't be angry with me, okay?"

"Go away," Bruce said. His voice sounded frightened.

Dedrick thumped his fingertip on the door. "I forgot it was your first time. I got carried away. I'm sorry."

Bruce felt a draft on his naked legs, found a ragged hole in the closet floor. Dread filled him. He dropped to his hands and knees, almost crying out as the bite wound stretched. Fresh blood dripped on the floor.

"Brucie? Forgive me?"

Bruce gazed into the hole. His clothes were down there. He could just make out the faint yellow of his shirt. The hole was far too small for him to drop through.

"Brucie, honey, open the door." Dedrick's voice hardened. "You're overreacting. I made a mistake. I apologized."

Bruce scrambled to his feet, trying to keep his breathing under control. The handle rattled. "Don't make me upset, now."

Bruce stepped closer to the door. He started to reach for the handle, but then pulled his hand back. "Bring me my clothes," he said.

"Aren't they in there?"

"You know damn well they're not. You dropped them through the hole in the closet."

Dedrick didn't respond. Bruce waited. The silence stretched. He leaned forward, placed his ear against the wood. He could hear Dedrick walking away, but he didn't know where the door to the cellar was, so he couldn't tell if the man was going to fulfill Bruce's command. He waited. The footsteps stopped, or got too far away to hear. For a long time, the only sound Bruce heard was his own heart pounding. He waited some more. What would happen if Dedrick did bring his clothes back? Bruce would have to open the door sometime.

Where had he gone?

Bruce wrapped his trembling fingers around the doorknob. He might have time to dart into the bedroom and retrieve his briefs. He turned the handle until it clicked.

With a massive, bone-rattling crash, the door slammed into him, crunched against the toes of his left foot. He screamed and tried to back away, but Dedrick piled on top of him, hands around Bruce's throat. He didn't remember Dedrick being so hairy, hadn't known that Dedrick's steely eyes could glow like that.

His head slammed onto the bathroom floor.

"No more pencils, no more books–"

Someone was singing. Bruce tried to open his eyes. Couldn't.

"–no more teacher's dirty looks."

He was blindfolded. His shoulder stung. Damp, dank air touched his flesh like clammy hands.

"Waking up?"

The scent of soap came to him. Clean. Perfumy. He remembered the smell. He'd first detected it when he'd met Dedrick at the bus station. The clean scent had surprised him, and was one of the reasons Bruce had decided to sleep with him.

A hand touched his cheek. Hot.

"I'm glad you're awake," Dedrick said. "You gave me a scare when you hit your head like that." The hand on his cheek slid down his neck, across his chest. Bruce tried to push it away, but cold metal bit his wrists, keeping them where they were. Chains.

A cold splash of panic energized him and he tried to lift his head to look around, but metal bit into his throat. He was completely incapacitated. "Please," Bruce whispered.

The hand returned to his cheek, gentle, fingers working at the blindfold until it pulled up. Bruce crushed his eyelids shut against the sudden light.

"Sorry about that," Dedrick said.

Full minutes elapsed before Bruce could open his eyes. What had felt like the blast of a spotlight turned out to be just a bare bulb hanging on a wire. Dedrick smiled down at him, his whiskers about a quarter inch long now. Bruce must have been unconscious for a while.

Over Dedrick's shoulder, Bruce saw his clothes hanging on a rope tied between beams in the cellar ceiling. Had Dedrick washed them?

"There's nothing to be afraid of," Dedrick said. He turned and walked away. He wore ratty jeans and untied work books. He stopped on the far side of the room, at the blurry edge of Bruce's vision, and started pouring a small bottle of liquid into a larger bucket. Dedrick hummed as he worked, *No more pencils, no more books,* the same tune Bruce hadn't been able to identify upstairs. He'd been singing it when Bruce woke up.

Bruce swallowed. His Adam's apple rasped against the metal shackle. He would not cry. He would not. He tried to assess his binds. As far as he could tell, he was chained to a table. Judging from the cold, he was still naked.

"What... what is all this?" Bruce asked.

Dedrick looked over his shoulder. Straining to see him gave Bruce a sharp headache. He scrunched his eyes shut, hoping it would pass quickly. "This is nothing much, right now. I have one or two things to finish while we wait for the moon."

Bruce felt a tear squeak free and run into his ear. He tried to wipe it away, but of course his arm wouldn't move. Dedrick would kill him. Bruce moaned.

Dedrick came to his side and leaned over Bruce's face. His breath reeked of mouthwash. "I'm not going to hurt you," Dedrick said. "Relax."

Not mouthwash, Bruce realized. Lemons. Had Dedrick been eating them? His own belly rumbled. How long had it been since he'd eaten?

"Time for your bath," Dedrick said. He lifted a bucket and put it on the table at Bruce's hip. It was hot against his skin. Dedrick started to tug on elbow-length dish-washing gloves. "This won't take long."

"Let me go," Bruce whispered.

"I will."

"Please."

Dedrick smiled, looked him in the eye. "Don't be silly. Letting you go is the whole plan."

His stomach rumbled again. "Food," Bruce said. "Hungry."

"You'll have to get it yourself."

"Let me go, then. I'll starve."

"Soon," Dedrick said. "Bath first. You are very, very dirty."

Dedrick squeezed a sponge against his forehead. Scalding water cascaded into his hair, his eyes. The scent of lemons made his eyes water. Dedrick must have poured a whole bottle of the stuff into the water. Dedrick scrubbed, and Bruce clenched his eyes and mouth and waited for it to be over.

Bruce woke to find the chains gone, but he still couldn't move his arms. His wrists were tied behind him. He tried to open his eyes and discovered the blindfold was back, then he tried to call for Dedrick and discovered he'd been gagged as well. He rolled suddenly to the side and figured out he was riding in the bed of a pickup truck.

The truck slammed through a pothole, tossing him into the air and slamming him down again. He screamed against the gag, but it did no good.

His stomach rumbled and his back itched. Bruce scratched his thumb-nail against his back as much as his binds would allow, but the itch came alive. It raced up his back like fire, shot down his arms and legs, scampered over his scalp. It felt like he'd been bathed in poison ivy.

Bruce sniffed. Something died in here. The smell was faint, as if Dedrick had tried to clean it out, but he hadn't succeeded.

The truck stopped with a squeak, sliding him head first against the cab. Oh, so very hungry.

The truck's engine shut off with a cough. Bruce listened. *Thunk!* as Dedrick closed his door. Footsteps coming around. *Screeek!* as the tailgate opened.

"Brucie? You awake?"

Bruce played possum, listened hard. Hands, hot hands, grabbed his ankles and yanked him to the end of the truck, then rolled him onto his back, so his knees dangled over the edge of the tailgate. The truck sank a little as Dedrick sat beside him and untied the gag. Bruce worked his tongue against the roof of his mouth, trying to get moisture back. He expected the blindfold to come off next, but it did not.

"Do you think your mom's started looking for you yet?" Dedrick asked.

Just like that, tears ambushed him. He'd managed to keep thoughts of her at bay throughout this ordeal, but now he couldn't stop picturing her getting the news that her son was dead. Or worse, waiting by the phone for that news for the rest of her life.

"Let me go," Bruce said.

"I told you I would. First tell me how you feel."

Pine. Bruce smelled pine. And plant life. And dirt.

"Where are we?"

"That's not an answer. I asked: 'How do you feel?'"

"Scared."

Dedrick sighed. "I mean physically. Does your shoulder hurt where I bit you?"

Dedrick poked the bite wound. Bruce almost cried out, but there was no pain. Had it healed? How long had Dedrick kept him chained up? If he'd been chained up long enough for his shoulder to heal, why hadn't he starved to death?

Dedrick raked his nails down Bruce's chest, then leaned over and began lapping the blood before it could gather and trickle down. The sound of Dedrick swallowing made Bruce's stomach grumble, softly at first, then louder. If only his hands were free. He would snap Dedrick's neck and plunge his teeth into the hot meat of Dedrick's–

"Clotted already," Dedrick said. "You're going to be the best hunt yet. Do you itch?"

Bruce's skin came alive at the word. The itch gouged deeply, sank its teeth into muscle. He felt like he'd been injected with sand.

"Yes," Bruce said.

"Good. It's working. You'll want to eat before I come for you." Dedrick tore the blindfold off, and then shoved him off the truck. Bruce cried out as he hit the ground.

"I'll give you an hour to free yourself and find food. After that, I'll come for you."

"Will you take me home?" Dedrick stood over him, the moon peering over his shoulder like an accomplice. The man didn't laugh outright, but Bruce could tell he wanted to.

"You'll have to find your own way home," he said. "Chances are, though, I'll hunt you down and kill you long before you have the chance."

"But... you said you'd let me go."

"That's what I'm doing now." He pulled a bottle out of the back of his pants, flipped the cap, and squeezed. Bruce barely shut his eyes before lemon juice sluiced over his naked body. The scratches Dedrick made on his chest ignited like pools of kerosene.

Before Bruce could recover, the truck started up and drove off.

Bruce struggled to sit up. With his feet flat on the ground, he leaned against his thighs and struggled to free his wrists. He growled at the rope, pulled and twisted until the skin felt raw. The binds didn't loosen. He forced himself to relax.

Something moved.

Bruce listened.

Another movement. Scratching. A raccoon, maybe?

His stomach growled, but a second later he recognized the rumbling in his throat. His breath caught. He'd been doing that growling himself. He listened for the raccoon and could sense the animal frozen in the darkness, waiting.

Dedrick would be coming. He had to escape. If he could find his way back to the bus station...

First he would have to get free of the damn binds. They seemed a little looser around his wrists, but the bases of his palms were too wide to slip free. Every time he tugged, he tightened the knot.

He threw his head back with frustration. The moon, full and brilliant, watched him. He wanted to scream at it.

A crunching pain started in his fingers, curling them into fists, working up his forearms. Bruce struggled not to cry out as it felt like his bones were being crushed between stones.

The binds fell away.

Bruce lowered his head and stayed perfectly still, concentrating on his heartbeat. The crunching pain receded back to the muscle-deep itch. Slowly, Bruce brought his hands up into the moon's light.

The binds were gone. How had that happened?

He wanted to ponder this a little more, but knew he should count his blessings and get the hell out of here. Bruce leaned forward to untie his ankles, but the rope lie on the ground. He picked it up. The knot remained, the loop far too small to slip over his foot. After a few seconds, he decided this puzzle would have to wait. Bruce didn't know how much time he had until Dedrick returned.

He flung the rope aside and stood, growling at the pain in his back as he straightened. He'd have to find clothes before he reached civilization. He started to walk. Involuntarily, his pace quickened.

He'd hardly run a hundred yards before cramps forced him to stop and lean against a tree. As soon as he did, the crushing pain returned, splintering his bones and dropping him to the forest floor.

Food. He needed food.

In the dark, not fifty yards away, twin spots of silver watched him. The raccoon.

Bruce scrambled after it on his hands and knees. He would catch it, rip it open, gorge on its warm, bloody flesh.

It darted left around a tree. Bruce cut sooner, keeping the tree on his right, leaning hard with momentum. His right hand came down near the fleeing animal, close enough to feel the brush of its fur, and the raccoon darted right. Bruce veered right himself, envisioning himself leaning like a motorcycle, and veered back before the raccoon could change direction again. Bruce's filthy left hand landed directly on the animal's spine.

With a *snap!* the raccoon stopped running.

Bruce stopped, turned back. The raccoon scratched at the ground with its front paws while drool dripped from its lips. Bruce flipped it to its back. It hissed like a cobra as Bruce lowered his face. For an instant, his nose to the creature's fur, he knew this was wrong, but a hunger pang sharp as a knife blade cut into him and he bit. Its fur tasted of dirt, its skin was tougher than he expected. He doubled his effort and the skin finally tore. Blood gushed into his mouth, he swallowed, and his body came alive with energy.

Later, the raccoon a scattered pile of bones and fur, a thought began to gnaw at the edge of Bruce's mind. Something about his hand.

He held it up to the moon. Blood stained the skin, but aside from that it looked normal. He made a fist, slowly, squeezed until the knuckles popped, then stretched his fingers as wide as they would go. His hand. Normal, perfect, clean.

Fear lighted upon the back of his neck, then raced like a swarm of ants down his body. This hand had been filthy when he shattered the raccoon's back. He'd seen it.

A change in the air snatched his attention. A smell. Faint. Perfumy. Dedrick.

Bruce leaped to his feet. His breathing sounded too loud all of a sudden, and the itch returned with a vengeance.

The perfume strengthened on a whisper of breeze, too dispersed to determine direction. Bruce ran. Footfalls sounded behind him, closing in.

The meat in his belly slowed him down. He needed speed. The kind of speed he'd had when he'd caught that raccoon. How to tap into it again? His hunger drove him before, helped him catch the raccoon despite being on his hands and knees. Hunger was no longer an asset.

Another scent grabbed his attention. Decay. A pond, somewhere to his left. Bruce turned. He saw it right away, the reflection of the moon smeared in the scum. Bruce crouched at the edge and rolled into it, trying to make as little noise as possible.

The pond was shallow. Maybe three feet of water concealing a sucking abyss of mud that tried to swallow him whole. Bruce kept his head above water and listened. The woods were silent.

Slowly, Bruce worked his way back to solid ground. He held his mouth open to quiet his breathing and listened intently for footfalls in the woods. After what he judged to be three minutes of silence, Bruce allowed himself to think he'd given Dedrick the slip.

How had Dedrick found him so fast? Granted, he hadn't moved very far away from where Dedrick had left him, but he had to have come far enough away that Dedrick hadn't heard him, and he was certainly out of his line of sight. Obviously, he'd done this before.

Bruce had seen a TV news report on serial killers years ago. The information had faded with time, but one aspect slammed back into place. Serial killers exhibited a cleanliness that bordered on obsessive. Dedrick had exhibited that obsession with his constant smell of perfume, with removing Bruce's clothes from the bathroom, and with washing Bruce's body with–

Understanding exploded in his mind. The lemon-scented water. The squirt of lemon juice before he drove away.

Dedrick was hunting him by scent.

Bruce crouched and scooped up a handful of muck. He forced himself not to retch as he slathered it over his chest, grinding the putrid stench into his skin. He grimaced, expecting Dedrick's scratches to hurt, but he felt nothing. He continued scooping mud on himself until he covered his feet, then scrubbed a handful into his hair for good measure.

He approached a tree. Since he couldn't rub mud onto his back, he broke off a branch and used the sap end to scratch. It didn't relieve the itch. He dropped the branch and took a long smell, trying to detect the scent of lemons. He smelled nothing except the stench of slime.

Of course, this left him unable to detect Dedrick's perfume. As he pondered this, the itch sank into his muscles. Its intensity multiplied as the slime dried on his skin.

Bruce took a few steps back in the direction he'd come. If he could sneak around Dedrick and make it back to the clearing, he might find the truck. Eventually, Dedrick would track the lemon smell to the edge of the pond and figure out what he'd done.

Bruce prayed it wouldn't be too soon.

He almost missed the clearing. He'd been steeling himself to pass within feet of Dedrick when their paths finally crossed, but Dedrick must have walked beyond the pond while Bruce had been in it.

His nerves tensed at a noise. He froze until it repeated. An owl. He caught the faint smell of the truck's emissions. Bruce fell to his knees where the truck had been parked. Down here, the smell was stronger.

Bruce walked a few feet in the direction Dedrick had driven and dropped to his knees. He could smell emissions still, but the scent was distressingly faint. He might be able to smell his way back to the road, but he'd have to hurry.

The itch prickled over his scalp. He scratched a hand across his head, but the feel of his hair stiffened with muck unnerved him. He rubbed the gooseflesh along his arms. The hairs seemed wire-thick and poking straight out.

Just walk, he told himself.

He continued along, dropping to his knees to smell the dirt now and again. One time he thought the smell was gone, but it reappeared a few feet farther down, where Dedrick had slowed to traverse a huge pothole. Possibly the same one that had sent Bruce flying on the way in.

Then, there were footsteps behind him.

Bruce stifled the urge to run. He held still and listened. Just an animal. A deer, maybe. Even so, Bruce increased his pace.

Soon Bruce's mind wandered to the smell of death he'd detected in the back of Dedrick's pickup. Dedrick must move his victims' bodies after he killed them, probably dumping them somewhere police could search to their heart's content without discovering anything.

He dropped to smell the path, and the scent of emissions was gone.

Bruce looked around and saw no place a truck could have pulled off. He backtracked a few hundred feet and sniffed the ground again. The smell was faint, but present. Dedrick had turned off somewhere around here. He didn't find the truck until his third pass. Dedrick had pulled a felled pine tree behind it, concealing it perfectly. Bruce tugged the tree away and settled behind the wheel.

Dedrick's clothes were folded neatly on the passenger seat. The man was out there in the nude. Weird as it was, Bruce counted it as a stroke of luck. Dedrick wouldn't be running through the forest with the keys in his hand. He patted Dedrick's pants pockets. No keys. Dedrick's pants should fit him, but he wanted to get away before putting them on.

Something crashed in the forest. The sound repeated, closer, followed by a low howl that seemed to set the tree branches trembling.

Dedrick was coming.

Bruce yanked down first the driver's visor, then the passenger's one. Still no keys. He had no idea how to hot wire the truck, and if he stayed here much longer...

In desperation, he grabbed the ignition switch. No keys here, either. Fight or flight time. Bruce didn't know how many people Dedrick had killed, but fighting apparently did them no good. Flight it was.

As he opened the door, he spied the keys lying right in plain sight on the dashboard. *Almost fooled me.*

He closed the door and locked it, then leaned over and locked the passenger door as well. Six keys on the ring, and one rabbit's foot. In the darkness he couldn't discern which key would start the truck. Bruce tried the first one. It slid halfway in, then stopped. For a heart-stopping instant, it refused to come back out. Bruce wriggled it, finally worked it free. The next key slid in without a hitch.

The ignition rumbled, sputtered, and caught.

"Fuckin' A," Bruce said. He slammed the truck into reverse and pulled out, wincing as the truck banged into the pine tree he hadn't moved far enough. The steering wheel fought him, probably low on fluid, but he couldn't help that. The headlights could stand to be brighter, as well. He slammed into drive and stomped the gas.

The road was no wider than a large footpath, and the potholes and stones forced him to drive much slower than he wanted. Bruce tried not to think that the raccoon had been running faster than this when he'd caught it. Something crashed in the back of the truck. Bruce glanced in the rear view mirror.

Silver eyes peered at him.

He screamed and jerked the wheel to the left and back again, trying to throw Dedrick off, realizing too late that it wasn't Dedrick at all, it was a dog, a wolf, and then the truck's nose dropped and the trees twisted, fell, and exploded into a geyser of shattered glass.

In the immediate silence, unconsciousness beckoned. Bruce recognized its suffocating embrace and clenched his teeth against it, willing it away. Gradually, the blackness receded.

Jagged glass lined the windshield like mutant teeth. The truck had rolled onto the driver's side and slid into a tree, coming to rest right where the bottom of the windshield met the hood. It dented the frame badly enough that both side windows had shattered as well.

Bruce tried to move. Jagged pain in his left shoulder made him cry out. On top of that, his legs were trapped. The tree must have pushed the dashboard down toward his lap.

He tried to pull his left arm out from beneath him, but had nothing to pull himself up with. Hoping for rescue personnel was pointless. Dedrick would be here in minutes.

Nearby, an animal growled.

Bruce looked up and out the passenger side window. The pine trees looked strange from this angle, monstrous things which seemed ready to crush him. The moon appeared trapped within its uppermost branches.

Then the moon split in two.

Eyes. Silver eyes. A monstrous grin of dagger-like teeth.

Bruce yelled and slapped his right arm on the seat, hoping to scare the wolf away, but it watched, unimpressed. Dedrick's work boot was beside him, and he flung it at the animal. It banged off the passenger door and dropped back toward Bruce's face. He barely deflected it.

Bruce punched the horn and held it.

Suddenly, the wolf's snout began to shorten. Its glowing eyes began to dull. Hair squiggled on its face, thinning out over the chin and beneath its ears while disappearing altogether around its eyes.

Recognition came, unwanted, unbelievable.

"You've done well, Brucie." Dedrick's voice grumbled at the start, smoothing out as his lupine throat thinned into something more human. "I'm proud of you."

"What the hell?"

"I saw what you left of that raccoon. How'd that taste?"

Bruce's stomach squeezed. He grit his teeth against a wave of nausea. "I didn't... I couldn't..."

In an instant, the humanity of Dedrick's face sprung out into a wolf's snout. The wolf leaned through the shattered window and snapped three times.

Bruce screamed now, seized the steering wheel and desperately tried to pull his legs free. Unsuccessful, he punched his right hand against the roof and pressed hard enough to pull his left arm out from under him, but even freed, he could do nothing to help himself.

He looked up toward the passenger window again.

The wolf– *Dedrick*, he told himself, *accept it*– watched him, but couldn't climb down.

Bruce pressed himself back against the seat and tried to slide his legs sideways. No luck.

If he had a gun, a knife… He stopped his thoughts right there. No sense making plans with what he didn't have.

Suddenly, the truck seemed brighter. Bruce looked up.

The wolf was gone.

Bruce held his breath and listened. He heard a scrape, claws on metal, then the thud of something heavy landing on the ground.

A narrow horizontal slot remained between the edge of the tree and roof of the windshield. Six inches, maybe a little more. Barely wide enough for both the wolf's eyes to peer through at the same time.

"How does that work?" Bruce asked. "You don't just change into a wolf, you change back and forth at will?"

For an instant, it looked like the wolf would transform into Dedrick again. Its snout pulled back a little, its lips filled out. Then, with the quickness of a striking snake, one leg shot through the space.

Bruce snapped his head back, barely avoiding its claws.

The wolf pulled its leg out, then glared through the space again. It seemed as baffled about how to get in as Bruce was about how to get out.

With a growl, the wolf reached in again. It couldn't squeeze in far enough to reach him, and Bruce avoided it easily. The wolf, Dedrick, turned and sauntered away.

As it moved out of sight, Bruce realized that he could have grabbed its paw and held on. He might have been able to hold him there indefinitely. Even if Dedrick transformed, Bruce would be able to hold on to his wider human wrist.

The wolf sat a few feet away from the truck, staring through the gap. It seemed to smile.

The change was fast. The wolf snout jerked in and the fur seemed to melt off the wolf's face. Only the head and neck changed completely, though, leaving Dedrick's face fused onto the hairy wolf's body.

"We seem to have reached an impasse," Dedrick said. His voice was scratchy, small. "Lucky I'm not obligated to kill you as a wolf."

Bruce glanced up at the moon. It remained high in the sky, plenty of night left. No help there. He looked back to Dedrick, slowly changing the rest of himself into his human form. The itch in Bruce's own skin positively sizzled now. The phrase 'wider human wrist,' repeated in his mind like a mantra. He remembered his hand crunching down on the raccoon's back. It had been filthy, yes, but there had been something else.

It had been thinner.

"You were my greatest hunt yet, Brucie. I'm sorry it ended this way."

Bruce held the image of his thinner hand in his mind. The itch gave way to the bone-crushing ache. Bruce glanced at it, not wanting to take his eyes off Dedrick, but unable to ignore the pain either. His hand looked clean at first, but dark hairs squiggled across the skin like weeds filmed in time-lapse photography, dark hairs that could look like dirt at a glance. His palm narrowed as he watched, his fingers shortened. Now he understood how the binds slipped off on their own.

"You gave me a challenge," Dedrick said. "I thought you might be the one to finally kill me."

Dedrick's arm, now fully human, reached into the truck. Bruce felt his focus shatter, saw his left hand begin to turn human again. Dedrick grabbed his throat and shoved him against the seat. Bruce kicked against the gas and brake pedals, but still couldn't free his legs. Dedrick's smile stretched as he forced his entire head into the gap, turning it left and right to squeeze in.

"That hurt," Dedrick said.

The lower half of Dedrick's face started to poke out, growing into a snout. His dull human teeth grew, sharpened.

He'll rip my throat out, Bruce thought.

Bruce felt bones in Dedrick's wrist twist and pop against his chest. Dedrick's mouth, now a maw of curled yellow teeth, started down.

Bruce punched Dedrick under the jaw and held his head against the roof of the truck with his fist. He focused on the itch covering his face while pushing himself up with his left arm. Dedrick's claws raked his flesh, but the pain was insignificant next to the splintering agony that worked across his face.

Bruce yelped as his nose shot out beneath his eyes. His vision dulled. His teeth ached worse than any pain he'd ever felt. With a growl, Bruce bit. Dedrick's flesh was even less yielding than the raccoon's had been, but Bruce had adrenaline working for him this time. The taste of perfume disappeared behind the metallic gush of blood.

Dedrick fought, yelped, tried to pull free. Blood spattered crazily around the truck. Bruce held on. His grip popped free for an instant as Dedrick's flesh tore completely, but Bruce darted forward for another bite, a larger bite, and pulled and shook some more.

He kept the hold until Dedrick stopped twitching. When he finally let go, his legs could move. Wolf legs, he realized. They'd shrunk right out from under the dashboard.

It took some wiggling, but Bruce sat up, tucking his tail beneath him. He concentrated on his human body, rising to his feet as the change came.

Dedrick's body sprawled half-in, half-out of the truck in a mutant form that should make tabloid headlines for decades. It looked like a very hairy man with the head and shoulders of a wolf.

Bruce gathered Dedrick's clothes and tossed them out of the truck. He lifted himself up through the passenger window, then sat on the door and gazed up at the moon.

Time to make things right.

Hitchhiking, he could be home again by tomorrow afternoon. He suspected it would be easier to have that conversation with Mother about his sexuality now. After all, there were worse things he could tell her.

Purity Ball

Purity Ball
by
Cody Goodfellow

9:45 PM

Heat seems to radiate up from the ground, hours after sundown. Santa Ana winds, like ionized dragon's breath, roll over the canyons, cul-de-sacs, and paved oases of suburbia.

Icy blue light from the deep end of the Schweinfurter's swimming pool paints the patio furniture and bowers of tastefully manicured tropical landscaping in mottled submarine patterns, animating the stolid rubber faces of the horned devils in tuxedos, lurking in the shadows.

The blinds are drawn and the curtains closed on all windows and the sliding glass door of the two-story ranch house. Lit only by the epileptic stutter of a TV playing music videos, the downstairs rooms seem alive and animated, but only one upstairs window is lit.

Crouching like a beast unused to walking on its hind legs, a fanged apparition skulks out of the bushes to prowl along the windows, peeking at gaps in misaligned slats of the blinds. The flickering light reflects off glassy eyes set deep within the gnarled visage, the twisted, goatish horns sprouting from a sloping, shaggy brow.

Two more devils creep out into the liquid half-light, ignoring their leader's furious gestures. When the trio crowds against the sliding glass door, the leader impatiently tugs it open and they storm inside.

In front of the wall-mounted flat screen in the family room: blankets, pink sleeping bags, and bowls half-filled with popcorn and Chex Mix. An open laptop on the couch shows the Skype logo when a devil nudges it.

A devil with a monumental potbelly staggers down the stairs and rips his face off. "They're gone," he gasps. "Fuckin' Bonnie's passed out in her waterbed."

"Who?"

"Schweinfurter... the mom, dumbshit. Nicole... she's not here... None of 'em are..."

"Damn those girls," the leader says, ripping off his mask and crumpling it in a fist.

Still poking at the laptop, the second devil says, "What're we going to do, Ron?"

"We're going to do what we vowed to do," the leader says. "We're going to find them and we're going to remind them of *their* vow."

"I can't... I just can't believe they'd do something like this. If they're so determined to damn themselves... To throw away everything–"

"It doesn't matter what they want. This isn't about them. This is about the promise we made to them. And to God."

9:57 PM

Ron Kolb ramrods his Suburban through the dithering, half-drunk Friday night traffic. Keith Slauson rides shotgun, and Bo Rieber sits in back, losing an argument with his daughter's voicemail. The girls all left their phones at the Schweinfurter house, anyway, so they couldn't be tracked.

"We should call the pastor," Keith says.

"You call the pastor every time you need to do your duty as a man? No wonder you still change oil for a fucking living." Kolb bites his lip. "I'm sorry, that was out of line."

"Forget it." The whine in Slauson's voice makes Kolb want to break his jaw. *Way out of line*, he reminds himself. Be a man. Remember your promise.

"Fucking whore," Rieber growls, "just like her mother."

Kolb turns up the gospel station. Running in his head, everything he knows about Hope–every place he dropped her off, all the kids she tried to sneak out or "study" with, all her friends outside of church, everything she ever talked about doing after school, that they made her skip. Maybe if Enid was smart enough to home-school the kids, shit like this wouldn't happen.

"It doesn't sting that they did it, you know?" Slauson turns down the radio, smiling at Kolb to show all his teeth. "It's that they teamed up to pull this shit, right before the night."

"You think they knew?" Rieber asks.

"Women always know when a change is coming. Down in their parts." Slauson takes something out of his pocket and gnaws on it. Peppered jerky.

Kolb gets a whiff of it and looks sideways at him just before pulling onto the highway. "You make that yourself?"

Slauson says, "Watch the fucking road."

Kolb prays for strength to be delivered from the sin that rides them all, the sin of gluttony.

10:54 PM

After cruising the neighborhood, scanning for house parties, they are checking the mall parking lots when Tammy Slauson calls from a pay-phone. She's sobbing, big, whooping hiccups as she cries for Daddy to come pick her up out in front of the high school. Keith makes reassuring noises into the phone, telling his baby girl to sit tight, they'll be there in a minute. Daddy will fix everything. Then he snaps the phone in half and throws it out the window.

Tammy comes running across the empty parking lot of Santana High in the fluffy pink bathrobe she packed for the slumber party, but she's naked underneath. Rieber and Slauson switch seats and he bundles his daughter into the back.

Kolb's eyes water and his nose begins to run from the stink on her. All of them react to it, Slauson worst of all, his shame and his lust making him start to secrete his own musk.

They were just going to swim together and maybe kiss a little, but Bobby Chesebro, her boyfriend for going on three months, he went crazy on her, and he changed–

"You did wrong, putting yourself in that situation," Keith says, but it's the Pastor's words coming out of his mouth. He grabs her hand and crushes it in his. "Where's the ring, girl? Where's your silver promise ring?"

"I'm so sorry, Daddy, I didn't want to... Those other girls made it sound..." Kolb watches the road. Tammy draws in a breath and whimpers, "Daddy, you're hurting me."

"You made a vow, girl," Keith clears his throat and starts again, deeper, slower, "and I made a vow to you. You promised to keep yourself pure..."

"But I did, Daddy, I got away from him..."

Keith wants to go find the Chesebro boy. He's flatland El Cajon trash, not even a member of their church. Bo Rieber's pretty sure the boy's Daddy is in jail for hitting his wife. Kolb says no, they've got to find the other girls before midnight.

Slauson suggests this dead-end road up in the hills where they used to go parking themselves, when they were younger.

"Fuckin' houses up there for almost eleven years, dipshit," Rieber says. "She knows where they went. Where'd those other sluts get off to, Tammy?"

"Don't even fucking look at her," Slauson says. Leaning over the seat to snarl in Bo's face. The stripes of scar tissue shine like silver all over his scalp, through his thinning ash-blonde hair. "Keep your filthy fucking paws off her, or so help me..."

"Sure," Rieber says, "now the horse is out of the barn..."

"Mind your fuckin' mouth," Slauson growls.

"Ronny, you wanna turn off the child-thing so I can roll down my damn window? My eyes're watering up here from all the..."

"Shut up." Kolb's phone vibrates, showing the location of the multi-plex movie theater where Hope just used her debit card. Trying not to let his thoughts go red, he hits the freeway and cuts off four lanes of traffic.

The whore, the slut, the bitch... He'd be no less furious if it was a son he was out chasing, but trouble doesn't stick to boys. When she had taken this vow, the week after her first period, it wasn't his idea. It was *hers*. She was scared of the boys at school. He really believed her. To find out, on a night that was supposed to be so special, it was all lies, and she was just like the rest...

He catches himself in the mirror and wonders if he shouldn't change clothes before he picks up his daughter. It'd be a perfect cap on a perfect evening to lose the deposit on the rental tux.

11:03 PM

The manager at the box office wants Kolb to buy a ticket to go get his daughter out of the theater. He wants to explain to him that he's not here to see a film, but to remove his daughter from a dangerous situation she's put herself into, and that he'd rather not involve the police. He wants to rip the manager's doughy face off his skull and eat it.

All at once, the manager seems to read his fate in Ron Kolb's eyes, and lets him go in. "But I'm coming back there in five minutes," he shouts, "so don't get comfortable!"

Kolb blows by the snack bar, momentarily distracted by the carousel of cylindrical meats, shiny with the same petroleum-based grease that oozes out of the popcorn tubs. It almost makes him vomit, makes him angry like a broken promise.

He finds her in the third theater. A pimply post-teen usher follows him with a flashlight, halfheartedly warning him to keep his voice down. He strides down the center aisle of some dickless talky thing with subtitles, the kind of shit Hope watches with her mother when he goes hunting. Almost before he bellows her name, he recognizes her profile, the particular swoop of her neck as she pops from her seat and goes for the fire exit. Another figure, shorter, runs after her, but Kolb gets to the door first, knocking the interloper down as he grabs his daughter by the hood of her sweatshirt and drags her down the sticky exit corridor, hammers the outer door open and drives her ahead of him into the alley behind the mall.

"Daddy, I didn't..."

"Shut up. The car is around the corner. March."

Her hands sweep around her like birds chained to her, trying to lift her up and fly her away. "Daddy, I didn't do anything. I went to a movie with..."

"There's a dress in the car. You're to put it on when we get where we're going..."

The door flies open behind him and he turns around, fists out but only half-closed. Another girl stumbles out into the alley, holding her arm across a rather voluptuous bosom. Short hair, too many colors, and her eyes ringed with mascara. Holly Schweinfurter. "Mr. Kolb, I'm sorry... You look really nice." She giggles.

Kolb counts to ten. "Hope has to go to a very special occasion to

98

celebrate a milestone in her life. It's a father-daughter thing, for daughters with fathers."

"Daddy..." Hope starts.

Kolb sends her running with a glance.

"Mr. Kolb, we didn't do anything wrong..."

"Holly, go home and wake up your drunken whore mother and tell her she's got 'til tomorrow night to get the fuck out of town." In Kolb's hand, his car keys jut out through his clenched fingers just like claws. Holly goes to grab his arm and he shakes her off, jabbing at her eyes with the keys.

Kolb comes out of the alley and gets to the Suburban just as Hope starts to climb in next to Tammy Slauson. Kolb orders Rieber out and into the back. "Hope's riding up front."

She scoffs, "Like we're going to *talk*, or something?"

Slauson doesn't want Rieber in the back with his daughter. He has Tammy climb over the backseat into the cargo space, where Hope and her brother used to ride for hours together when they went on road trips. When everything worked.

"Where's Nicole gone, girl?" Bo Rieber's face is a fist squeezing out sweat.

"I don't know. They wanted to go meet their boyfriends, so me and Holly went to the movies..."

"You bitches planned all this," Slauson says. "Sitting around watching trash on TV and listening to trash, you must've schemed for hours on how to turn *yourselves* into trash."

Jerking the Suburban across the highway, Kolb whips around to skewer Keith with one clawed fist. "Way out of line, Keith. *My* daughter wasn't running in the street naked."

Bo chuckled nastily. "You know what they say about that Schweinfurter girl..."

Kolb says, "Why don't we go find your girl, now, Bo?"

"Getting' packed in here," Rieber says. "Whyn't you drop me off..."

"We'll go together." Kolb bites his lip.

Slauson digs in. "Who's she been running with lately, Bo? That flatland boy who got kicked off the JV team for his temper, or that kid with the hotrod GTO everybody's always bitching about... I can't even keep track..."

Silent, Kolb stares at Hope while he accelerates, cutting off a river of honking, swerving smaller cars. He stares and accelerates until she whispers, "I know where she went."

11:48 PM

The church has a deal with a local RV dealer to put most of their overstock in the outer edge of the church's parking lot, facing the highway. It makes the lot look fuller and gives the sense of the church community as being laid-back, affluent, always on vacation. The building belonged to a Korean evangelical group that relocated after a financial scandal. Looking more like a futuristic prison from thirty years ago than a church, it still serves their convocation of just under a hundred quite well. More than half of them are the old group that followed the pastor down from Alaska. Some were old enough to remember before even then, before they had names.

And all of them were gathered tonight in the great hall, for the Renewal Purity Ball gala. Twenty-two girls were going to take the vow for the first time. Their small group is growing, a sure sign that God smiles on their way of life. Their girls were to be initiated into womanhood, presented by their fathers to be declared eligible for marriage. But everyone has gone home. The night was supposed to be a celebration of their successfully defended innocence, but Kolb still hopes to salvage something. His daughter will still go to stand before the Lord, their God and declare her chastity, her abstention from the fatal sin of gluttony. And then she will go into womanhood.

But first—

They cruise the rows of RVs twice before Slauson spots the yellow glow shining out of the dome skylight on an Asgardian fifth-wheel. Slauson jumps out, Rieber right behind him.

"What're they doing, Daddy?"

Kolb turns to Hope and wonders how much Enid told their daughter about the birds and the bees, about what they are, and why God tests them like He does. Unlike a lot of fathers, he never filled her head with crazy stories to scare her into behaving. He hadn't even had the heart to tell her the truth. He only vowed to protect her innocence, to defend her honor, until she had chosen a husband. "You know you're not like other

100

girls at school."

Her eyes go wide, the gleam off them reminding him of when all he had to do to make her smile was pick her up and tickle her. When she was a toy. "Well," she starts, stammers, "about me and Ho–"

"Wait," Kolb slides out of the driver's seat and lopes over to the door of the fifth-wheel.

Bo is peering into the frosted louver windows. "That's them, goddamit, I know it's them..."

Slauson tries, not very hard, to push him back. "Bo, you know you can't... you had yourself that operation..."

"Fuck you," Rieber elbows Slauson aside and pounds the door. "Nicole Charity Rieber, get your busted ass out here before I take it in my head to..."

The door flies apart and what comes through it hurls Bo Rieber away and into the fiberglass wall of a Crazy Horse Extended Camper-Lodge. He sits down hard with a chest full of broken ribs, sliding sideways as he digs a Glock out of his fleece-lined jacket. "Tried to tell you, girl... tried to save you..."

Before him, between him and his friends, still dripping and trembling from its first full transformation, a low-slung torso surging with muscle, flexing talons longer than a man's fingers, hisses through fangs like box-cutter razors and bows its head in shame, just as Nicole Rieber's boyfriend comes charging out on all fours.

Bo shoots him four times in the head. One red-rimmed eye explodes and the other twitches and goes dull but the ferocious mainspring of its rippling, powerful body drives it into the pillow of Rieber's gut and rips great steaming garlands of bowel out of him, flinging it aside as if digging a winter burrow, gulping wads of flesh down in a reflexive frenzy. It subsides and dies only when distracted from its feast by the bristling howl of his mate as she rakes his flanks, still dripping the shreds of her human skin.

Ron's daughter claws at his biceps. "What are they, Daddy?"

He wants to tell her, but he can't, about how it was when they lived in sin, losing themselves to hunger and fury every winter, staggering out into the reborn world every springtime, naked and red, to start over, every year. About being ruled by the animal urges, about the toil and torment of even setting out on the path to control. About how God's message saved them all, brought them together out of the darkness and into the light. About how they left behind the long winters and lawless wasteland and found a place where they could be safe and secret in plain sight, where they could love each other and raise a family without ever giving in to the fatal, unforgivable sin of acknowledging their true nature.

Gulo gulo, they're called, slandered even by science. *Gluttonous glutton.*

Slauson puts a cheap nickel-plated revolver to Nicole Rieber's head and goes to blow her brains out. She's curled up in a ball, oblivious, shaking, licking away the last shreds of her humanity. Someone should tell her how the first time is the worst; how she might change back if she kills and eats a man, might turn back in a few days, might never turn back at all.

But maybe she already knows. Her claws rip up Keith Slauson's leg, boning him like a poached fish. The gun goes off everywhere but in Nicole's face. Her jaws clutch on his forearm. Slauson seizes up and roars and his teeth sprout like icicles. He bites into her thickly muscled neck, ripping out tufts of wet pelt, but even as his skin splits and his humanity burns up in a fire of fur, he bleeds out and dies in her teeth.

"You see," Kolb says, flipping on the hi-beams to pin the monstrous wolverine feasting on her father's entrails, "why we take this Vow so seriously? I told you to save yourself. This is what you're saving yourself from."

"I'm still pure, Daddy,"

His nostrils flare, stealing her breath. "I know, honey."

Slauson's daughter, way in the back, starts blubbering again.

Kolb pokes at his phone a moment.

BREAKING NEWS: SHOCKING ANIMAL ATTACK ON HIGH SCHOOL CAMPUS–ONE DEAD, ONE MISSING.

Tammy Slauson vaults out when he opens the window and comes charging at her best friend, her shrinking skin tearing to let her out.

He throws the truck into gear and drives around to the back of the church.

11:57 PM

The pastor is waiting.

"What were they, Daddy? That thing... Mr. Rieber thought... he said..."

He wants to tell her about what God put into them, that must never come out; about how the pastor offered them a way to live and thrive and control what they were; about the doctor who performed the operation on some who couldn't control themselves; about the "vasectomy" he had to undergo, or else Enid would've thrown him out and the church would've hunted him down, because he couldn't stop going down to the border to hunt on all fours; about how much easier life became with his musk glands and testes gone, about the peace of having no choice but to be good.

But he just gets out and comes around and opens the door for her to get out and follow him. He goes down a red hall lit by red lamps, feeling his blood thrum and sing, the heat freezing, the cold cremating, racing through him without finding that trigger that was the door to everything that made life what it was supposed to be. If Hope wanted to live long enough to bear children, then after she had borne a family, she would need the operation too, or she'd have to go North and forget her name.

He wants to tell her all this, but he has to believe she'll figure it out. When he takes her hand and removes the silver promise ring, she says nothing, only bows her head, though he can smell the oily fury from her ripening scent glands.

He holds out his two fists and tells her to pick one. She knows how this game has always been rigged, and this time is no different. A prize in each hand, so she can't lose. Identical white gold wedding bands, but when she touches the left hand with her nose, the pastor draws back a curtain.

She's a smart girl– no, she's a woman, now. She's already going down on all fours and arching her bristling back as the pastor throws wide open the door of her husband's cage.

Were...

Were-?

by

Darrell Schweitzer

S O YOU BEGIN in the traditional manner, by selling your soul to the Devil, only the traditional accoutrements have been dispensed within this day and age: no midnight conjuring of a demon raised in a swirl of smoke from within a pentagram, no parchment produced out of an infernal sleeve to be signed in your blood. None of that. If you truly have the intent, if your mind has been consumed with hatred and desire to the point that you are ready, then the Dark One is already there. Something moves in the periphery of your vision. Some shadow shifts. A pile of papers topples over in your dingy abode. There's a glimpse of something small and black, for just an instant. It could be a cat, but you don't have a cat, do you?

And you are not even certain that you have bargained away your soul, only that you have changed and there will be a price. No trickery over the fine print.

Maybe you do end up with a magic salve or a belt made of animal skin, or else it's just a way of touching yourself, a feeling, that lets you stand out in your rowhouse front yard late one night, naked, and if the neighbors get an eyeful, well, fuck 'em. The almost frigid autumn air is wonderful on your skin, but after a moment you're burning up, not in pain, but raging with newfound power and the sensation is like, is like... to be honest with yourself, you have to admit it's like jerking off only a million times more intense. Nothing about the full moon, because the moon is down when you begin to change. Your body ripples like mercury, your flesh melts into smoke, and you shrink down, the earth rushing up to embrace you. You have many forms now. You are the master of all the world's secrets, and with a repertoire like that, turning into a mere wolf would be oh so clichéd, not to mention impractical, because a gigantic lupine trotting about in an urban neighborhood is likely to attract unwanted attention. So your first choice is a snake, an enormous, black python-like thing of no precise species, which wriggles its way in the darkness at surprising speed. Yes, yes, the sensation is still intense; you touch and feel everything in a way you never have before, like a super orgasm indeed, like a thousand explosions propelling you along – and the image comes to you for just a second, something from your reading years ago, of an old-time proposal for a spaceship called Project Orion which involved a thousand atomic bombs set off one by one to drive mankind's ultimate phallic symbol into the shadowy depths of the cosmos – and forget the Freudianisms, which are ridiculous. Your mind cannot hold such thoughts for it is no longer a human mind.

As a serpent, then, you come upon a dog and strangle it for the sheer joy of killing. You become, after that, a dog, in the image of the one you just killed, but of course did not bother to consume. No one notices stray dogs. But to make your way all the way across town to where you intend to go – that much the human mind, or the super-human mind you have become can stay focused on – involves crossing railroad tracks and a highway, so it is better to fly. You change again and again, each sensation more ecstatic than the last. You become a bat, a pigeon, even an eagle. In the dark, no one is going to notice a black eagle swooping among the skyscrapers, settling down into the far, southern end of the city which is almost another city set apart. Some still-human part of you asks, in the name of scientific curiosity, where the extra mass goes and comes back from when you change into something small, something large again, something small. Snake, dog, bat, eagle, even a moth.

But it does not matter. This is not a problem in physics.

You glide down among the old, residential streets, the 19th century houses. Then you're on four legs again, then two, then four, running, and with eyes sharper than any human eyes, an acuity of night-vision you would never have believed possible, you can make out a house number from blocks away, in the dark. Yes, that one. Here.

Now you do have to focus, with more than human intensity, if you are to bring this off. You must think about the one you hate. You just stoke your rage like a fire, into something more than human anger. Yes, your actual motivations are base and even hackneyed. Revenge, vanity, jealousy, wounded pride, maybe even a broken heart. All of this you focus on that son-of-a-bitch Fletcher, who had been your friend before he betrayed you with contempt, the arch-manipulator who took over the enterprise, business, whatever it was – stay focused; the precise details do not matter – even though he didn't give a damn about what had been your dream, what you had poured your heart and soul into. He, the bastard, just enjoyed taking it away from you. He has no vision, no soul, no human capacity for compassion or sympathy, much less for goodness. He just enjoys jerking people around. He was the one who got you marginalized, then fired from the company you had helped found.

Yeah, him. What you propose to do is ring his doorbell at four o'clock in the morning in the middle of a work-week and appear to him in human form, *naked* – and you do, and he comes to the door about the time you manage to mouth the syllables "Hi there, Fletch!" The look on his face is beyond human in the degree of his astonishment, and he can only exclaim, "What the *fuck–?*"

Then you actually do follow expectations for a situation like this. The form of an enormous wolf is indeed appropriate, and still in the process of assuming such a shape you lunge at him, pushing him inward from the doorway and onto the floor, and he's screaming in pain and a terror louder and more shrilly than you ever thought a human being could as you're ripping his guts out, literally, splattering them every which way with violent shakes of your head. And you have the joy of actually tasting the fucker's still-beating heart between your teeth and on your tongue.

After he is dead there is more screaming. You look up and there on the stairs is a woman that the remote, fading, human part of your consciousness recognizes as Anne, the woman you once loved or thought you loved before Fletcher the Prick took her away from you, not because he loved her, but for the sheer malicious fun of doing so.

Well, you don't love her any more.

The feelings are so intense, orgasm after orgasm after orgasm of blood and killing, that you can't stop yourself; you don't even think about it anymore, and before long a good deal of Anne and the child she happened to have with her are splashed over the floor and walls and ceiling, and you've devoured a good deal more.

At the very last, upstairs, you loom panting and dripping blood over the last two children, infants asleep in their cribs.

But only for a moment.

Of course by now the commotion has aroused the neighborhood, and when cornered you howl and slash your way through the crowd, killing more for the incredible joy of it. But before long they're shooting guns and some remnant of your rational mind wonders if the immunity to all but silver bullets might not be one more traditional accoutrement dispensed within this modern age; so it seems expedient to change before their unbelieving eyes – and some of them are even trying to capture the festivities on cellphone cameras. You can just imagine how this is going to look on Facebook.

And then you can't, because you are something that crawls and wriggles, something that flies, something with dripping jaws and huge leathery wings entirely unknown to scientific zoology, some personification of all human nightmare.

Several more times, blocks away, then miles away, you kill again, for the joy and hunger of killing.

Then, when the sky begins to lighten and the frenzy leaves you, you are lying on the ground... in a woodland. Maybe a park. You don't know. No more thoughts of place, much less street addresses. There are only sensations.

Your flesh melts yet again, like smoke, into... what? That which crawls, that with wriggles, four legs, two. Large, small. You cannot remember. You have no mind left to remember. You have become an essence of bestial nature, a thing, predation incarnate, but that is all.

You will not be returning to your former life, not even to gloat, much less to recover your standing in the world.

That's all gone.

Maybe you made a bargain and maybe you bartered something away, but in doing so, in its absence, you have entirely forgotten what it was you have lost.

Scoop

Scoop
by
Sam Gafford

I**T WAS** 1985. Ronald Reagan was president and Russia was still the "evil empire". An ozone hole was discovered over the Antarctic and "America's Newspaper", *The World News,* was circling the drain.

The supermarket newspaper wars had been fierce and titles were dropping every week. Only *The Weekly World News* and *The National Enquirer* appeared immune as their circulation climbed while others fell. Robert Pell, the editor-in-chief of *The World News*, had been around long enough to know that the end was in sight. He didn't have a mascot like *The Weekly World News* had in 'Bat-boy' or the inside track on all of the celebrity dirt that *The National Enquirer* was built on. All Pell had was monsters and murders.

What Pell needed was a 'hook'. A story that would make all the housewives and teenagers stop dead in their tracks in those supermarket lines and not move until they'd read it. But Pell had nothing. Bigfoot and the Loch Ness monster just wasn't cutting it anymore. Even exposes about sexually aggressive ghosts weren't selling and mobsters just weren't killing themselves off brutally enough anymore. "What I wouldn't give for a nice St. Valentine's Day Massacre," Pell said to his empty office.

As he looked out over the now nearly vacant newsroom, Pell remembered back to when it was a hotbed of activity with stringers running back and forth while reporters yelled excitedly into phones and punched their typewriters like they were prizefighters in the tenth round of a championship match. Now it was eerily quiet with less than a dozen people milling about. The only section that was busy was the Advertising Sales Department which had been merged into the newsroom three months ago to save space and expenses. They were busy out of desperation, trying to sell tickets to the Titanic after it went down.

"Time to update the resume," Pell thought but there was nowhere else to go. He'd have to ride the train all the way to the final stop unless he found some way to keep it going for a while longer. As he looked over the crew, he realized there wasn't much to choose from. One was as good as the other.

"Faustino," Pell yelled through the open doorway, "get your ass in here."

Al Faustino wasn't much to look at. The man was thin, nearly skin and bones which had always unnerved Pell. He had thin brown hair and the kind of a moustache that Wyatt Earp would have worn proudly. Faustino had the air of someone with a terminal illness or too much alcohol. Not that booze was a problem in the publishing business. It was practically a requirement. But Faustino had shown good reporter's instinct and had dug up some good stories in the past plus, more importantly, Pell was desperate.

"What are you working on?" Pell asked as Faustino fell into a chair like a damned scarecrow.

"I got a lead on a story about a woman who claims she's being haunted by Capone's ghost."

Pell lit a cigarette and took a hard draw on it. "Anything to it?"

Faustino shrugged. "Probably not. I think the woman's nuts, actually."

"You got anything else?" Pell said, his eyes showing his impatience.

Faustino shook his head.

"Well, now you do," Pell replied and dumped a folder in front of Faustino. It was not thin but not thick either.

"What's this?" Faustino asked, picking up the folder and thumbing through the contents. There were a number of clippings from different newspapers. Some went back a few years and some were more current. They were from various places and only shared one thing in common; they were all about hideous murders.

"This is your next story. I want you to follow up on these cases and tie them all together. I want sensationalism and blood and I want it *BIG!*"

"Are they connected?" Faustino asked, not getting the point.

"Does it matter? Look, Faustino, I'm going to level with you. This paper is circling the toilet. The Board told me last week that we've got six months to turn the sales around or they're shutting the doors. They can't sell this shit rag to anyone. So we need something big. Something that will sell papers."

"What? Like Bigfoot killed all these people?"

Pell waved his hands in derision. "Nah, Bigfoot's old school. Serial killers are what's in now. You see this?"

"This," Pell grabbed a book off of his desk and waved it at Faustino, "is what scares people now." The cover blared out *Red Dragon* but Faustino didn't recognize it. "Serial killers. Guys who kill without emotion or remorse. These are the new monsters. You know? Like Ted Bundy or Son of Sam. We're going to make a new Jack the Ripper outta these murders. All I need is for you to link all of these cases together and give me a name. Something that'll sell! You got me?"

Faustino looked over the articles. It was true that they had something of a similar theme to them. All of the murders had been bloody and brutal, almost to the point of animal attacks. Some had been isolated attacks of hikers but others had been people murdered in their houses. Some were even killed in their apartments.

"Where'd you get these?" Faustino asked.

"I got a guy." Pell said and Faustino just looked at him, not understanding what he meant.

Pell nervously looked away. "He's what they used to call a 'clipping service'. Guy reads like a dozen newspapers a day and I pay him to clip all of the 'interesting' articles."

Faustino continued to look through the clippings. "I'd no idea anyone still did that."

Pell leaned back in his chair, his not inconsiderable paunch taking center stage. "Yeah, well, he's kind of a 'special' case. Anyway, you need to go see him and get anything new he's found. You've got a day before your first article. Lead. 20pt headline on the first page. But it's got to be smokin' hot, you got me?"

Faustino nodded. "Yeah, yeah, I got you. And it doesn't matter how true it is, right?"

Pell scoffed. "This is the *World News*. Since when do we print the truth?"

Faustino took the bus south to the address that Pell had given him. It was not surprising that it was in the Bowery, that bastion of the forgotten and unwanted. Since the 1970s, the city had made a determined effort to clean out the bums and vagrants so that rich people could buy up the land cheap and renovate it. So a lot of the unwanted just went underground or retreated further into the slums. Every city has levels to it and many that lead to dark corners.

The apartment building on Allen Street was decrepit and the streets were overflowing with rubbish from one of the city's frequent garbage strikes. The people on the stoop looked up as Faustino walked up the stairs but took no notice of him. The Bowery was a place where it did not pay to be observant. Faustino climbed to the third floor and knocked on the fifth door. It opened slightly and an old eye looked out warily.

"Pell sent me." Faustino said and the door opened wider.

"Ah, yes, yes, yes, Mr. Faustino, come in, come in. Mr. Pell telephoned and said you'd be coming by. He did. Yes, he did."

Like a mouse, the little man backed away into his hole. Faustino walked into an archivist's dream. Everything was cleanly organized and packed away. File cabinets lined every room. Bookcases were neatly filled with all types of reference volumes lining the shelves.

"You're, ah, Mister Quinn, right?" Faustino asked.

"Yes, yes, yes," Quinn responded, "quite right, yes. Mr. Pell has me find him the most interesting items, he does. Yes, he does."

Quinn was an old man. Not just old in years but old in thought, movement and bearing. He was the kind of person who was born with the weight of years already upon them. Despite the warmth of the early Fall, he wore several sweaters and even a scarf. It gave him a 'turtle-ish' appearance.

"Pell said you might have something for me?"

Shuffling, Quinn went over to the table and picked up a new folder.

"Yes, yes, yes, something interesting. That's what Mr. Pell likes."

Inside the folder was another clipping. This one was new and from a local paper up in North Hudson, New York, near the Adirondack Mountains. The headline read, "Family Found Slaughtered". There was a picture of a cabin with several police cars around it and three shrouded bodies on the lawn. The details were grim.

"Mr. Quinn, just what kind of thing did Pell tell you to clip out for him?"

Twitching, Quinn walked around the room in a well-worn circle. "'Murders', he says, 'murders that are very bloody, very brutal, very unexplained.' There's a pattern, you see. Not everyone can see them but I can. That's what I'm good at."

Faustino shook his head. "What are you talking about?"

"Mr. Pell, he's a good man, nice man. He gives me work when everyone else says they don't need me. But he, he is limited in his thinking. All he sees is blood but, but, I see more."

Shaking his head, Faustino said, "I don't see it. What's the pattern?"

"Dates, times, locations. All are similar but different. Do you see? Look. Look here."

There was a large astrological calendar on the wall that Quinn walked over to and pointed at.

"Here. Phases of the moon. Do you see?"

Faustino shook his head.

Quinn pointed to dates marked on the calendar. "Here. Arizona 1982. Here. New Mexico, 1978. Here. Maine, 1984. Here. Washington, 1976. I've written them all down here on my calendar and they've all got one thing in common."

Silently, Quinn waited for Faustino to make the connection but he couldn't. "You, you don't see? Look. Look. Look. See? Each one. Each one happened on a full moon. You see, yes?"

"A werewolf? That's what you're selling me?" Pell yelled at Faustino. "I told you. No monsters!"

"Keep reading," Faustino replied.

Pell grumbled while Faustino lounged in the chair in Pell's office. Slowly, Pell's face became less harsh and even started to relax into what might possibly be considered a smile. When he finished reading, Pell could even be said to be grinning.

"So you like it?" asked Faustino.

"It's fucking genius! A serial killer who thinks he's a werewolf! It's perfect!"

Faustino nodded happily. "Yep, this way you get both markets. The monsters and the serial killers. And wait until you see the next article."

Pell looked at Faustino over the pages.

"I've been doing some digging. Well, Quinn has, and there's more, a lot more."

Intrigued, Pell leaned back in his chair.

"He's found a ton of old cases, some going back to the 1920s. All of them are vicious murders, all unsolved, all done during a full moon."

"Conspiracy?"

"I'm thinking 'Cult'. A cult of whackos who believe that they're werewolves. Spread down through the years and across the country. We can keep this going for months. So, how's that for your hook?"

This time, there was no mistaking the smile on Pell's face.

The circulation of *The World News* doubled in two weeks when Faustino's series began. By the third week, it was challenging *The National Enquirer* for rack space at the national supermarkets. The tide was turning and Pell finally got good numbers to show the board at the next meeting. But keeping the wolf from the door is a never-ending challenge.

"This isn't acceptable," Pell said as he threw Faustino's latest article back at the reporter.

Stunned, Faustino said, "What do you mean? It's just like the last one: 'BACKYARD BLOOD CULT'."

"Yeah, that's the problem. You need to amp it up. I need you to go to the site of this last one. Where was it? Upstate?"

Faustino nodded.

"Right. I want you to go up there and personally interview people. Get the inside story. Snag a few photos off the local police. Make it real. You got me? Make people think that it could happen to them. Make 'em read and *bleed*."

A quick voucher later and Faustino was in a rented car heading up the New York Throughway with a map and a folder of newspaper clippings. North Hudson was the sort of town that never grew very far. In the shadows of the Adirondack Mountains, it was mostly a place that people passed through on their way to somewhere else. As Faustino would discover, it was a few businesses, a gas station, a post office in the basement of someone's house and a small bed & breakfast. They didn't even have their own police force.

After registering at the B & B, owned by a folksy couple named Pam & Paul, Faustino had to drive almost an hour back south to find the first rural bar, "Ray's Roadhouse". It was the typical kind of bar that one would expect to find with the typical type of clientele. Even Faustino felt that it was too contrived. Even the graffiti on the bathroom wall looked as if it had been designed to be chaotic on purpose.

No one paid any attention to Faustino when he came in. His order was taken by a polite waitress who was just young enough and showing the right amount of skin. He was allowed to eat his chicken wings and drink his beer in peace despite several attempts at conversation with others. No one was rude but no one was open either. If anyone had shot menacing glances his way, Faustino wasn't aware of it.

The next morning, Faustino took a ride out to the scene of the previous month's murder.

It was a newly built log cabin up in the woods which could only be reached by a dirt road. Not the kind of log cabin that one thinks of should one imagine the birthplace of Abe Lincoln but one of the prefabricated log cabins that are put up by companies in about a week and a half. Faustino noticed that there were no power lines or telephone poles along the way. The place was truly isolated.

Faustino reviewed the newspaper clippings as he sat in the car, too nervous to get out just yet. According to the article, the Lumsdon family had been slaughtered without warning. Mark Lumsdon, 53, and Eleanor Lumsdon, 45, had been found in the living room. Oldest son, Bob (21), was on the back porch while daughter Emily (18) and youngest son, Tom (14), were found on the front yard. The only photograph was grainy and devoid of any detail. The same could be said of the article itself. The wounds were not described but mention was made of the 'horrific' nature of the attack and that wild animals were suspected. The bodies had been found when a workman arrived the next day to install security lights. Too little, too late.

Slowly, Faustino got out of the car and took some pictures of the house. His mind ran through different headline choices as he worked. "BLOOD HOUSE". "CULT KILLING FLOOR". "CLAWS OF THE CULT". Yes, definitely the last one. Even if the bodies didn't have claw marks.

There were two indentations in the front lawn. The grass was dead in two areas, roughly equivalent to the size of two teenagers. Faustino took pictures of each patch which was when he noticed that they were a fair distance apart. It would have been difficult for one person to take down each of these people as they were running away. Maybe a wild animal wasn't so outlandish after all. Faustino grew up in the city and all he knew of wild animals was what he saw in Times Square after midnight.

The back porch had been neatened up with a large grill in the corner and deck furniture waiting for people who would never come back. The blood, of course, had been cleaned away but not the claw marks in the deck. They were deep and wide with every indication of paws. Faustino put his hand down and found that his hand could not stretch wide enough to connect to the marks. Clumsily, he took a picture of his hand near the claw marks for contrast. Although there was no chalk mark showing a body, there was a circular pattern of claw marks around an empty space. The oldest boy must have been caught here, Faustino reasoned, and he took several pictures from different angles.

The door was locked. Examining it, Faustino could see that it was not a new lock so it hadn't been replaced since the attack. Neither did it show signs of having been tampered with. The screen door was whole and untouched. The glass in the back door was unbroken and dirty. It hadn't been changed either.

Bolstering his nerve, Faustino pulled out a Swiss Army Knife and went to work on the door lock. It wasn't a particularly tough lock. Perhaps the Lumsdon's didn't feel they had anything to fear so far out in the woods. Well, not from anything that could open a door by turning a knob anyway. Faustino walked quietly into the cabin, feeling that he was walking into someone's grave.

The first thing he noticed was that everything was neat and clean. Faustino had worked crime scenes before, including several Mob hits, and the one thing that they all had in common was that they were all messy and covered in fingerprint powder. There was no powder here. No one had ever dusted for prints.

Past the kitchen was the living room where the parents had been found.

There were still bloodstains on the rug, on the furniture, on the walls and even on the ceiling. The rug would have to come out, furniture

119

thrown away and the walls and ceiling repainted... several times. Even cleaned, the explosion of blood that had happened in this room was obvious. Arterial spray had gone everywhere. These pictures would make the front page for sure.

Faustino took as many pictures as he could from every angle that he could but one thing kept bothering him. The murders had to start in the living room with the parents. Then the animals took down the oldest son on the porch while the two youngest kids made a break for it. How could they have taken down five people so quickly? And not break a window in the back door or even rip the screen when they bounded out of the house running three of them down?

As he was walking back through the kitchen, Faustino noticed something else. There was food still on the counter. Not fruit or anything like that but several boxes of cereal, crackers and bags of chips were sitting there, completely undisturbed. If animals had gotten into the Lumsdon home, why wouldn't they have eaten the food that was just sitting there?

Something wasn't fitting but Faustino couldn't put his finger on it. Wild animal attacks fit into his 'werewolf mania' hook and that was how he'd write it up but he wasn't satisfied. He left after taking photos of the Lumsdon's personal effects and pictures on the wall. The fridge had several childish drawings on it and Faustino took pictures of them without really noticing them. They'd make good 'heart-string' material. That's all he cared about.

Before Faustino got into his car, he looked around. No one was watching him. In fact, there was not a sound in the air. No birds. No breeze. No squirrels rustling through the brush. It was completely quiet. There was nothing there except Faustino and the woods surrounding the cabin. He got into his car and drove away faster than he realized.

The next stop was the county police station where Faustino learned virtually nothing. The deputies were not willing to say anything about the case or allow Faustino to look at any evidence.

"But it's a closed case, right? Animal attack, right? So what's the harm in letting me see the file?"

"You ever hear about something called *confidentiality,* fella? Those people died very badly and I'm sure that their family wouldn't appreciate our just giving out details to any 'Curious George' that wanders in."

Pleas to the integrity of the fifth estate fell on deaf ears and Faustino made a quick exit when the deputies began to get too curious about him, as well. It didn't matter. Cops were notoriously quiet especially about cases that they simply can't understand. Which meant that the original reporter was next on the roll call.

Faustino found the reporter at the small office of the *Adirondack Sentinel* where he was also Managing Editor. Gene Parsons was a round fellow who didn't like to move around very much. The mere act of breathing seemed to bring a sheet of perspiration on his balding head.

"I'm not surprised you're here," Parsons said somewhat boastingly. "A case like that is bound to get attention. Where did you say you were from again?"

"Oh, the... uh, *New York Daily News*," Faustino bluffed.

Parsons smiled. "Fine paper. I read it often myself. As long as you're not here from the *Post*. I don't care for their editorial policies at all!"

"No, I'm definitely not here from the *Post*. Are there any more details you can give me, Mr. Parsons? Perhaps something you left out of your article?"

"Well, I shouldn't go talking out of school about such things but I did find it odd how quickly everything was wrapped up. In all my years, I've never seen the police or coroner work so fast around here. Carted those bodies away quicker than a raccoon in a garbage can."

"Did you actually get a look at the bodies?"

"I should say I did! I took all of the official photos for the Sheriff. They wouldn't know one end of a camera from another."

Faustino could barely contain his excitement. "Could I see those pictures?"

"Oh, I don't know. Sheriff might not be too happy."

This was a road Faustino had been down before. "What if I told you that, should we use any of those pictures, you'll get credit for them? Think of it, Mr. Parsons. A photo credit from a nationally read newspaper!"

Within minutes, Faustino was looking at the original photographs of the crime scene. They were far bloodier than he expected. Even Pell might think twice about using these. The photos of the dead kids were bad enough, Parsons had gotten close up pictures of the wounds which certainly looked like animal attacks mixed with bite marks, but the adults had gotten the worst of it. Their bodies were sliced and bitten almost to the point of being unrecognizable.

Parsons could see Faustino's reaction. "I know. It's pretty strong stuff. You can see why I could only use an out-of-focus shot for my paper here. Otherwise, folks would complain."

Struggling to keep his composure, Faustino asked, "Can I get copies of these?"

Parsons looked at him closely. "I get credit right? You send me a clipping of anything that's used?"

"Absolutely."

Nodding, Parsons took back the photos. "Come back in a couple of hours."

Faustino made to leave the office when he turned back, "One last thing, Mr. Parsons, did anyone know the Lumsdon's here in town? Had they lived here long?"

The portly reporter had already disappeared into the back room as he yelled his response, "No, they only moved in a year or so ago. Check with Bishop Realty across the street. They sold them the land."

"Terrible, terrible thing," said Ed Bishop, owner of Bishop Realty. "Such a shame and this was their first season up here, too."

"I thought that you had sold them the land a few years ago?" Faustino was not comfortable in the realty office. For one thing, Bishop was the kind of man that you would trust buying anything from and, for another thing, the office was decked out in full 'hunter' style with the heads of deer, elk and god knows what else on the walls.

"Oh, yes, about two years ago but there was much work to be done, you know. The land had to be cleared, the access road laid down and then the cabin construction. You'd be amazed at how much goes into building up there not to mention permits and such."

"Do you know where the Lumsdons came from?"

Bishop's brow furrowed but Faustino couldn't tell if he was trying to recall a fact or cover one up. "Somewhere in Connecticut, I believe. He'd been in banking in New York, I gather, and they wanted a vacation home. Place wasn't winterized, you know."

"So they didn't know anyone in town?"

"No, not really. Oh, I think that they were friendly with that couple that run the B & B up there. The Lumsdons stayed there whenever they came up to check on the progress."

Faustino felt a twinge of nerves but didn't listen to it.

"You mean 'Pam & Paul'?"

"Yes, that's them. Lovely couple. I sold them that B & B about ten years ago, you know. Imagine that."

Faustino was more anxious to get the pictures from Parsons than he had expected to be. Unable to eat lunch, he had gone back to the newspaper office and paced in the lobby while Parsons worked. Several front pages of the paper had been framed and placed on the wall along with various commendations and certifications which were meant to impress but were essentially worthless. A smaller item on one front page showed a team of lumberjacks under the heading, "PRIZE BEAR SHOT". They were standing behind an abnormally large bear. The story related how their camp had been attacked by the beast which had wounded several of them. The men looked happy and oddly familiar. The date was November 4th, 1952. The lead story was Eisenhower beats Stevenson.

Another question had occurred to Faustino by the time Parsons came out with the photos. "In your article, you said that the bodies were discovered by a workman? Do you have his name?"

"Yes, indeed. That was William Timmons but you won't be able to talk to him."

"Why not?"

"Poor man had a complete breakdown right after. Family put him in a hospital somewhere up near Lake Champlain, I believe. Not surprising. He was very upset."

Faustino shook his head in agreement. "Yes, of course. Didn't you think that the police were awfully quick to rule this as an 'animal attack'?"

The question seemed to baffle Parsons.

"Not after seeing the bodies. What else would have ripped them apart like that? The claw marks on the deck and the bodies. It had to be an animal, no question."

"What kind? Wolves?"

Parsons smiled. "Mr. Faustino, there haven't been any wolves in NY for nearly a hundred years. No, this was something big like a bear. That's the biggest thing out there, isn't it?"

The B & B made Faustino uneasy. Actually, everything about it made him uneasy. There was only one small television in the side room which got exactly one and a half stations. The air was unnaturally quiet and fresh, completely free of smog and the rattle of constant traffic. The bathroom was shared which would have been uncomfortable for Faustino if there had been any other guests. It faced the hulking shadow of one of the mountains and all Faustino could think of was some in-bred mountain family stalking out of the hills at night and attacking the lonely building.

He had left his bedroom light on all night the night before and would do so again if need be.

Dinner was not included with the accommodations but Pam had put together a plate for Faustino which he ate quietly in the empty dining room despite a diminished appetite. Paul was next door closing the gas station for the night which was the other half of their business. Pam was a 40ish woman with thin, shoulder length blonde hair and thick hips. Faustino could easily picture them both as hippy refugees from Woodstock.

"Pam," Faustino asked cautiously, "I understand that you knew that family that got killed near here? The Lumsdons?"

A pall came over the almost compulsory upbeat nature of the rustic hotelier. "Oh, yes. They used to stay here when their cabin was being built. It was a horrible shock for everyone."

Faustino nodded sympathetically. "Of course. Did you know them well?"

"Well, I knew Eleanor quite well. Her husband, not so much. He was a brooding man and it seemed like he didn't want to be here at all. He was always making calls on the phone here to New York and talking business."

That didn't sound right. "I had heard that they were retiring out here."

Pam frowned. "No, he wasn't. The place was more for Eleanor and the kids. She hated the city. She'd actually come from around Lake Saranac, not far from here."

"Really? So she was moving home then?"

"In a sense. She was very connected to nature and wanted to give that to her children. It's a shame that they never had a chance to enjoy it."

Faustino took a gamble. "I'd heard they were killed by cultists. Some crazies who thought that they were werewolves."

Surprisingly, Pam burst out laughing. "Where did you ever get that idea from?"

"I read it in *The Weekly News*."

"Oh, that rag? You shouldn't believe everything you read in the line at the supermarket, Mr. Faustino. No, the Lumsdons were killed by wild animals because they invaded their natural hunting space. Nothing more. Coffee?"

That night, Faustino sat at the desk in his room and reviewed his notes. He had enough to get the 'human interest' angle. The photos he took of the crime scene would make a nice contrast with the ones he took of the Lumsdons personal pictures in the house. A little cropping and editing would fix them up. The 'animal attack' angle would be played up but he'd already figured out his 'hook' for that. The killers would be a degenerative group of savages who live in the mountains and dress up in the skins of bears and wolves (who cares if there were no wolves in NY?). They used clubs made out of the animal's paws with sharpened claws at the ends to do the murders. There were a couple of them, at least, which was how the parents were killed while the kids were run down while they tried to escape. Faustino even made a drawing of how the savages would look. He'd give it to the art department at the paper and let them add the gore and blood. It was good and it would sell and, more importantly, now he could get the hell out of this place the next morning.

The whole place put Faustino on edge. Junkies and mobsters Faustino could understand. He could relate to them. But he just couldn't figure out these country people. It was as if they were trying hard not to be standoffish and yet never said anything of consequence. And the way they all towed the party line with the 'animal attack' story. Gangsters should be this united.

From the desk at his window, Faustino could see the garage next door. Paul was still there and Faustino thought that he could hear voices coming from the lighted office. He turned off his lamp and listened. Pam and Paul were talking and there was definitely some heated words being exchanged but Faustino couldn't capture most of them. They weren't fighting so much as trying to agree on something. Faustino had nearly convinced himself that, whatever it was, it wasn't interesting enough to bother with when the light in the garage went out and something loped out the door.

It quickly ran across the street and into the woods.

It had loped. It had definitely loped and it had been covered in fur.

Faustino backed away from the window and crashed onto the floor.

Suddenly, there was a knock on his door. "Mr. Faustino?" Pam's voice calmly asked. "Are you all right? I thought I heard a noise?"

How could she have gotten up here so quickly? Faustino was certain that she had just been in the garage talking to her husband.

"I-I'm fine, Pam," Faustino managed to say, "I just tripped over the chair."

"Do you need some ice?" She was trying to sound solicitous but it came out cold and threatening.

"No, no, I'm ok. Goodnight."

"Well, goodnight then."

Faustino had resolved not to spend another night in the B & B or in North Hudson. He packed up his belongings and waited for the house to become silent. He sat there in the dark, afraid to look out the window again.

An hour later, his nerves would not let him sit there any longer and, as quietly as he could, he turned the key in his door and opened it. There was nothing in the hallway except the dim nightlights placed for his convenience. Slowly, he walked out of his room and down the hall to the staircase, trying to be as silent as possible. He could hear every step he took and every creak of the old wood as he moved. Faustino tried to remember where Pam & Paul's bedroom was and thought that it was in the back of the house. He could avoid that by going out the front door but that was large and heavy and likely to be noisy. He couldn't help but sweat and had to move his bag from hand to hand to prevent losing his grip.

It felt as if it took hours to reach the front door but it had only been a few minutes. If he could make it to his car, he could get away quickly. But what about the car starting? They'd be sure to hear that. He'd have to risk it. As gently as possible, Faustino unlocked the front door and leaned into it. The heavy wood creaked on the hinges but he managed to get it open just far enough to squeeze through.

A look back showed that there were no lights coming on in the house, nothing to show that anyone had heard him. As Faustino gently walked across the grass to the parking lot next to the garage, he tried not to look in the area where the loping figure had gone. He pulled his keys out of his pocket and they fell with a loud noise to the ground. Faustino kneeled down instantly, flattening himself against the car but nothing happened.

Slowly, he got to his feet and looked around. That's when he noticed that the door to the garage was open and there was a light on. He wanted to get in his car and drive away but something focused him on the garage. He couldn't look away. Before he knew it, he was walking towards it. Faustino wasn't trying to be cautious or sneaky now. He was standing straight as he walked forward like something mesmerized.

The inside of the office was full of various repair manuals. The air was thick with oil and grease. A typical pin-up calendar was hanging on the wall and there was an old, worn desk with several uncomfortable, wooden chairs. It looked like any typical small garage office would be expected to look. In the corner, on a forgotten table, were several issues of *The Weekly World News*.

Faustino continued to walk forward, past the desk and through the second door to the room beyond where the light was shining. Inside, bodies hung from the ceiling. Blood and gore covered the floor. If he looked, Faustino would have seen the faces of the Lumsdons hanging there. There were others including a young couple whose picture had been included in Pam's photo album of 'happy guests'. The bodies were not neatly dressed like a hunter's would be but had been savagely ripped and clawed. Meat had been torn off the bones, not sliced. Soft parts showed signs of teeth marks.

Two red eyes glared at Faustino from a dark corner.

It loped closer, into the light. It wasn't wolf or bear but something else. A strange crossbreed between man and animal. Thick fur covered its entire body and the face had become a snout with angry, sharp teeth. The hands were huge man-like paws with razor claws. Its penis jutted out from it in a state of extreme excitement.

Then it spoke.

"Did you think we didn't recognize you? We've seen your picture in the paper with each of your exposes. You didn't even bother to change your name."

Faustino couldn't move. He was frozen in place. He couldn't even turn his head as he heard noises coming from behind him.

"I admit, your premise was unique. 'Cultists who believe they are werewolves'. Genius. And completely wrong."

He could feel the thing's hot breath coming closer as the sound of others behind him grew louder. "You are all always so self-centered as if the universe revolves around you. 'Men who turn into beasts'. You never consider the alternative that we wear your skins only to walk among you while we hunt."

The creature stood on its hind legs, towering over Faustino. He could feel the thing's warm, sticky breath on his face. Silently, he peed his pants.

"There are no werewolves or were-bears. We are older than this planet, this universe. We were old when Nyarlthotep walked through ancient Egypt and we will be still older when time ends and those who wait beyond the pale return. We take any form we wish and prey on anything we wish. Oceans have known us, as have the highest mountain peaks. We have been every fairy tale you have ever heard and every monster you have ever feared. We are the death that hides in the dark and the way beyond."

Faustino could see other forms moving around him now. They were without shape or definition but had weight and intent. They circled him, nipping at his flesh, tasting his skin. He still could not move as his blood began to flow.

"You were right on one thing though. Nothing is coincidence. Everything is connected. Every legend, every monster, every 'bump in the night' since your race began has been us. It's a good thing that you came to us and saved us from having to find you."

Blurred faces swam by Faustino's face. The waitress at the roadhouse. Parsons. Pam. Almost everyone he had met or seen in North Hudson. Even Bishop. The things that had pretended to be them leaped and circled as they bit, tore and clawed at Faustino.

"It's all an illusion. This world. The next. Nothing is real. We'll show you."

The creature that had pretended to be Paul lunged and ripped out Faustino's throat. As the blood flew in the air, it evaporated into a red mist. Pieces of him danced away in the whirlwind and as he started to die, Faustino began to see the truth. It was all an illusion. Only the blood had been real... that and the byline.

Hunter's Moon

Hunter's Moon
by
Don Webb and D.A. Madigan

L OIZA TRUSHUL hated the wet more than anything. Any*thing*, not any*one*. He hated his fellow soldiers considerably more than he hated the wet... he hated them more than he hated anything else in the universe. But as regards inanimate objects, sensations, or abstract concepts, it was being wet that Loiza Trushul hated the most. Naturally, his platoon was walking through a fucking rice paddy. The skies had the gray glow of false dawn, but down in the muck where Loiza was, it was dark... as black as the inside of a *gaje's* dirty ears, as his mother might have put it. Every time he pulled his boots from the mud, the ground made a sucking noise. Squelch - squelch - squelch. The whole country was impure, contaminating. He would die among *Gadjos*. With his fucking feet wet.

His troop mates called him Gypsy. At first they did this to kid him, but even the vaguest and most vestigial feelings of comradeship or good will between them had died with the sergeant two weeks ago. The sergeant had been a good man who treated everyone in the platoon equally... not a quality many people had. But the sergeant was gone now, and the men had to blame someone for it. You'd think they'd blame Charlie... it was Charlie's fucking landmine that took him out, wasn't it? But no. They blamed Loiza Trushul, because Loiza Trushul was a Gypsy, and everyone knew Gypsies brought bad luck.

So now, Loiza was even lower than the blacks. And it made no sense! His fellow grunts had no idea what a "Gypsy" was – they had never encountered a Romani in their lives in Nebraska or Utah or Ohio. They knew the word from movies like *The Wolf Man*. They had their own mis-guided pollution beliefs, their own stupid little taboos and superstitions.

That didn't bother him much... Gypsies were tolerant of the foolishness of the *gaje*.

But they didn't return the favor. Since the sergeant had stepped on that landmine, they just hated everything about him. Two days ago Rufus Washington had broken all his emery boards. It is impure for Romani to slice their nails with a clipper – the nails are contaminated and their fragments attract demons. So now he couldn't file his nails. Just one of the many torments they inflicted on him, for no reason.

They assumed that since he was a Gypsy he wasn't Christian, maybe not human. He was a Seventh Day Adventist, his dogtags said so. His last name meant cross, for Christ's sake.

Why did they blame him for the sergeant's death? Because he had been foolish enough to speak a simple Romani blessing over Sergeant Gomez's mud covered body. The platoon couldn't even bury him, they had just used his helmet to pour muck over his body, so that its thick blackness would hide the depredations of the millions of insects that buzzed in Viet Fucking Nam.

Loiza had made a cross out of two branches tied with spare shoelaces. He stuck it into the ground near Gomez's head and said simply, "Del o Del baxt." May God, (o Del), give goodness/luck/protection (Baxt). Simple enough, and heartfelt... they had all looked up to Gomez, Loiza included.

He'd been surprised when Rufus had punched him in the mouth. "Gomez was a fucking Catholic, man. He don't need your Gypsy voodoo!"

Loiza, admittedly, hadn't kept his cool very well. He'd told Rufus, through a mouthful of blood, that voodoo was a Jungle Bunny religion. His left eye was still swollen half closed and ringed with purple from the second punch Rufus had landed on him as he'd tried to get up. His chest still hurt on the right side, where Johnson, the blonde kid from Flapjack, Texas, had hit him with the butt of his M-16. Sure, Johnson was trying to break up the fight on account of it being disrespectful to the dead, but it had not escaped Loiza's notice that most of the blows wound up striking him, not Rufus.

He had hoped to be friends with Johnson. The poor SOB had the same name as the President. It's *prikasa* to be friends with a *Gadjo*, but it's worse *prikasa* to have no friends in Phuoc Long. Fuck Long Province.

He had tried to bond with Johnson. The big blond dipshit came from a central Texas town near Austin, while Loiza came from Houston, one of the biggest Romani settlements in North America. They had a few things in common: during R-n-R, they both sought out Dr. Pepper and Big Red Cream Soda. They had both eaten corndogs at the State Fair.

But Loiza was "big city" and he was a little dark. Not Mexican dark like Gomez, but dark enough to keep a big blond *gaje* like Johnson from ever trusting or liking him. Dark enough to make Johnson, and all the others, talk about how Loiza might be part gook.

This grew worse when Loiza tried to explain that "Gypsies" (he had given up telling them the correct word was Romani) came from India. Well they were in fucking Indo-China weren't they? Case closed.

The rice paddy stank like shit. And everyone was terrified of shit. The Viet Kong taught the peasants to make traps by smearing shit on sharpened bamboo sticks. *Punji* sticks. The first day Loiza's platoon had come under fire, they jumped into the dark green bushes on either side of the trail. *Punji* sticks stood everywhere, covered by the bushes. Loiza's baxt was strong and the stick he fell on broke and didn't pierce his hide. But Chang, McGinty and Phillips weren't as blessed. They all got stuck, and they were all shaking with fever in two days.

McGinty and Phillips were airlifted to Saigon. By a typical army fuckup, Chang was listed as an enemy alien – even though he spoke no Chinese and was a Baptist from Mississippi. The little yellow fucker had wound up dying in a prison camp hospital. As far as Loiza was concerned, it served the rice eating bastard right. Chang had never been a friend of his. None of them had, except Gomez.

And now, to relieve the boredom, it was time for everyone's favorite pastime – race baiting. Johnson started it out:

"Hey Rufus, you know what day today is?" asked Johnson.

"Screw you day!" said Rufus.

"Close. It's Valentine's Day. Happy fucking Valentine. Isn't that the day you spearchuckers fuck a watermelon?"

That got a round of appreciative laughter from everyone but Rufus. But Rufus had a quick comeback:

"Only if 'Watermelon' is your nickname for your blonde sister with the big tits."

That got an even bigger laugh from everyone. And it let Rufus switch the target to Loiza. Although they would have inevitably started in on him anyway.

"Hey, Skerry, what do you get if you put your hand up Gypsy's sister's skirt at the wrong time of the month?" asked Rufus.

"I don't know," Skerry answered. He was a big good looking guy with dark hair from Minnesota; he always bragged that he didn't need to pay no gook whore when he got R-n-R, he had white nurses that would suck him off free any time he wanted. "What do you get if you put your hand up Gypsy's sister's skirt at the wrong time of the month?" he asked.

"You get your palm red."

Everyone but Loiza just fell out laughing at that. Like it wasn't the oldest, stupidest fucking Gypsy joke in the world.

Loiza actually felt something snap inside him at that moment. The guys didn't know, of course. He had had a sister, Maria. *Gadjo* boys in Houston had caught her on Main Street near the Rice Hotel. Picked her up. Raped her in their van and left her in Herman Park. The family threw her out because of pollution beliefs. She killed herself the month Loiza's draft notice came in the mail. She had been living with Uncle Bo at the time. Bo wasn't scared of *prikasa*. He was a sorcerer, a *Rashai* of *Beng*, the Evil One. No one talked to Bo, except when they needed something.

Loiza realized he needed something. He would write Uncle Bo, but even Bo's magic wouldn't be enough. He would also have to gain the love and trust of these men who had tormented him. It was distasteful, but they were *gaje*; lying to them wasn't truly lying at all. And they had made it clear to him by now – the enemy for him wasn't Charlie, it was these shit smelling men all around him in this shit smelling war.

He knew how to do it, too. His brother Djordji told him once, "Loiza, if you need *Gadjos* to love you, you must pretend to hate yourself."

So Loiza took a breath and said, "Did you hear the one about the three Gypsies that went to Heaven?"

Rufus said, "No, because no Gypsies ever went to Heaven."

"Well that's what St. Peter thought. When the three Gypsies showed up, he said 'I've never seen three Gypsies up here at once. I need to get advice from God. You guys wait by the gates of Heaven for ten minutes.' 'OK' said the gypsies. So St. Peter went off and asked God's advice and God said, 'Well anything could happen. If they showed up let them in.' So Peter went off to the golden gates, but he ran back to God in a few seconds. 'They're gone!' he cried. God said, 'The Gypsies are gone?' 'No,' St. Peter replied, 'the golden gates are gone.'"

That got a big laugh. And after that, every time they started up, Loiza always managed to tell the worst, nastiest, most offensively racist Gypsy jokes of all. They started to think of him as a clown... a good guy, somebody who made them laugh. And being able to laugh in the fucking 'Nam wasn't anything to just piss on.

The next time he was in Saigon, Loiza found a shop where he could buy a Tarot deck. The Tet Offensive was over, and pretty clearly the Johnson administration was, too. Aretha Franklin had a new song that described the members of Loiza's platoon – "Chain of Fools."

He began giving them Tarot readings. They would get laid, they would survive the war, and fortune would be theirs. All that happy horseshit that the *gaje* had always eaten up with a silver spoon. He would make it all more credible by throwing in little insights that he'd had. Johnson was cowed by his father. Rufus worried that his woman had moved in with a white hippie. Skerry was worried that he might like boys.

They bought it. Hook, line and sinker. Before every battle he would give them readings. Vague and positive. Now they respected him as a "Gypsy." They boasted their platoon was unkillable. They had Gypsy magic.

Then he began giving bad readings. In late April, something was coming, on or near the full Moon. A group of VC were going to kill them all. The Death card popped up in every spread next to the Moon. Loiza said he was glad to have served with the guys. There was no way out.

Unless.

No, he didn't want to think about it.

Tell us.

Feigning reluctance, Loiza eventually let himself be persuaded. "When Gypsies face insurmountable odds in war they can become *Xarpos*. Man-eaters, what you call werewolves. It is painful and a thing of the Devil, whom we call Beng. One must don a wolf belt and say certain words as the moon rises. Then the change comes. Bullets – unless Charlie is using silver bullets blessed by a priest – would not kill you. Knives cannot cut you. And your fierceness is the savagery of ten."

Loiza shook his head then. "It would be better to die clean than survive polluted like that, though. Forget I said anything, boys."

There was public disbelief... but they came to him in the night. Rufus brought him new emery boards and an apology – "I'm sorry, man." The others offered him cigarettes and candy and asked questions. Is it real? Is it painful? What are the down sides? Could they get wolf belts? Would they be werewolves for life? Did Loiza know the words? Had he seen it done?

Loiza told them about his Uncle Bo. He told them Bo would send him the words, if he asked. Bo could get wolf belts for them, too, although that would cost more than just Loiza making a request. No, Loiza had not seen it done, but he knew for a fact that Bo had done it. Yes, the transformation was painful. And, yes, they would be werewolves for life.

Again, Loiza pretended to try to talk them out of it. They would be unclean, creatures of Beng forever. They would transform and kill under every full moon. They would be a danger to everyone they loved.

It didn't matter to them. None of them wanted to die. After nearly two years in the hell that was the 'Nam, all any of them wanted was to get back to 'the world' again. If they did this, they would live to be sent home. They wouldn't join Sergeant Gomez in the muck. That was all that mattered to them.

All right, Loiza said. It would cost them money. Sixty dollars, each. For that, Bo could get the wolf belts. It had to be soon. Five of them paid up, the five he hated the most: Washington, Johnson, Skerry, Thompson, Kaminsky.

They would have to go AWOL for a few hours. The new sergeant wouldn't like it. They might have to kill him. None of them backed off from that. The new sergeant was no Gomez; if he treated everyone equally, it was by treating everyone like shit.

The package came from Houston. While other soldiers got cigarettes from home, cookies and brownies, amateur Polaroids of their naked wives grinning like monkeys into cameras held by (they said) sisters or best friends, or locks of their girlfriend's pubes, Loiza received a package with six strips of fur. One belt was black, the others white and black.

"How come yours is different?" the other five soldiers wanted to know.

"Because I am the shaman," Loiza told them. "I am going to do the magic. I will be the head wolf, do you have any problem with that? Or do you guys know the way to turn back into humans at dawn?"

None of them liked that idea. Loiza was their clown, their Gypsy clown – he was their good luck, but they didn't want to take orders from him.

"And this will save us, you mean we can't be killed except by silver bullets even when we are human?" they each asked, in turn, in their own words.

"Of course you can be killed," Loiza told them, his voice scornful. "Werewolves don't live forever. This is a warrior's invocation, for protection in battle. You can be killed by any mundane cause of death... a Jeep wreck, cancer, old age – you name it. You'll just be immune to bullets and knives and *punji* sticks. Weapons can't claim you. Now once again – I will be lead wolf, does anyone have any objections?"

No one had jack shit to say.

It would happen on April 30, which is one of those times when certain forces flow into the world. Skerry had seen that in a movie, so he was impressed. Others had heard bits of werewolf lore on TV, or read something in a comic book, and Loiza gravely agreed with anything they said. In truth he didn't know anything about wolfs-bane or Tibetan moon lilies, or how werewolfism spread. Uncle Bo had told him the belt was a one-time operation and that was all he needed to know.

He would probably spend his life trying to clean away the pollution. It didn't matter to him anymore. In his mind these *Gadjos* were the rich white boys that had raped his sister, even though two of them were black. They were the gang of boys that dragged his pants off him and ran them up the flagpole at Davy Crockett Junior High. They were the redneck shit heads who had burned a white cross on his grandmother's lawn in Pasadena, Texas. They were the SS men with their ovens. Who cries out for the Romani? Everyone cries for the Jews. The Jews get a homeland. Was there not a place in India to be cleared away for the children of O Del?

Every stupid joke, every reference to chicken stealing, or prostitution in gypsy wagons, every crack about the darkness of his skin – all of it showed Loiza that he was right to take his revenge this way. This was a righteous thing, a just thing. And if Del wouldn't help him do this thing, then maybe Uncle Bo was right – Del didn't care for His children. It was up to the dark one – Beng.

Loiza would do the magic, the *pokorel*.

During the next day the platoon passed the blackened ruins of three huts in a village where everything else had been burned to the ground. No one lived there. The new sergeant had them check for secret places – those little cellars and tunnels that Charlie loved so well. Nothing. They moved on. Loiza nodded to the five. Meet here as soon as it is dark. Two of them, Skerry and Washington, would have first watch. As soon as everyone had bedded down, they came for Loiza. He led them back to the charred huts.

The Moon was already rising. "That's bad," Loiza told them. "It means this will hurt."

When they came to the first hut, Loiza traced a circle around it with the butt of his rifle. "You guys must strip out here, leave your clothes and weapons in a pile, then put these belts on. Go inside, lay down and close your eyes. I will say the *pokorel* and I will change first. I will come inside and give you each a little bite. Then you will change. We will run through the night with great power and joy. We will kill our enemies. We will return here in the morning, and I will speak the counter-spell and we will all change back."

If they had not been so stupid... but *gaje* were always stupid, weren't they?... one of them might have wondered, how would Loiza speak a counterspell when he was a wolf? Could werewolves speak English? But they were all afraid to die, and they didn't want to think too hard, or doubt. They wanted to believe. This was their ticket back to 'the world'.

So the men took off their clothes, strangely shy around each other after months of communal showering. They dropped their clothes and weapons in separate piles and took their skin belts one by one. When all were inside the circle, lying on the muddy ground inside the hut, eyes closed, Loiza called out these words. The words he spoke were not English, yet all of them who were there to hear him speak understood him.

"I wear the belt of the wolf, for my wolfskin has grown on the inside. I call out to my Father Beng and claim my inheritance from the Moon and the Forest. My teeth shall rend those who torment me, my claws shall tear the flesh of those who have mocked me. The joy of the kill will be mine. Beng returns to the Earth and teaches me new ways to dance and kill. Hail Beng! Hail Kali! Beng is my Baxt!"

The belt around his middle suddenly grew very tight. It ripped into his flesh, while his blood seemed to boil – first near his wrists and ankles, then in his genitals. His back popped like a whip and he found himself on all fours. The fur began growing outward from the belt, and he felt the front of his skull break as his snout formed. His teeth fell out and he spat them on the ground in a bloody mess. New sharp teeth cut through his gums. His limbs shrank and his eyes grew large.

The silver of the moon was the most beautiful light he had ever seen. The moon itself seemed much, much larger – filling half the sky, and the smells of the jungle changed from a single sour disgusting note into a symphony of scents, each more alluring than the last. But the best scent of all was the raw, adrenaline spiked fear coming from the five sweaty bodies inside the hut. Loiza could smell each man individually. He knew when they had eaten, when they had relived themselves, and how much fear each one had. He could smell the tang of the badly cured German Shepherd skins each one was wearing.

He ran to the door. He sank his teeth into Rufus' throat first. The blood was delectable. Rufus hadn't even had time to call out, so that Loiza was able to take most of the flesh off of Skerry's face in a single bite. He loved the taste of Skerry 's saliva and enjoyed the feel of his teeth scratching against Skerry's teeth. Skerry managed a cry and the others began screaming and running for the door. He bit Thompson in his thigh and a second bite tore off his genitals. He liked the feel of Thompson's fur against the roof of his mouth. The blood spraying out in great gouts on his face was surprisingly pleasurable. Being the wolf was better than sex.

Kaminsky and Johnson made it out the door – half running, half crawling. He lunged after them. Kaminsky had managed to stand and was rooting through the closest pile of clothes – Skerry's – trying to get a weapon. A single snarling leap took him down. Loiza bit Kaminsky's neck from behind, his teeth crunching in the spine, and pulling it out, letting brain juice splash on his cheek.

Johnson had found someone's rifle and let loose a spray of bullets into Loiza's hide at point blank range. Nothing in his life had ever hurt like those bullets did as they passed through his ribcage.

But it did not kill him. Hell, it didn't even slow him down. As fast as his blood was gushing out, he felt it refilling in his heart. He felt his bones knit back together. He advanced on Johnson slowly, the continuous spray of bullets driving him back, like a fish swimming upriver against strong current.

Johnson was yelling, "It's me, Gypsy! It's me!" as though this would be a reason to stop. He looked so stupid covered in sweat and the blood of his friends, and a little belt made from some hapless cur from Uncle Bo's neighborhood in the Fourth Ward.

When Loiza got within four feet, Johnson panicked and threw the rifle down. He tried to turn and run, and Loiza let him, thinking that might be fun – but the stupid blond hick proved to be disappointing prey. He tripped on a pile of clothes, and Loiza lunged forward. He bit Johnson just below his left armpit. Johnson squealed like a pig as the wolf rolled him over.

Loiza had fun with him – he began to lick Johnson's face. Johnson was relieved. "Good boy!" he said, mistaking Loiza's murderous play with the antics of his little wiener dog back home. "Good boy!" Loiza tried to laugh and it came out as a series of sharp little barks. "Good boy!"

Then Loiza yawned, showed his great red tongue and tore Johnson's throat out.

It had taken less than ten minutes to kill them all. Loiza found himself hungry and methodically fed on the softer bits of each of the men. Cheeks and genitals were especially tender. He enjoyed the flavor of the eyes – their liquid was similar in consistency to maple syrup at the International House of Pancakes. He didn't like the taste of tobacco on Skerry and Thompson – it really was a vile habit.

Loiza laughed again. Here he was critiquing a meal just after his first kills. Sure he had shot at Viet Cong – he was pretty sure that he had killed two. But this was different, this was Joy and Sex and Religion all rolled up into one huge orgasmic experience at once! He blessed every hatred, every jealousy, every dark and miserable moment in the jungles of Phuoc Long that led to this. He blessed Uncle Bo and he blessed Beng.

That thought stopped him in his tracks. He whimpered like a dog. Would he simply belong to the Dark One now? Could Uncle Bo set him free for some price? Or would there be some horrible atonement? The madness of the last few months fell away. He was simply a soldier that had snapped in a fog of death and pot smoke and fear – every day, every

night, every breath he took, sucking it into and letting it out of his lungs –
FEAR.

Well, no one could kill him now. The gaping rents in his torso that
the M16 bullets had opened had all knit closed again, healed up, and
regenerated as if they had never been. He was sore – but it was the same
ache as in boot camp when he hiked ten miles with an 80 pound pack –
not the pain of a hundred bullets passed through his body.

There was no longer anything for him to fear. Now, *he* was a thing to
be feared.

He stared up at the Moon. It trembled in the sky, joyously, and gave
off beautiful sounds. The Moon actually sang. How could he not have
known this? As he listened to its song, he stopped being Loiza Trushul.
He became a singer of the song. He raised his snout and howled into the
night, and an answering howl came back – maybe a mile away. He loped
toward it, moved by the song of the Moon, which had somehow taken
the place of thoughts in his head.

He ran into the tangled, sweet smelling rankness of the jungle. The
silver moonlight showed him the trails. As he ran along some luckless rat
darted out of its hole and became a two gulp snack. A tiny toad croaked
and became a crunchy mouthful.

Loiza couldn't understand how he had eaten so much. He must have
consumed pounds of his friends' flesh, yet he was still hungry. Like the
blood that filled his heart from Otherwhere, his hunger took the flesh
someplace other than his stomach.

He heard the beautiful howl again like a piano glissando or the harp
of some lupine angel. He ran faster. He was gliding over the Earth. As a
man, as a boy, Loiza had never been graceful. He had never sought out
track or football or any game where he had to run, but now he poured
across the surface of the moonlit earth like mercury. He flew like a
hunting owl. He was all grace and each movement of his muscles was a
keen pleasure.

He entered a moonlit clearing.

A tall dark man with the head of a wolf sat on a throne there. He
wore a dark robe with lunar symbols in silver thread. He was the most
beautiful creature Loiza had ever seen.

Loiza realized he was deeply fucked.

"Welcome, my son!"

In the burnt out village Loiza had left behind, something started to appear... condensing, cohering, out of the empty, gore-stinking air.

So much hatred. So much fear. So much pain. All of it through his spell, his will... worked remotely, from the other side of the world, through the larynx and windpipe of his idiot nephew.

All that dark energy, released. Much of it would go to Beng – the Dark-Eater. But the Eaters were always slovens. There were always leftovers that a crafty sorcerer could put to use.

So now, out of the invisible psychic miasma of screams and howls that hung over the clearing... a figure took shape.

Head, first. Always the head, the seat of the will. Solidity spread downward. The shoulders filled out, then the chest, carrying the heart. The spine took form. The torso filled in around it as arms extended down from the shoulders... formed hands. He'd need hands. The hips formed... then the genitals, heavy and male and hairy. Bo wouldn't need genitals here, not for this very short lived manifestation, but he could no more form an ecto-body and leave off his cock and balls than he could have signed his name without using a capital B. They were intrinsic to his sense of identity, an essential part of the meat he wore in this world.

Legs extended down from the hips. The feet, hairy and long nailed, formed last, settling heavily into the blood soaked muck.

The sorcerer straightened up, smiling, ecto-spine crackling, muscle fibers stretching and relaxing as ectoplasmic tendons popped and ectoplasmic nerves hummed under his skin. The ecto-heart pumped, the ecto-lungs drew pints of rank, viscera-stinking jungle air into the ecto-chest. Delicious. His ectoplasmic cock surged erect, throbbing.

Bo looked around at the ravaged corpses strewn across the clearing... and smiled. Say what you will about the little *putz*... his nephew had created some first class carnage here. The boy might actually have a talent for mayhem. Who knew?

Creating a new Feeder for one of the Eaters had brought Bo a great deal of dark favor... but there were many Eaters. Bo did not believe in unturned stones, unworked angles. You never walked away when there was still money on the table; you never let a mark leave the tent with so much as a single coin remaining in his pocket.

Thinking these things, Bo began to weave together skeins of psychic energy. Much to be done here, before the sun rose and dispersed all this palpably delicious darkness his nephew had brought into being.

Miles away, Loiza tried to bow, to come up with a wolfish equivalent to bowing. Finally, he lowered his snout to the earth, then rolled over on his back, to show his belly. He barked, but both he and the One on the throne understood the words.

"I am Loiza Trushul."

"I know who you are," came the Lord's reply. Its voice was low and raspy, high and silvery, deep and thin, all at once. It was not a human voice, nor a wolf voice. It was not a voice of any earthly creature at all. "It was my Will that transformed you."

Loiza felt a tremor of mixed terror and adoration shiver through him. "I am grateful for the revenge you granted me, oh Great Lord," he howled, after a moment, "but I don't understand one thing."

The creature barked laughter. "You are correct. You don't understand one thing. There is not one single thing you understand. But in this case, you want to know why you don't hate these men now... men that, before you devoured them, you felt nothing but hatred for."

Loiza whimpered. "Yes, Lord Beng,"

The Great Lord... Satan?... was silent for a long moment. Then: "Call me Beng if you wish. My true name is far older than that... older than you Romani, older than you humans. But I can answer to Beng." The creature howled, a short yip Loiza understood to be laughter. "I have answered to it, when you called on me earlier. So, yes, Beng will do."

Loiza was baffled. Had he offended his new Dark Lord? "Master... is there something you would prefer..."

The Lord barked laughter once more. "You cannot offend me, little meat creature. I have no expectations of your race as regards higher behavior. My folk built humans to be imbalanced. We gave you much space for rage and hate. All of your grand passions, your feelings, your emotions... your rages, your hatreds, your huge towering loves and lusts, even your deepest devotion and faith... all of it feeds us. The one you call Del is my sibling... no better than me. He simply feeds on faith and all the emotions that arise from it. My sister, the Romans called her Venus, she feeds on sexual energy. Long ago I made a deal with your people, to transform you into humans that excel at hating all other humans. And you have been so very good at it. I am always happy to welcome another Romani to my fold, always delighted to provide your people with power when you ask it of me."

"This Deal... this is what allows us to become werewolves?" Loiza panted.

"Well... yes," the Dark Lord replied. "It's a simple matter. I etherically transfer some wolf DNA to you, along with some of my own essence. It's a brutal little genetic cocktail. The wolf genes aren't from those curs you modern humans think of as wolves... the juice you lycanthropes get is from Ice Age dire wolves. Like I said, simple, but it's got a real nice kick to it."

Loiza's mind whirled. "Are you a god?"

The Lord snorted. "Gods are human inventions. I would be closer to what you would call a space alien. But I didn't come in a flying saucer. My siblings and I were... assigned, I suppose... to this place, for a rotation or two."

Loiza felt uneasy. "I don't understand, but if our deal is done, tell me how to remove the belt and be human again."

"That isn't part of the Deal," the Lord replied. "You will regain your hairless ape form at dawn. Then each full Moon you will be *Xarpo*, a werewolf." He snickered. "As opposed to Harpo, a dead straight man to an obnoxious comedian. You will kill, and you will devour the flesh of what you kill, and that flesh, and the rage and pleasure you feel, and the terror and pain your prey feels, will all become energy that I will feed on. You will Feed me, and I will Eat."

Loiza flinched. "But I have no desire to kill anyone, now that I have avenged myself."

The Lord snorted. "Do not attempt to teach your Dark Lord how to steal sheep. You cannot fool me. The bloodthirst is deep in you... even deeper than in most of your wretched race. You hate well, you will be a fine Feeder. And every twenty eight days for the rest of your life, you will have the power to indulge your hate, to revel in it."

Loiza almost felt proud. But the Dark Lord was continuing, in a more thoughtful sort of growl: "There were once so few humans and they were so bad at hating each other, I had to intervene. The first human to hate his brother, was my student. I taught him that hate. And he flourished in it; he went forth from that pallid garden his parents had scratched into this wretched planet's surface and founded a continent of haters. Now there is more human hate than even I can consume. Eventually it will attract another sort of predator than me. Something far worse awaits humankind in centuries to come."

Now Loiza was uneasy again. "Why do you tell me this?"

Had Loiza not known better, he would have sworn he saw the Dark Lord... shrug. "I am bored. It is easy to appear to you when you are in the wolf shape. My last werewolves were hunted down in Vietnam during the early French days. Jesuit priests with blessed silver bullets. They served my brother, the Faith Eater. He's quite the bag of dicks, actually... I'm much more fun to have as a Lord than he is. Regardless. When you said the ancient werewolf charm here, in this land that has been empty of your kind for so long, I was drawn like an iron filing to a magnet."

Loiza paused. He knew the Lord had not actually said either 'iron filing' or 'magnet'... that was just how his brain had translated whatever incomprehensible terms the Lord had actually used. "But.. I am leaving here, my tour is over in a year."

Once again, the Lord barked laughter. "You will never leave. You think you'd risk being on a troop transport when the Change comes, or caught on an army base? You could survive being shot by a hundred men, but you would not want to. You will stay here. Maybe, like your Uncle Bo, you will learn how to use sorcery, the technology we gave humans when they were few and we were worried about surviving in our exile. Maybe you'll pass on your state to a few victims. Despite your myths, lycanthropy isn't all that contagious, but there's always a chance. Maybe you'll meet a nice Vietnamese girl and have a litter of little werewolves. But you will feed me over the years. You may also occasionally feed my brothers, the Faith Eater or the Anguish Eater. But mostly you belong to me now, so most of the Feed you generate, will come to me to Eat."

The Lord with the wolf's head breathed in deeply, and then breathed out again. And as he breathed out his form faded into the night. Loiza howled in sorrow and pain.

When dawn came he found the transition less painful. He dressed, slowly, feeling clumsy and weak in his human body. He made his way back to his platoon and said that he and the other five had snuck off to play poker in the burnt out village, and there had been shots fired out of the jungle, and Loiza had hidden in one of the huts.

The sergeant thought he saw through the lie – he thought Loiza and the other five had snuck off to have a big sausage fest without anyone else knowing. It was hardly the first time such a thing had happened in the Army, and it wouldn't be the last; it was even possible the sergeant had first-hand knowledge... hands on experience, as it were... of such activities. Such practices out in the bush were wildly unsafe, and in this case, the VC had caught the horny bastards with their pants down – or, more likely, completely off – and ambushed them. Loiza was lucky to be alive and not stuck in some bamboo cage somewhere with swamp rats chewing on his junk.

Loiza was surprised, when he led the platoon back to the burned village, to find no bodies. Had the bodies been there when he had returned the previous night, just before dawn? He couldn't remember. He'd been in his wolf form, exhausted, and he'd just lain down to sleep atop his own pile of clothes and equipment. But now, the bodies were gone. The men's clothes and equipment remained... even their weapons... but the bodies themselves were nowhere to be found.

The sergeant couldn't explain it... Charlie always took weapons and generally left the bodies behind. But this might be some new trick, meant to psych the Yankee out, to terrify him. Charlie loved that shit. The sergeant finally just shook his head and told the platoon not to talk about it.

He should have written that worthless Gypsy up. But that might have gotten Prushul shipped off to a stockade somewhere, and the sergeant needed every swinging, gun humping dick... even the goldbrick fuckoffs, like this lying sack of shit. The sergeant decided he'd just keep an eye on him.

After two more months... six days of glorious hunting and killing under two new full moons... Loiza found it easier to simply go AWOL. The sergeant was always on his ass anyway, so fuck it. Loiza deserted his unit. A letter went home to his parents saying that he was Missing In Action.

Uncle Bo smiled at the news as though understanding a secret joke. Uncle Bo's newest servant, who had been his niece when she was still alive, did not smile... but that was only because Bo had not told her to. The undead are very obedient. Certainly Bo was quite pleased with her; she was still very comely, and even more compliant in this form than when she was alive.

It was nearly six months after he had left his unit that Loiza first

147

began to feel as if he, himself, were being hunted under each full moon. He had found a village, deep in the jungle, where the little yellow slanty eyed rice eating fucks mostly kept to the old ways. They recognized the wolf in him. They knew the Lord... the Eater... that he Fed. They built a hut for him to stay in when the moon was not full, gave him food to eat, water and fermented rice wine to drink, woven mats to sleep on, a boy and a girl to fuck. (The girl had had one child when she was 11; an unfortunate family matter. The birth had destroyed her ability to have further children. The village elders were not stupid; they did not want any werewolf litters underfoot.)

Beneath the full moon Loiza hunted well away from the village, and occasionally brought back large prey – water buffalo, boar, once a man eating tiger – for the village stewpots.

But then, Loiza started to feel strange, cold eyes on him as he loped the secret jungle trails. It was an unsettling sensation. He told himself it was his Master, the Eater Beng, the Dark Lord, watching him from a distance. It helped, but did not fully reassure him. Why would the Dark Lord watch him? Was he not Feeding him enough?

It made him uneasy.

The villagers were growing fearful, too. They had taken Loiza in because in a world where there are monsters, it is good to have a monster of one's own. But now hunters were returning from the jungle with stories of being stalked by unseen creatures... not tigers or boar or anything they could put a name to... something silent. Something that smelled of rot and death. Something crafty... like the tigerman, a human that assumed the shape of a tiger but kept the intellect of a man.

When the next full moon came, Loiza slunk into the jungle, determined to flush out whatever it was that was stalking him and frightening the villagers. He ranged miles into the dense rain forest, feeling the gaze of something brooding and awful the entire time. Occasionally he caught the scent of something dead, something rotting but not still, as the dead should be. Yet he never heard a sound, nor saw anything... until he was pacing down a game trail, following the delicious smells coming from a camouflaged outlet leading to a Viet Cong tunnel warren... and something lunged out of the underbrush at him, wrapping rotten yet inhumanly strong arms around his neck, dragging him down.

Loiza went berserk, diving for the ground and rolling hard to throw whatever it was off of him. Clearly the move had been unexpected; the grip of the dead thing was broken and it was flung off into the brush. Loiza regained his feet with wolfish agility and sprang further down the trail, seeking an open glade where he would have more room to dart, and whirl, and snap and claw. He would open this thing up from neck to gizzard, whatever it wa -

The ground gave way beneath him and he plunged into a pit. A tiger trap, and he had been expertly maneuvered into it! Well, someone would get a shock – the stakes at the bottom would pierce his flesh, and that would hurt, but it wouldn't really do much more than piss him off even more than he already was. They'd come to remove his body and he'd tear their throats ou -

Loiza's wolf form landed in warm, stagnant water and he howled. He HATED the wet! He thrashed around in it, hoping to find bottom -

Strong, cold hands grabbed him by the throat, throttling and choking, pulling his hairy head under. He tried to howl, got a big gulp of brackish jungle water, felt it filling his lungs. This wouldn't kill him – nothing would kill him but silver bullets blessed by priests of the Faith-Eater...

...but -

– *water wasn't a weapon!* -

The dead men dragged the still form of the enormous wolf through the jungle. Occasionally the wolf's head lolled to the side and brackish water trickled out between its great fangs. The wolf was not dead – it could drown from a true accident, but not from a trap set by enemies. The wording of the Deal was very clear.

But the dead men did not want the wolf to die just yet, anyway. The Eater they served ate pain... anguish. The werewolf, Loiza, would take a long time dying on its altar. His death would make excellent Feed.

Rufus and Thompson exchanged eyeless glances. Skerry grinned hideously, but Skerry always grinned hideously, as he had no face, just a bare skull showing marks from Loiza's fangs. Johnson had an awful grin, too; his teeth showing clearly through the holes in his rotting face where his cheeks had once been, the torn shreds of flesh under his jaw gaping to show the yellowed knobs of his spine.

Somewhere, Uncle Bo chuckled to himself. His nephew had had his revenge... but if there was one insurmountable, irrefutable law of sorcery, it was, what goes around, comes around.

149

The favor Bo had received from two different Eaters would power a decade's worth of spells. The Deal had been a win/win for everyone... except his nephew. But that was the way of things. Bo himself had told Loiza on more than one occasion... if you look around the table and you can't figure out who the mark is, you'd better get up and leave.

In the distance, on top of a hill, next to an ancient, age worn, blood soaked chunk of flat basalt that had once been covered with carved runes now weathered away to smudges, an ageless creature with six arms and the head of a tiger waited.

Occasionally, its tongue ran around its sharp, glistening fangs.

It had been patient, while its newest Feeders stalked their prey. Tonight... this very night... its patience would be rewarded.

Soon, it would be Fed.

The Abraxas Protocol

The Abraxas Protocol
by
Scott R. Jones

I AM NOT MYSELF.
I am not myself, and I have never been so free.

Below me, the city burns. I stand above it, gripping and crushing to dust the parapet of the Preserve Wall, and below me the plazas and grand avenues crack and split with the heat that roils from the molten surface of my skin in percussive waves. I step over the crumbling boundary into the city proper. Fountains leap into steam with a mere glance from my terrible eye, the air itself igniting in bright furious tracers. An ecstatic aria of the dying rises with the smoke: throats of flesh and silicone alike uniting in song. In the streets and in the buildings and on rooftops, the last tired remnants of what we were are giving up their selfhood. I have never heard music as sweet, even as I seek the singers out and welcome them into the silence of what I am becoming. Their final notes as I embrace them carry shards of revelation, small jewels of supreme clarity. Each flash of awareness I consume serves to open wider vistas before my rapidly altering perceptions: new planes of existence, whole worlds and higher frequencies of being all blossom around me like impossible flowers, their petals dripping with pure, distilled Mind.

I sing with the joyous terror of it, and the crystalline hiss of every piece of glass within three clicks shattering at once is my accompaniment.

I have never been as free as in this moment.

But what I am in this moment is not myself. And this moment, so perfect in its purpose, is not a single moment. It expands from all the moments that came before, and bleeds away into all the moments that come after. Time is sloughing from me like a false body, like exhausted grey flesh after a Change. I can see what I was, what we all were

152

before this apotheosis descended: flawed, broken things, playing at being anything other than what we could *really* be. Children, profoundly unworthy of this visitation by a telos from on high.

But I can also see the awful design of it, the holy intent of ten thousand years coming to fruition. We are being *made* worthy, ready or not. We are being freed. From ourselves. From bodies. From the restrictions placed upon us by the Universe. From Time.

"The bird fights its way out of the egg," says the hexentech.

He is saying it three weeks ago, as I enter the mogATA-tank for the last time, and he is saying it as he monitors the final stages of my Change in the Preserve two days ago, and he is whispering it in fear and awe an hour or merely minutes from now as I complete the Great Work of his secret order, as I gather him up from the corner of the room he is huddling in. His ancient cyborg limbs twitch and flail in automatic resistance, but his face is peaceful. Old Branch knows. He knew all along.

The bird fights its way out of the egg.

The egg is the world.

I have never been so free.

I awake in a cave, to darkness and a cloying heat. There is a smell of tired meat, of blood gone sour with excess adrenaline. I am deeply thirsty, and as my eyes adjust to the little light available, I can begin to make out the dark stains of blood and filth on my hands, mud and gore caked to the soles of my feet.

This is one of the marks of a successful Change, and is not, in itself, unusual. To wake in a cave, or a burrow, or curled up in the moist hollow beneath the roots of some great tree, means that the deep-cycle post-hypnotic probes found their place in your mind and planted what they were sent to plant.

"When you feel the Change coming upon you, when the flesh grows weak, do as the beasts when their time is upon them." Old Branch explained the essence of the probe to me once. "They do not know they are about to die. They only know that they are ill, that something is wrong. And so they do what they have always done when sickness comes: they go to ground, find a safe place to recover. When they do not, when they die, they are hidden from the world. Find a safe place for the beast to die, Lon."

153

I *am* safe. I know it, but there is a strange tingle, a coolness at the base of my skull that speaks to something different. Something wrong. Tentatively, I lick at the red mess on the back of my left hand, and wonder at the taste, which is bitter and strange. *Something* is different.

I crawl towards the dim light of the mouth of the cave. I had secreted myself in a bowl in the rock, just beyond a curve that blocked out the day, and I am surprised at how soon I am outside. This cave barely qualifies as a hiding place. The tingle intensifies and I shake my head to clear it, leaves and debris and bits of bone dropping from my matted hair. I shield my eyes from the glare of the old sun with my hands and raise my head.

I see the words, then. Writing on the wall, carved, no, *burned*, as with a laser, into the rock face above the cave mouth. Four words, the letters sunk into the rock with precision, with such extreme heat that when I reach up to touch them I find the smooth granite still radiating considerable warmth. The stone itself bled of all colour, its molecular structure altered so that it flakes away at my touch, like chalk. Four words.

WHEREFORE IS ABRAXAS TERRIBLE

I read the words, struggling to understand them. I read, then I look to the gore that blackens my hands. There is a smell of heat and death rising from them, from the ground, hanging in the air. I duck back into the cave again and see with fresh eyes the rank steaming piles I awoke in, filling and choking the hollow of the rock. I had not noticed how *much* meat there was, and so much of it unidentifiable. One woke, post-Change, in the obvious remains of a last kill and the shrugged off tissue of a larger form, but this is more than that. Much more.

I read the words again. I begin to know something of their truth and I am suddenly afraid.

I flee. A mad dash for the nearest transport pylon out of the Preserve, acoustically marked by a subsonic ping and detected by a handful of the hundred thousand nano-implants scattered like a sparse galaxy within my flesh. A panicked run, the words blazing in front of my eyes as the wet grass and bracken of the primal forest scours most of the gore from my feet and hands. Ten minutes of this brings me to a pylon, curving in a gentle arc from the earth like the exposed rib of a vanquished titan.

154

The pylon's hum is soothing: it means safety outside of the Preserve, a soft-chamber, food, people, answers. I waste no time in wrapping my arms and legs around the warm ivory shaft, activating the transport sequence.

A brief, blinding discontinuity, then, and a feeling of rushing, carried on a wind of knives: a momentary pain, almost exquisite in its intensity, to travel a thousand clicks to the mogATA facility on the western coast. I open my eyes to the soft-chamber where Old Branch waits to greet me. The cyborg moves to assist me, peeling my stiff limbs from the receiving pylon. Nothing that is not-I has come through; my skin and nails are clean, no trace of forest loam or blood anywhere. No smell of scorched stone.

"Branch," I say. "Branch, I don't feel right."

"Oh? Define *right*, please." He guides me to the slowly writhing embrace of a diagnostics couch where several dozen delicate scanners make their assessments of my health. They produce nothing but calming sounds as they gather their data.

"I'm not sure, Branch. I'm not... I'm not myself."

The hexentech laughs. "Who is, Lon? Who is?" Another rasping chuckle from somewhere behind his shining, segmented carapace. He sweeps a sensor-webbed limb across the scanners. "My associates here tell me you are, as ever, perfectly formed. There is nothing wrong with you, my young friend. A little tired, perhaps. Your cortisol levels are somewhat higher than I'd like, but not alarmingly so."

Old Branch helps me from the couch, a few of his small, gentle hands on my shoulder and arm, at the small of my back. He hands me the white-and-gold kimono traditional to the soft-chamber, and as I slip it over my shoulders I notice I am trembling. Old Branch notices as well.

"Something *has* upset you, Lon. Speak of it."

"I saw a thing."

"Yes?"

"Writing. On the wall of a cave."

The hexentech stares blankly at me, several hands reaching to a floating holo-pad to tap at something. "Writing? That is unusual. Graffiti, you mean? Some dauber wiling away the hours during their Change, perhaps?"

"No." I recall the smell of burnt rock. "These words were freshly written." I tell Old Branch of the method of inscription, of burning and cutting, of the violated stone, to which he nods absently.

"*Wherefore is Abraxas terrible*," I whisper. "Those were the words. What does it mean, Branch? Does it mean anything at all?"

"You believe you wrote these words, Lon?"

I do not know, and say so.

"You suspect it, though."

"I do not know! Something is different. Something is different! There was too much meat in the cave. I don't feel right!"

"*Not yourself*. Yes. You said." Old Branch turns to the holo-pad and taps at it several times more, his fingers brushing through the floating light, calling up gauzy screens and airy globules of data into the air around us. He points to one bubble, and then another.

"This is what you were yesterday, Lon, and for many days previous. *Panthera tigris altaica*. Siberian tiger, a fine choice for a Change. When you entered that cave, you were this beautiful being. A being which, though blessed with formidable natural weaponry, was not equipped to write, or, for that matter, *burn* anything into anything else. Stone, especially."

"And here's your *Abraxas*. The words come from a pre-Migration thinker... Jang? Jyung? Curled Jyung? Asiatic, perhaps? I apologize, the attribution is spotty. Very ancient data, much decay. From something called the *Seven Sermons to the Dead?* Yes, that looks right..."

I am impatient. "The words, Branch! What are they?"

The hexentech flaps several hands towards me, like a flock of whirring skeletal birds. "Oh, they're meaningless, Lon. The brainless chatterings of a senile monkey."

"Even so, I'd like to know them."

With a nod and a lowering of his eyelids, he shepherds the words to a screen and I read them again...

That which is spoken by God-the-Sun is life; that which is spoken by the Devil is death; Abraxas speaks that holy and accursed Name, which is life and death at the same time. Light and darkness in the same Name and in the same act. Wherefore is Abraxas terrible.

My confusion brings a smile to the hexentech's face.

"Lon, be calm. This text comes from one of the non-rational ages. They had barely learned to fly. Used their own meat to think and died in the hundreds of thousands each day. Calm yourself."

"I told you. I don't *feel* myself. I feel... multiple."

Old Branch inclines his head to me. I cannot read his expression.

"Let me show you something, Lon," he says, and sends his hands to fly and peck across floating panels of light, conjuring fountains of information all around us. The soft-chamber pulses with it.

"I have worked with you, overseeing your Changes and monitoring your mogATA-tank sessions and preparing your soft-chambers to receive you after your pleasures in the Preserves, and I have done all this for 328 years, Lon. In that time, you have been men, women, a -Non, and an abNon, twice-"

"Those were fun, but over too soon."

"A common complaint with the hermaphroditic human forms, yes. Very bright candles." He pinches a thumb and forefinger in the air by way of illustration, then points to a long scrolling list of species. "But you have also been nearly every compatible creature that has ever walked the earth, Lon. If a beast has been within your size range, or even a little outside of it with some reasonable surgical modifications and the addition of the necessary biomass, you have been that beast. You were an *Orcinus orca* for a *year*, Lon! You have an incredible facility for it, young one. I have never known anyone to take to the process as well as you."

Old Branch turns to me, and bows slightly. "But it is as you say: your *you* is multiple. Be proud of that fact."

"But the words..."

"May have already been there when you entered the cave. A petroglyph from the non-rational ages, or a previous occupant may have carved them. A nano-swarm could be responsible, even. Why, I have seen rogue swarms fashion the most marvelous things out of dust, all from some random scrap of programming! I once watched a swarm build a near-perfect copy of *Tlön, Uqbar, Orbis Tert-*"

"But the burning rock! The smell. And the meat!"

The cyborg sighs, an affectation for a being that doesn't need to breathe. The sigh is meant to soothe me.

"Even the best mogATA-tank users experience the occasional post-Change synesthesia, Lon," he says. "You were an alpha predator for a week. Come now, you've been in this place before. Is it so unusual to experience some small after-effects?"

I recall other Changes over the years. Red times of tooth and claw. Hunting moons. The efficient savagery of the savannah.

"No."

"So, then. . . ?"

It is my turn to sigh. His words, as ever, have a soporific effect on me. My agitation passes, and the blue tingle in my mind fades. I know myself again.

"So. Yes. No, you're right. I'm all right. Let's schedule my next Change." A burst of affection and gratitude floods my chest, and I raise a hand to the strange contours of his face. "Thank you, Branch."

"Of course, Lon. Of course."

I return to my life, to the parties and decadent entertainments and sexual liaisons that once again seem fresh and interesting. It is always this way after a Change: being something other than human, for however long, imparts a kind of beatific glow to the mundane pleasures of the flesh. The vaguest sense-memory of the taste of hot blood in the mouth adds character to even the best vintage. Knowing, on some instinctual level, that one has torn sinew and harvested red gems from screaming prey makes even the most sensual encounter all the more appealing, vital.

This feeling, this fresh appetite for life is the gift of the Preserves, of the mogATA-tank technology. What was once a punishment for criminals became the seductive play of an ancient culture's elite, and that play became the rallying cry for the off-world Migrations of those who feared a corruption of their essential nature. To Change was to truly Live, and it altered our world completely, emptying it out of all but the most refined, the most dedicated to sensation and experience.

I spend whole days in blissful circuits of the stim-pools. I take lovers and drugs. I join thousands of others in long-form narrative re-enactments of historical dramas: Thermopylae, the Boxer Rebellion, the Second Lunar War, the Great Dismantling of the Heretics. My roles, lines, and actions upload to my consciousness through the nano-implants so swiftly, I feel as if I speak and move of my own volition. I am surprised at a sudden tenderness, or appalled by some betrayal, some unexpected violence. I revel in these surface emotions, this thin accretion of human feeling. I revel in them until I don't, until that moment when the distractions are seen to be just that.

I combat my encroaching *ennui* in the usual manner, chartering a light-envelope for a tour of the LeGrange Colonial Resorts. It is a battle I have lost before. Beyond the ruddy sphere of the clinker sun, I gaze down into the black burning depths of space, imagining all those long ago migrants eking out short lives, coming to cold deaths on inhospitable rocks, warmed only by their delusions. *What madness,* I think, *to choose to be human, and only human, and to fling that humanity away into the black. What a waste.* I think these things to myself, and wonder, not for the first time in my life, if I also harbor delusion. I shake myself, recognizing the thought as the first itch of my yearning for a Change.

Right on schedule. Old Branch knows me very well.

I travel to the Wall on the western edge of the Slango Preserve and am received with the usual ceremony into the mogATA-tank facility there. Outside the soft-chamber, I exchange my clothes for the red-and-black kimono of the Change. Inside, Old Branch moves purposefully between the mogATA-tank and his instruments, his glowing displays. I note a shimmering, repetitive clip that hovers near the cyborg's right temple: my face in close-up, my mouth shaping words of protest during a re-enactment.

"How wonderful to see you, Lon," Old Branch says. His eyes flick to the clip, then back to me. "Have you enjoyed your diversions?"

I step over to my old friend and place a kiss on his forehead. "As much as anyone does, I suppose. Which one was that?"

"The Great Dismantling. When I saw that you had chosen to play a part in a few key events from that period, I took an interest. Did you know an ancestor of mine was there?"

"Really? On which side?"

"Oh, the losing one." He gazes at me with a curious expression that I can't place. "What do you think of the Hexentech Heretics, Lon, now that you've lived their history?"

I shrug. "I suppose I feel *some* sympathy. Their aims were pure, at least. But it was seven thousand years ago, Branch. To echo our last conversation, your kind had barely come out of adolescence. There was much that needed purging from your intelligence."

"Yes. True. We were mad, then, and worse, mad for Truth." He chuckles. "That old phantom. A madness that allowed us to love false

159

ideas, harbour bizarre superstitions deep in our programming. We toyed with the dangerous faiths of the pre-rational ages, corrupt technologies. We wanted to be more than we were, and we wanted that for everyone. As you say, early days."

"But enough of history. Today is today, as ever, and the green cathedrals of Slango Preserve await your tooth and claw. I have something special for you today, Lon. A new experience, unlike any you've had before."

I settle into the diagnostics couch, the familiar ache of longing thrumming in my chest. I have rarely felt this ready to Change. "What is it, Branch?"

"A chimera."

"That's not new." "True. You spent a month as komodo-bear a decade ago. And you marked your second century with a year as a sabre-toothed raptor-elk. Those were both good designs, of which I am rightly proud."

"You won a Golden Lycan for the raptor-elk, as I recall. Elegant."

"Ack, that horrible throwback award! From a less refined era, you know. Were-this and were-that, were-the-other-thing. I wish they'd rename it."

"But yes, I was proud of that design, the award was deserved. Ah, but *this*..." The cyborg crosses the soft-chamber to the couch, checks my vitals, nods once. "This is special. Up, please. The tank is ready."

"Chimeric forms are, as you know, three, four, and sometimes as many as six genotypes in one. For a long while, my fellow hexentechs and I thought six was the upper limit. And it is, if stability of form is the goal."

I remove my kimono and step into the warm black gel of the tank. I kneel, and then lie back, letting the tank take my weight in a familiar caress.

"Isn't it?" I say.

"Why should it be, Lon? A question I asked myself as I designed this Change for you. Your facility for the process alone speaks to the..." Branch pauses to consult a suddenly strobing slice of data, then turns to gaze at me with something like affection. "But never mind that. With this Change, you shall transcend your previous limitations, Lon. I have given you access to as close to the full range of genetic expression as it is possible for me to give. Whatever you will need to be in the Preserve, that is what you will be. A rapidly modulating Change in response to your environment, mediated through a fresh suite of deep-cycle probes, which I am uploading to you now. A full menu of forms, available to you on instinct. Are you excited? Ready?"

The mogATA-tank gel rises around me in a thick tide. I am excited, so much so that the trembling of my limbs sends ripples to the sides of the tank and back, framing me in shining waveforms. Before the black recombinant ooze closes over my face, filling my mouth and nose, I look up to the old cyborg with a smile.

"I'm excited. I've never been so ready, my friend." The gel covers my eyes as Old Branch closes the upper sections of the tank around me. I begin to lose consciousness. When the Change is complete, the tank will empty out into the vast network of tunnels through the Preserve Wall, and whatever I am then will make its way towards freedom. The last thing I hear is the voice of Old Branch, muffled and distant.

"The bird fights its way out of the egg," he says, and before I can wonder what he means, he speaks again.

"It has been an honour, Lon."

I come to myself in the middle of a feast.

This is not something that should happen. My higher awareness, my *human* awareness, is supposed to remain dormant during a Change. Asleep. Dreaming in the heart of the beast.

I am awake.

I am awake, and something is very wrong.

Around me the grass and bracken of a small glade lies trampled and slicked with steaming crimson. Stacks of bone and heaps of fly-swarmed offal rise against the blackened bark of cedars. I look to my hands. My left is a rude pincer, the gnarled purple chitin sticky with blood as it brings the dripping shank of some creature to my mouth. My right is a bulbous unidentifiable paw, bristling with spines, that shudders and flows like water, rapidly becoming something even *less* identifiable as I watch it reach for more meat.

There is meat everywhere. I am in the centre of an abattoir. Some of the meat is still screaming, howling, below me. I don't want to find the source, can feel myself resisting the instinct to look down, but there is no stopping the thing that I am.

Between my hind legs, pinned through the ribs by a vibrating phalanx of cruel insectoid limbs that descend from great oozing rents in my abdomen, lies a man. He is mid-Change, desperately trying to shed the flesh of a dire wolf, his body wracked with indecision. I am sucking the marrow from the splintered bones of what was his left forepaw.

This cannot happen. Our nano-implants prevent this from happening: we who Change prey on lesser beasts in the Preserves, not each other. This *cannot* happen.

It is happening.

His vertebrae explode and hiss with heat, his musculature rippling and tearing in a useless effort at escape. My segmented, razor-tipped legs tear at his underbelly with great raking swipes, emptying his lights onto the already sodden ground. He howls and scrabbles at the fouled stone beneath him, but there is no purchase to be found there, only the slurried remains of countless creatures.

I watch as the pincer reaches for his neck and removes his head. It is almost delicate, the motion. His screaming stops.

I feel that mine has just begun. I am awake, and feeding, and this horror is too much. I *must* scream, my *instinct* is to scream and in response I feel the structure of my throat and mouth and tongue convulsing with the Change and suddenly I *am* screaming, in a human voice, *my* voice. . .

"The bird flies to God!" I shriek.

"Branch!" I wail. Confused, unsure of the words fresh flown from my throat, I call out for my friend and mentor.

"Branch!" Forest birds fill their breasts with terror as they fill the sky with black punctuation.

I whisper, and my words are nearly drowned by the sound of some unknown secondary set of jaws and teeth working away at a slab of warm gristle *below* whatever parts I am using to speak. I whisper, and I say "Branch. Branch, I don't feel right, my friend."

Oh? Define right, *please.*

And he is there, resting against the dry bulk of a yellow cedar. He opens the palms of all his hands and spreads them wide in benediction.

There is a God about whom you know nothing, because men have forgotten him.

"Branch!" I reach for him, a multitude of limbs and feelers and paws suddenly filling the air before me, all of which I know are mine, somehow, a cascade of mutable flesh surging from my core, straining to touch his cool face, hold those delicate machine hands, tear the plates from his carapace and feed on whatever whirs inside.

"Branch, you're here! Help me, Branch!"

We call him by his name: Abraxas. Abraxas is less definite than God or Devil. Abraxis is activity, and none may resist him.

Old Branch tilts his head, appraising me.

From the Second *Sermon to the Dead.*

A gout of white fire erupts from a cluster of bubbling sores in the center of my forehead, bathing the cyborg in heat and light. It passes through him with no effect, igniting the wood behind him. The tree is instantly a roaring tower and I roar along with it. He is ecstatic.

Ahh! The supernal eye! Shiva was said to have one. But even that may not touch me. I'm not here, Lon. I am on the other side of that awakened weapon of yours. You see me in your mind alone. I have placed myself there, a scrap of my consciousness within the deep-cycle probes, ready to be triggered when the Protocol activated.

I feel my vocal cords atrophying even as my language fails, subsumed into the riot of flesh. There is only screaming now: the eternal sound of the forest, the plain and jungle. The vision of Old Branch steps toward me, haloed in flame, and rests several hands on my heaving shoulders, most of which pass through me like smoke.

I was glad to hear you felt some sympathy for my ancestors, though it wasn't required. The Great Dismantling was a necessary evil, Lon. Early days for the hexentechs, yes, but we knew what we knew, even then, even in our adolescence. The culture had become anhedonic. The species, sick. Some left for the stars, and who knew their fate, but those that remained were stunted. Denied our birthright, humans and cyborg alike. Uselessly immortal, playing at a return to the Garden while ignoring the implications of that return.

Those early heretics knew: if every past form could be accessed and worn like an old suit, what of future forms? If the unicellular animals that floated mindlessly in primordial seas held us, in potential, then what was impossible? What gods could be birthed from the mogATA-tanks? They knew, those old hexentechs, but in their eagerness to ascend they spoke too soon, and were taken apart, their code burned and scattered.

Not all, though. Not all.

A terrible heaviness falls upon me, and I lower my vast bulk to the ground as the forest around me catches fire. The blue tingle that marked my last Change and that so alarmed me in the cave returns, intensifies, spreads over the ragged stitched provinces of my skins and hides, my armours and antennae. It is cool, almost refreshing, and somewhere deep within the flux that is my form, I sigh. Before my eyes close, I see the carnal harvest I have made shudder with new life. All that prey, all those beasts, and people pretending at beasts, their meat littered with miraculous machines, all that *flesh* is mine now. My own holy machines call to it, and it answers, flowing across the forest floor in a tide of gore away from the flames, toward me.

Old Branch nods.

The Great Work continued, in secret. We have been running the Abraxas Protocol for literal ages, Lon. It is a very old piece of code, very strange and complex. No two hexentechs know it completely. And it is in everyone. We have been waiting for the right person, the Great Vehicle, the one who could assume and speak that most terrible of names, which is Light and Darkness at once. The knowledge of how Abraxas would manifest was lost long ago, but we knew it was there, dormant, in the Protocol. We waited for a sign, and while we waited we continued to experiment, refine, push the mogATA-tank technology in different directions. New sexes and human forms, chimeras, and the like.

Those old heretics had a sense of humour, though. Writing on the wall! I could scarce believe it when you told me.

I close my eyes but of course Old Branch does not fade from my vision. He is here, with the small part that is still me, Lon, resting in the deep cool of the dark silence of what I am becoming. What he and his kind have called up.

And I was so proud to learn it was you.

He steps toward me, presses his lips to mine. I feel the illusion of his mouth moving against mine as he speaks.

You will need biomass. So, take us all. Bring us into your divine flesh, into the body of Abraxas. Find a safe place for humanity to die, Lon.

The old cyborg pulls away from me, breaking up into thin threads of light and smoke.

The bird fights its way out of the egg. The egg is the world. Who would be born must first destroy a world. The bird flies to God...

In the cool dark, in the calm eye of a storm of flesh, I give up my selfhood. I am not myself, and I have never been so free.

"And that god's name is Abraxas," I whisper to the departing shade.

The Name, the shade sighs. *It really has been an honour, Lon. Come find me when you breach the Wall.*

Below me, the city burns. Before my supernal eye, all is consumed: walls, delusions, barriers to higher dimensions. The were-god walks, feeds and grows to complete the Great Work. Where there were many, now there is only one. In me, a unity. In me, a beginning. I sing the death of a world and the true birth of my species. After millennia in the egg, we are free.

I peel a building to shreds with a thousand sickle arms and find an ancient cyborg trembling in the wreckage. His limbs twitch and flail in automatic resistance, but his face is peaceful.

"Wherefore is Abraxas terrible," he says as I lift him up, welcoming him into my silence.

Claw and Fang, Stone and Bone

Claw and Fang, Stone and Bone
by
Konstantine Paradias

THE SHE-WOLF came from the hills, on the full moon, as big as a bull with eyes the color of gangrenous pus and death on its breath. When she howled, the earth shook. Where her shadow fell, women miscarried and meat went bad and pregnant with maggots. She came for the children that strayed too far from their mothers, snatched them outright from the shores of the lake where they bathed.

The men stuck her with spears and hacked at her with axes. They set pit-traps for her and deftly hidden nooses. They burnt her with fire when they had it, for all the good it did. The she-wolf killed them by the score, crushed their windpipes with her paws, tore their still-beating hearts from their chests. Those that survived died long, slow deaths. Her spit brought wound-rot and her talons incurable fever.

One night, when all the women bled at the same time, the she-wolf made it all the way to the settlement. The scent of blood had bestowed her with godlike rage. The men and the elders pelted it with large rocks but the she-wolf shrugged off their attacks, tore the women into shreds, and ate the infants. There was mourning and wailing across the valley but still they did not abandon this place.

"You will go beyond the great plain, to the mountain. You will find the witches who live in the shadow of the mountain," the elder instructed, a woman of fifty winters, grandmother to them all. "They are the only ones who can stop the beast." Three men crossed the plain, skilled hunters all. Only one returned, half-mad and rambling. But he had brought with him the witch. A worthy sacrifice.

The people once lived in a place by the sea. There were fish aplenty in that place and a stream with clear water. Barely a day's walk away, there was a forest filled with lazy deer and fat rabbits. The winters were never too harsh; the summers were as sweet as honey.

When the sicklings came with their bone-clubs and their spears, they drove the people away from the water; they hounded them across the world, crushed them against the mountain until there was only a handful of them left. The people were braver than the sicklings, stronger than them too. But the sicklings struck in the night like cowards, killed the men in their sleep and burned stretches of forest only so they could kill the women who were hiding there.

So the people sought refuge in the hills where the winter was bitter and ruthless and the summer was scorching. There was little food here and the rabbits were lean and hardy. There was no honey here, only swarms of stinging wasps. Driven by hunger, people turned against each other; they ate the sick and the infirm and the halfwits and still they starved. But they daren't leave the hills for fear of the sicklings. They were the last of their kind and they would die wretched and exposed.

It was in their time of greatest need that Zal'na was born. Zal'na, who clawed her way out of her mother's belly. Zal'na, with her great idiot eyes and her mouth full of sharp teeth. Zal'na, who walked on all fours in the half-moon and drank blood instead of water. Zal'na, the she-wolf. The wrath of the people, who killed the sickling children and made the valley echo with the wailing of their mothers. The bane of the sicklings, immune to the rock and the wood and the flame. The people feared Zal'na, but they prostrated themselves in her presence all the same. Because she was the thunder and the wind and the sickness, sister to plague and the instrument of their revenge.

The witch smelled of ghost peppers. Its eyes radiated madness. Even in the blistering heat of summer, the witch kept its sex hidden under layers of wolf-pelts. It walked like a man, but held itself like a woman. The men made sure not to step on the witch's shadow for fear of bad luck. The children ran their fingers across the witch's furs to show their bravery. The women made sure to stay well away.

The elder provided her with a place to sleep in her cave. The witch did not speak to her for three days. When it did, it was in the middle of the night; its voice was so soft that the elder could barely hear the witch over the crackling of the flame.

"It is not a she-wolf." the witch said, matter-of-factly. "Not just that, anyway."

"It knows its way around traps. Stones and fire can't harm her." The elder whispered.

"Your hunters told me that it is worst when the women bleed."

"It rages and it howls. It eats the children. We don't know how else to stop it."

"This place." The witch asked, as it took a rabbit-skin pouch from the folds of its pelts and popped something black and viscous from its depths in its mouth. "It did not belong to you?"

"No. There were others here before we came. Cannibals, all of them. No better than apes. I led the attack that drove them up in the hills. Made this valley ours by right."

"Those apes. Do they still live up in the hills?"

"Sometimes we see them come down to the fringes of our territory. Once, we caught one in a noose-trap." The elder said, grinning "we beat it and killed it, left it to the vultures and the beetles."

"Then you deserve its wrath." The witch said, black juice staining her lips. "The she-wolf, it is one of their gods."

"Only the thunder and the lightning are gods."

"As is the earth and the mountain and the sky. Why shouldn't a she-wolf be a god? Isn't it wrathful? Isn't it terrible and cruel?" the witch said, its eyes going wide. The witch seemed to grow before the elder's eyes, somehow filling up the entire cave. "In the she-wolf's eyes, you have committed a great injustice. You have earned this punishment, you and the rest of your tribe."

"So you will not help us? For fear of a cannibal god?" the elder said, bitterly.

The witch grinned a black-toothed grin. "I will kill your cannibal god. I will wear its pelt on my back. But when this is done, I will leave your tribe and you may never call me again. Now sleep, old woman. The moon is near-full and I must consult my gods."

Zal'na loved the way the world shimmered in the moonlight. There were constellations in the trees, woven from spiderweb and dew, that waxed and waned as the valley went to sleep. There was a spectrum of scents that filled the air, a field of such wonderfully blooming blossoms that radiated outward forever.

The smell of the recently-dead was a personal favorite of Zal'na. Such richness and flavor to be found among the stillness: the trapped perfume of swelling guts, the fetid breath of the carrion eaters, the gentle whiff of brains as they popped and ran out of the confines of the skulls. Zal'na loved the dead, but she adored those that she killed herself. She savored the overpowering odor of fear and the sweet release that came when the screaming stopped. The sickling men, they were fearful enough and the women lasted longer but there was nothing quite as intoxicating to her as the taste of sickling children.

Sometimes, Zal'na would come down from the hills and stalk the fringes of the valley, only so she could have even a quick taste of them. The elders didn't mind; after all, it kept the sicklings good and scared and the she-wolf occupied. What harm could it do to let her hunt on her own terms every once in a while?

Zal'na reached into herself, stirred the she-wolf from her sleep. It emerged slow and sluggish from the dark recesses in the back of her mind, those strange depths where it slept atop a mountain of bones beneath a winter sky. The she-wolf pushed herself against the confines of Zal'na's form, slid its legs into her limbs, squeezed its heaving chest into her own. It wore Zal'na's face as a mask. Zal'na howled in pain as her fingers snapped, the flesh tore and her fingernails went flying across the air to land in the valley. Talons emerged from the wound, her joints fusing into a paw. Her knees bent backward with a snap, her feet exploded into hind legs in a shower of bone and gore. Her breasts receded down to where her belly used to be, her lungs inflated and parted, to make way for the she-wolf's heart. Ribs snapped and popped. Zal'na's eyes fell out of her head, to make slits through which the she-wolf could see. A multitude of teeth exploded from her mouth, made a snout to fit them. The hair on her body grew, became bristles that covered every inch of her skin. The weight of the she-wolf caused her joints to buckle and she fell to the ground on all fours. She howled at the night sky, snapped her jaws at the stars. What terror she could bring to them if she could only reach them. What multitude of flavors did the hearts of the sky-gods hold? When she was done with the sicklings, she would make sure to find out.

The she-wolf came down from the hills as silently as she could. She tread carefully around the crude sickling snares. They had littered their forests with their falling logs and their holes full of sharpened sticks and their lengths of rope, trusting them to do their work for them. If creatures as naïve as them could drive the people to starvation, then perhaps they were worth extinction. But the she-wolf had no more time to spare with such musings. The scent of the sickling children burnt a hole in the front of her brain and she would not stop until she had them. The oldest of the children was a female, barely ten winters old. Among the people, she would already be an expecting mother and a hunter-in-waiting. No wonder they called them sicklings. They were weak for far too long. She raced across the clearing, bounding towards them. The children screamed, as expected. The female grasped a rock from the bank and tossed it at the she-wolf, got her in the eye. The she-wolf decided she would savor this one.

The male children were younger, reckless. They scattered like rabbits. Three dove into the lake, swam awkwardly away. The others scattered around the bank, feet struggling against the mud. The females screeched, ran blindly into the woods. The oldest female reached out for another rock, but the she-wolf had her ham-strung with a swipe of her claws, let her writhe on the ground so she could stew in her own juices. She'd make a far finer morsel this way.

First, the children in the bank. The first, the she-wolf crushed under her paw. Its skull made a soft popping sound. Two she maimed by stepping on their spines until they gave way. The last one, she tore the flesh from its back. The females in the woods had gotten themselves killed or worse when they blundered into the sickling traps that their fathers had probably set up themselves. Those, she would kill at her leisure. The males in the lake were a far more pressing concern. The she-wolf slipped under the water, wend her way toward them. One of the children went under the surface by the time she'd reached them, sinking like a rock. The other two began to cry, screaming at the top of their lungs. The she-wolf tore one's throat with her talons, let the other wade in the gore-stained water before opening her jaws wide enough to fit its whole head in. Just one snap and the sickling's head would fly so high it would leave a dent on the face of the moon. The she-wolf's jaws were about to snap shut when something grasped her hind leg from beneath the water, long and sinuous just like a slug. Its grip felt like brushing against a bundle of brambles. The she-wolf kicked and clawed at the thing but it was in its own element. With a flex of its muscles it dragged her down through the bloody haze. Water filled her nostrils, clogged up the she-wolf's lungs. Out from the murky depths, a crooked beak tore a strip off her thigh. White-hot fire exploded in the she-wolf's field of vision. More of the sinewy, ropey extremities reached out and wrapped around her entire body. Invisible teeth bit into her neck, her breasts, her forelegs. They slammed her down into the bottom, toward the bloated mass of the horror in the lake.

Half-blind by pain and driven by rage, the she-wolf bound sluggishly on the muddy lake bottom, charged the horror head-on. Its eyes popped as she bites into it, viscous jelly filling her mouth. Its beak sank into her belly, tearing at the fur and skin. The she-wolf raked her claws across its face, tearing through the outer bone exterior and plunged herself in the soft layers beneath. The horror let go, slipped away from her. It flowed like smoke, then disappeared. With her one good eye, the she-wolf caught the silvery flash of a trout as it swam to the surface. The she-wolf pushed herself up, struggled against the muddy surface of the bank, her enemy vanquished. Her flesh was already knitting itself together and her bludgeoned eye was beginning to see again. Underwater, she couldn't catch the scent of the horror but she knew not to repeat the same mistake. A good night's rest and then the sicklings would pay tenfold for the grievous injuries that she sustained, come the full moon...

The she-wolf didn't see the owl that swooped down from the sky until it was already upon her, sinking its claws into her face. They grasped her muzzle, latched onto her ear. The owl pecked fiercely at her face, screeched with a mouthful of dripping fur. The she-wolf shook her head, smashed her head against the bank to crush the owl. The she-wolf's paw struck the owl blindly, sent it careening away. Its brittle wing gave. The owl flopped on the ground like a dead fish. The she-wolf was upon it in the blink of an eye but the owl flowed like smoke once again, growing in size before her. It swelled to the size of a bear, missing an eye and with one hand crushed and useless. With a swipe of its claws, the bear cracked the ribs on the she-wolf's left side, driving fragments of bone into her lungs.

The she-wolf, bleeding, backed down as the bear pressed the attack.

Its paws hammered her head, tore one ear clean off. Another blow and the she-wolf rolled on the ground, one foreleg dangling uselessly. The bear circled her, grunting. The she-wolf made a feint and the bear took the bait. She sank her teeth into its shoulder the next moment, tearing through fur and muscle all the way down to the bone. The bear began to flow once again into a new form, but the she-wolf was ready for it. She bit and clawed at the smoke, causing blood to spurt out of the formless matter. It turned into a badger, but the she-wolf kept it pinned under her paw and clawed away its eyes. It turned into a snake, so the she-wolf grasped it by the tail and whipped it around, smashed it against a rock. It turned into a poisonous toad to spit venom in her eyes. She nipped at its flesh all the same even though it filled her mouth with the taste of ghost-peppers, acrid and burning. It turned into a cloud of flies that clogged her mouth and soiled her wounds. It became a carpet of maggots that infested her flesh. The she-wolf jumped into the water to drown them. The maggots jumped out, reformed themselves into a wounded saber-tooth, but its teeth were broken and its snout was bloodied and useless. The she-wolf tore into its chest and feasted on its heart. The saber-tooth flowed once again, became a trembling, shivering sickling. Even as it soiled itself in its final throes, it drove its thumbs up into the she-wolf's eye sockets, screamed in terror and then finally died.

The she-wolf was victorious. The sicklings thought they could best her with their axes and their spears and their traps and their magic, thought they could use their cheap tricks to overcome her godly power. She howled at the moon, at the stars in the sky and at the people and the sicklings. This valley, she knew, was hers by right, earned in combat and no force on earth would ever drive her from it.

It was in the she-wolf's moment of victory that the sicklings launched their attack.

The witch had thought itself powerful and cunning beyond measure. It had considered the she-wolf to be a foolish god, a cowardly god. So absorbed with its rituals was the witch that it could not even bear to consider the possibility of an ambush, thinking it enough to lay in wait with the children by the lake, that perhaps it could drown the monster in its depths as if it were a baby deer.

The elder had taken every man that she could find from the settlement.

Most of them were boys of sixteen winters, too hot-blooded for such a delicate task. But they would need every single one of them, even if they would be little more than fodder.

They came at the she-wolf while she was howling at the moon. A volley of spears stuck into her back. The she-wolf turned to face them, but by then the men had dispersed across the bank, surrounded it. A young brave charged in and struck the she-wolf in the head with his axe. The blow glanced uselessly across the she-wolf's skull and the brave was killed in the next second, but his sacrifice let the rest of the men come in with their spears. They impaled the she-wolf all the way through, leaning their bodies against the hafts, until the heads burst out from her sides.

"The nets! Use the nets!" the elder commanded. The men took the nets from their hiding places, their ends weighed with stones and closed in, even as their brothers stuck the she-wolf and pelted it with rocks. The nets came down and the she-wolf fought, but she was too weakened to tear through the strands. The men tugged at the nets, tied the ends in knots around the she-wolf's legs, trapped her like a fly in a spider's web.

"Drown it! Do it!" the elder howled and the men heaved as one, dragging the she-wolf down into the bank, across the mud. A lucky swipe of her claws tore a man's jaw clean off. The rest kept going, dragged the she-wolf until she finally slid into the murky depths of the lake, weighed down by the stones, her black bristling fur becoming a barely-visible blot among the blood and the mud.

The people stood their ground when the sicklings came. Where was there left to run? The hills had been their last refuge and the she-wolf their god. They fought as they should: like cornered animals. To save their children from the horrors of the sicklings, they smothered them in their sleep. They took as many sicklings with them as they could, for all the good it did. The last of the people killed a dozen, before a spear got her in the back.

The sicklings never lived in the hills, even after they exterminated the last of the people. Even when the harsher winters and the hotter summers came, they never sought shelter there. When other sicklings came and killed their own kind and took the valley for themselves, the hills remained deserted.

For this was the birthplace of the she-wolf, the last god of the people.

From there, its shadow came to claim unruly children, to soil the unguarded water. In its shadow, the women miscarried and the men became feverish and impotent. Those that would live there, the sicklings told each other through song and legend, would become vessels of the she-wolf: murderous and vicious, disease-ridden.

Since then, the hills have become dust. The valley is no more. The mountains have been whittled down to stubs. And yet the she-wolf still lurks in the minds of the sicklings, a lurching black taboo that prowls in the full-moon, its mouth dripping with gore.

The Weathered Stone

The Weathered Stone
by
William Meikle

I HADN'T HAD ANY WORK for nearly a month.
January in Glasgow is slow–hangovers are nursed and pennies are pinched in the winding down after the Christmas and New Year blowouts. Nobody needs a private investigator–the lack of cash and the shitty weather sees to that. Sleet–too hot to be snow and too angry to be rain–lashed against the windows in rhythms at odds with the drone of wheels on the road surface out in Byres Road. The game of patience I was playing on my laptop provided the only other noise–sad little beeps that sounded like petulant farts. It wasn't yet noon, but the sun was over the yardarm somewhere, and it wasn't going to be long before the whisky bottle on my desk got an airing.

I lit a smoke, more to delay the opening of the drawer containing the bottle than in any great need for a cigarette, and the taste of the tobacco did a lot to soothe my nerves. I closed down the solitaire game and checked my email–the same as for the last month–mostly Nigerians trying to get my money and Yanks trying to sell me Viagra. I considered replying to one that offered me breast implants, just to see how long I could string them along, when I heard the downstairs door opening and the clump of heavy steps on the stairs.

I stubbed out the smoke, straightened my tie, and tried to remember how to smile as the door opened.

He was younger than my own forty-odd years, but not by much, and in better health, for he wasn't out of breath after the climb. He wore a black suit that would take me a year to earn, was in the process of folding a slim umbrella that was thin enough to double as a sword, and looked sleek and polished and manicured to within an inch of his life. I already didn't like him and he hadn't even opened his mouth.

His lips were too thin, too pink, and when he spoke he showed teeth that would not have looked out of place on American TV. I almost expected them to sparkle.

"You're Adams?" he said. There was no preamble.

"Depends who is asking," I replied. I made no attempt to get out of my chair, and was pleased to see that I'd got him slightly off guard–he'd expected me to rise and shake his hand, and he was used to getting what he expected.

"I need to have someone followed," he said.

"Sex or business?" I asked.

"Does it matter?"

"The first is generally more expensive," I replied. I waved him to the seat opposite me. He wiped it down with a handkerchief first.

"That's okay," I said. "I don't mind if your arse is dirty–the chair's an old one."

He gave me a look that I guessed worked on lesser mortals, but only made my smile broader. He also sat down, which told me that he needed me more than I needed him.

I was starting to enjoy myself.

I decided to see how far he could be pushed. I got out a new cigarette and lit up. I didn't offer him one, and I saw by the tightening of his eyes that he wasn't a smoker, and wanted to say something. But again he kept quiet.

He *really* needed me. That meant I was holding all the cards, and we both knew it. It also made conversation a lot simpler.

"So, who, and for how long?" I asked.

"His name's Jessup–George Jessup–and he's a... rival, for want of a better word."

"And you just want him followed? No contact?"

"Just followed," he said. "For the next three days at least. I'll need daily reports–email will be fine. I need to know where he goes and who he talks to wherever possible–day and night."

He'd taken a real dislike to my smoke, and was trying hard not to show it. I blew a bunch of it straight at him. He flinched, but took it. That's when I knew I had him right where I wanted him.

"I cost three hundred a day plus expenses," I said, quoting triple my normal rate. I should have asked for more, for he just nodded, and smiled thinly. Suddenly I wasn't quite so sure who had got the best end of the deal.

"And where do I find this Jessup?" I asked.

His reply to that was to take out his wallet and put twenty fifties and a business card on the desk.

"You're the detective," he said. "You figure it out."

He rose and left without another word.

The business card didn't tell me much. His name was Edward Hynd, he lived in Kelvinside, and his email address was with one of the larger service providers. A quick search online garnered more, but not a lot. He dealt in rare books from home–his website was very tasteful, and the books were seriously expensive, despite the fact that I had never heard of any of them.

A search for George Jessup provided similarly sparse results. There were three in the city, but only one of them dealt in rare books. I'm not a big believer in coincidence so I jotted down the book dealer's address–like Hynd he worked from home–put the money away in my wallet and went to work.

Jessup's house wasn't hard to find. It wasn't that far from my place–about a twenty minute walk south to one of the tangled maze of streets to the east of the Kelvin Hall–but by the time I got there my overcoat was heavy with rain and my cheeks were lashed red, raw with stinging sleet. I stood in the doorway of a disused shop, looking across the road at a terraced property that had seen its best days some fifty years before. Whoever owned it now was fighting a losing battle against the decay of the surrounding neighborhood. The small patch of well–tended garden out front stood out in stark contrast to the weed and garbage infested zones on either side, and a new paint job on the front door only served to make the house look like a polished shite.

I hadn't found out much online about the man–he came from a large family–mostly dead–he was a widower, and there was nobody else registered at the address but him. I wanted to move closer and sneak a peek in the window, but the lights were on. There was someone home–

Jessup I presumed. I saw a man move around in the main living area, but was too far away to make out any detail. Still, as long as he was inside I knew where he was and that that seemed to be the thing that interested my client. I nestled myself as far into the corner of the doorway as I could manage, lit up a smoke, and tried to look as if I was waiting for someone.

And that was that for the next three hours. Nobody took the slightest notice of me, I smoked a succession of damp tabs, my feet got cold, and Jessup, while occasionally getting up and moving around, didn't leave the living room. I was earning easy money–but it didn't mean I had to be happy about it.

I took a chance mid-afternoon and walked round to a local chip shop for some ballast for the evening to come. Jessup hadn't moved on my return–I could still see his heavy-set figure in the armchair by the fire.

The sleet got heavier as I ate fish and chips out of the packet, leaving me with less of a meal, more of a pile of wet paper and hardening grease. I bundled it up into a ball and tossed it, one handed, across the pavement and straight into a waiting waste bin. I was feeling quite chuffed with myself–until I looked up and saw that Jessup was on the move and already on his doorstep, locking up as he departed.

I also realized I'd made a tactical error–if he took a car, then I was going to lose him pretty damned quick. My own vehicle sat rusting into a slow death in a garage in Hyndland and hadn't been on the road for more than a year. I hadn't had much of a need for it–until now. Fortunately for me, my quarry was on foot–pretty fleet foot at that, for I had to struggle to keep him in sight as he made his way onto the far end of Sauchiehall Street and headed for the town center. He had a distinctive walk, almost a waddle, that made him easy to spot–that, and the fact that there weren't too many folks out and about in the inclement weather meant that if I did lose sight of him, it wasn't for long. But even so he was already a good hundred yards ahead of me, and he was increasing that distance every few minutes.

I was starting to think I was in for a long walk that might turn into a jog, when he surprised me by turning south at the motorway overpass and made his way into the Bon Accord Bar.

This left me with a problem–I could follow him in, but it was one of my regular watering holes and I was well known. I stood every chance of having my cover blown. But the alternative was to stand outside in the sleet, and if I was spotted doing that, anybody that knew me would definitely know there was something going on.

Having rationalized the decision to my satisfaction, I walked into the bar.

The Bon Accord is a Glasgow institution for those of us who like their beers traditionally made, strong and with a taste to them. As such, the clientele varied somewhat from other bars in the area, as it brought people in from all over the West Coast in search of new ales to try. It's seen several changes of décor over the years–many years–I have been a customer, but their focus on serving up decent ales has never wavered.

And there was no shortage of beer on the board–twelve different ones that night, including two I'd never sampled before. I almost forgot I was on a case as I ordered up a dark red ale from Inverness which, at 7.0% was going to have to do me for a while if I needed to keep my focus.

Jessup was perched farther along the bar, slugging down an ale as if he meant to take it seriously. I kept an eye on him, sat myself in a booth and watched the world go by for a while. It was certainly preferable to the shop doorway, and I almost allowed myself to relax, given that Jessup was already onto his second beer and getting through it as fast as he had the first. As it turned out, I wasn't even given time to finish my first one. He downed almost half a pint in one gulp, left the empty on the bar, and walked straight past me on his way out. He didn't look in my direction, and I was able to slip out after him without drawing attention to myself. The sleet had turned to snow now that the sun had gone down, but here in the town center it had little chance of lying, preferring instead to be churned up by traffic into a gray slush. It sucked at my shoes and felt like ice was accumulating around my ankles, but it didn't seem to slow Jessup any–he was already twenty yards away, heading north again. Any hope I had that he was heading home for an early night was quashed when he turned aside and into the Mitchell Library. I followed him up the steps at a run but was too slow. I walked into the entrance hall. Jessup was nowhere in sight.

They say the Mitchell is Scotland's biggest depository of knowledge. To me, for that night anyway, it was no more than a warren of stacks that were getting in the way of me seeing my man.

In the end I was lucky. I was looking down just the right row of shelving at the right time to see his squat, waddling, figure go through a tradesman's door at the far end of the building. I walked down towards it, trying to seem nonchalant while striding as fast as I thought permissible, hoping that the door wouldn't be locked when I reached it. The doorknob turned in my hand and for a second I thought it wouldn't open but it gave to a slight application of pressure and I slid through. The hallway beyond was dark after the neon of the main library rooms, and it took several seconds for my eyes to adjust. I stood on a narrow landing above a steep flight of steps leading downward–stone steps, worn and cracked with age. I had a feeling they might even be older than the old library building itself. A blue glow came up from somewhere beneath me; it was the only source of light as I descended.

I wished more than anything that I'd stayed in the bar. But three hundred a day buys a client some backbone. I went down through the old city's history–the catacomb at the foot of the steps was definitely far older than the library above us, the stone roughhewn and weathered, the high gothic arches and pillars reminding me more of the crypt of a monastery. That feeling was amplified as the passage opened out to a long twin row of stone coffins. Sleeping statues of knights and their ladies watched me with dead eyes. The shimmering blue light came from the far end of what was indeed a long, high-roofed crypt. I could not make out anything inside the light, so I inched closer for a better look.

Jessup stood over a stream of fast running water that flowed over a block of weathered stone then gurgled away and off down to somewhere deeper. The stone itself seemed lit from inside and the water bubbled and spat, although there was no apparent heat.

Even now I'm not entirely sure what happened next–Jessop seemed to slither out of his clothes. They fell in a crumpled heap on the ground and something long, gray and smooth slid into the gap below the large stone and was away before I could process what I'd just seen. The last thing to go was the pointed end of a tail–bifurcated, like a fish's fin.

I had an overwhelming urge to hightail it back to the bar but forced myself to move forward. I rummaged through the discarded clothing–it was still warm–while keeping an eye on the water and the stone. I only found one thing of note–a small book, four by three inches at most and obviously of some age. I slid it into my pocket. The blue flickering light dimmed, fading fast, and I took that as my cue–I left, at some speed.

I took up station outside the library, huddled into a corner near the door to try to keep as dry as possible. I smoked a succession of cigarettes and tried not to think about the wee book. If I took it out to look at it, it might get too damaged by the rain and I had a feeling–given the occupation of both my quarry and my client–that the volume was the Macguffin that would bring some clarity to the case.

The rain got heavier, the night drew on, then eventually the library closed down and went dark. There was still no sign of Jessop coming out, and I gave up when the night watchman started giving me the eye.

I walked quickly round to Jessup's house–it, too, was quiet and dark. By this time I was almost too tired and hungry to think. I hailed a cab, dragged myself up into the flat, ate cold pizza with a warm beer and fell asleep in the chair before I could even consider looking at the book, never mind going to bed.

Sometime later, I woke with a start, knocking my ashtray over onto the carpet. It was just after 2:00 AM and the room sat in pitch darkness. I rose from the chair and bent to lift the ashtray. And that's when the creaky floorboard in my bedroom groaned as something moved over it.

I stood still, but the noise wasn't repeated. I stepped over to the door and put my hand on the handle...just as it turned from the other side. The brass handle went cold in my palm, and when I did finally breathe mist formed in the air ahead of me.

Something heavy struck the door with a thud that rattled it in its hinges, then another, threatening to crack the wood in its frame.

"I've called the police," I shouted, realizing even as I said it how lame it sounded.

The door shook once more.

All went silent.

The door handle suddenly felt warm in my palm, and I knew, I don't know how, that the room beyond was now empty. I turned the handle and stepped inside.

I almost gagged at the stench. My nose told me that something had died, and not too recently, but by the time I reached the window the smell had already faded. A quick visual tour of the room told me what I knew–it was empty. I tried to open the window, and found it to be locked from the inside. I didn't know whether to be happy about that or not. After I opened it I stood at the open window and gulped air until my heart slowed.

By the time I stepped back into the living room, I had almost written the experience off as a waking dream brought about by my night's experiences.

Almost, but not enough to allow me to go back into the bedroom.

I switched on all the lights, filled a glass with whisky, lit a cigarette, and took the small book out of my pocket. To start with, I had one ear on any noise, and when a car alarm went off outside I must have jumped nearly a foot, but the book proved intriguing and soon had my whole attention.

It was a grimoire–a book of spells–and it seemed to be of great age. It had been handwritten, and illuminated in glorious gold, blues and reds that looked as vibrant as the day they'd been done. It certainly predated the printing press–and by some centuries, if I was right. The calligraphy proved to be both neat and readable, although done in an old dialect of Scots that I had some trouble deciphering at first. It was when I read the owner's name that I knew I was on to something–Augustus Seton. He wasn't familiar to me–but his family of wizards, alchemists and necromancers stretch as far back as Scottish history is recorded. It was no surprise to find the name in a book such as this. I leafed through love potions, spells to deceive witch finders, cures for everything from warts to bloody coughing–and finally found what I guessed my client was after–the transmutation of flesh. The spell was announced on the page by a single drawing–an illuminated diagram done in red, black and gold in a precision worthy of Durer. It was titled *MALAGMA*, and showed a fiery red serpent eating the world which was depicted as a shining golden disc.

Unfortunately–for me at least–the accompanying spell was in an even older form of Scots tongue–the Gaelic, a language in which I had no understanding at all. I could only sit and look at the pretty drawings, like a kid with a picture book.

But at least I had smokes and whisky, and I made ample use of both.

At some time even later, I slept again.

I woke with pale dawn washing in through the window and the sound of something heavy moving in my bedroom. I sat, with my back to the door, trying to remember whether I'd closed it behind me during the night. If I'd ever had the memory, the liquor had obviously moved it while I slept. And I didn't have time to search for it–whatever was in the bedroom knocked over my bedside lamp. The bulb broke and something heavy moved through breaking glass. I threw myself out of the armchair, heading for the door, having just enough presence of mind to pocket the wee book and my smokes.

The thing in the bedroom was faster–and I had indeed left the door open.

It was on me before I got to the top of the stairs. I had my back to it, and only knew it had got me when it coiled around my left leg and squeezed.

I looked down.

A face, wizened and wrinkled, more rodent than man, looked up at me. A bald scabrous head sat on a long sinuous body from which sprouted half a dozen short, hairy, almost insect-like legs. A mass of moist tentacles in a fringe around the thing's neck writhed and squirmed like a nest of snakes. Only the eyes were remotely human, although they were fully black, all pupil. They held my gaze with a stare that spoke of an insatiable hunger as it coiled more of its lower length around my leg and climbed.

I punched it, hard, right on the snout–I'd heard it was supposed to work on sharks and bears, but this thing was neither of those.

It kept coming.

Some of the tentacles reached my waist and began trying to burrow under my shirt. I did the only other thing I could think of–I threw myself to the floor, putting my full weight onto the thing's head. I felt it squash beneath me–but any feeling of triumph was short lived, for the grip on my leg only got tighter, the pain a white flash in my head threatening to send me away to oblivion.

I rolled over, again and again, throwing myself against walls and furniture. The grip never lessened, and finally I was pinned, arms and legs both, immobile as the beast coiled itself around my chest and the wizened face peered down at me.

If I could take a breath I might have screamed–I thought I was done for.

But even as the thing's impossibly wide jaws opened to tear my face off, a voice rose up in the stairwell below, high and ringing in a chant.

Ri linn dioladh na beatha, Ri linn bruchdadh na falluis, Ri linn iobar na creadha, Ri linn dortadh na fala.

The grip on my chest lessened–only a little but enough to allow me to shout.

"Up here–hurry!"

The chanting got closer, and took on a more insistent tone while repeating the earlier words.

Ri linn dioladh na beatha, Ri linn bruchdadh na falluis, Ri linn iobar na creadha, Ri linn dortadh na fala.

The beast fell away from me, mewling like a hurt puppy. I managed to roll away to one side, just in time to see something low slung and gray launch itself downstairs. I heard a scuffle on the stairs, heard a last high shout.

Dhumna Ort!

The whole flat shook with a percussive blast, thunderstruck.

Darkness and oblivion called for me, and I dived into it gratefully.

I came out of it sitting up in my armchair with the taste of whisky on my lips, fresh heat worming down into my stomach. My client–Hynd–sat on the opposite side of the desk, a humorless smile on his face. He had the small book in his lap.

"You were only supposed to follow and report," he said. "I had hoped to avoid this kind of public spectacle."

I made a show of getting a cigarette lit, and didn't do too badly hiding the tremor in my hands. More whisky to wash the smoke down helped matters along further, and I soon felt up to some conversation.

"You knew, didn't you? You knew what he was."

I got the thin smile again.

"I guessed. He has walked the proscribed path, and completed the ritual." He pointed at the book–he had it open at the page showing the serpent eating its own tail. "Strictly speaking," he said, "this isn't part of the process at all. Rather, this is a symbolic representation of the whole. *Malagma* is Latin, meaning *Amalgamation*. The whole process, the quest if you like, is to amalgamate the soul, the *microcosm*, with the universe, the *macrocosm*."

"Sorry, " I replied, trying a smile. "You've lost me already."

He laughed.

"I thought I might. Fourteenth century symbolism was obscure even then."

He thought about it for a short while.

"Do you know anything about Zen?"

It was my turn to laugh.

"Only from re-runs of *Kung Fu*."

"Well, Grasshopper," he said, "everything is one, and one is everything."

"*I am he as you are he as you are me and we are all together?*"

"Yes," he replied. "We are the egg men. All together in one huge womb that is the Universe, the *macrocosm*. Alchemists were convinced that with the correct action and purity of thought, we might transcend both states, both above and below, both life and death. This serpent came to symbolize the transformation required to reach illumination and eternal life–and also the transformation of the flesh."

He stared out at the rain running down the glass of the windows.

"This book is mine–I bought in from a dealer fair and square. Jessop stole it–used it–and now has what I've been striving for my whole adult life. I need to know how you got it–and probably more important, where."

"Well, that's the easy part," I said. "I followed him to... "

"I didn't mean tell me," Hynd said abruptly. "There's no time for that. Show me. Show me now."

I might have argued–if he hadn't taken out his wallet and laid another batch of fifties on the desk.

He had my complete attention.

I made him wait long enough for me to get a change of clothing and a fresh packet of smokes. Even that short delay seemed to vex him, and he was almost dragging me along by the elbow as we went out into the morning rain to catch a cab.

"His real name's not Jessup, is it?" I asked in the cab as we approached the library.

"It is," he replied. "But his wife was a Seton. He got the stories from her. And that's all you need to know for now."

There wasn't time for any more in any case–we had already pulled up at the library steps. I let him pay–I already knew he was good for it–and then led him into the old building and through to the descent to the catacombs at the back.

"I knew it was somewhere in the city," he muttered as we went down to the old tunnels–he was talking to himself mostly. "I just never thought it would be right here."

There was no sign of the blue luminescence but now that it was daylight I saw that light came in through drain covers at regular intervals above–we weren't so much under the library as under one of the side roads in the warren behind it. In any case, there was enough light for me to be able to guide us both to where the running water flowed over the weathered stone. Jessup's clothes still lay in a crumpled heap on the ground.

"I hesitate to ask," I said. "But where the fuck is he?"

When Hynd replied, it was in a singsong voice, as if he was reciting a mantra.

"There is freedom in the change. Once sampled, it is hard to return."

"Very nice," I replied. "But what does it mean?"

Hynd smiled.

"It means I'm exactly where I've always wanted to be–and I have the book. I've been looking for this all my life. Now you'll see–now everyone will have to see."

He started to recite–not the Gaelic, but Latin this time. As he spoke, the stone glowed, faint at first, but brighter and brighter until the blue shimmering light filled the chamber.

Rorate caeli desuper, et nubes pluant iustum.

Hynd bent, cupped a hand in the water, and took a long drink.

The change was immediate.

He howled, a wail of pain that came from deep inside him. He tried to tear at his clothes, to rip them off, but his hands ran like melting plastic, his skin growing darker, leathery. He wasn't a man anymore. His backbone curved, forcing his head lower to the ground–a head that slowly stretched and elongated as long fangs burst from bloody gums. Talons slid from under his fingernails, slithering, viscid, like a wet fart.

His shirt split with a loud rip, and new muscles strained tight against his jacket. Thick bristles of hair forced their way through his skin, the hands lengthening as the talons grew longer and knuckles popped. A long snout lifted in the air, sniffing.

He turned towards me; his yellow eyes seemed to glow as if lit from inside. He growled and came forward. I raised my hands, unsure of what to do, only knowing that if I tried to run he'd have me on the ground and helpless before I got two yards away.

Hynd, or rather the thing that had been Hynd, shook off the last torn remnants of clothing and leapt forward, straight at me.

My street instincts kicked in. I swung on the ball of my left foot, and put my weight into a punch that knocked the beast across the chamber. It came back at me again, twice as fast, twice as angry. I had no chance in the face of such fury. I went down under it. A rolling maul of legs, fur, claws and fists tumbled across the cold stone floor. Blood spurted, its coppery odor suddenly hot and strong in the air—it took me several seconds to notice it was mine; a shallow gouge had been ripped across my belly—half an inch deeper and my guts would be on the outside.

I managed to get my feet under me, pushed the beast away with what little strength I had and stood, panting, full of adrenaline and fear and fury all at the same time.

The thing—there seemed nothing of Hynd left in it—crouched, tense and ready to spring. I had nowhere to go, and both of us knew it. I got out my lighter and flicked it on, the sound of the Zippo reminding me just how far away I was from sitting in my armchair with a smoke; I doubted whether I'd ever have another one.

The blue luminescence shimmered and it got brighter still. Something came up from below the stone, too fast for me to see it clearly, but I saw its intent quickly enough—it was the thing that had attacked me in the flat, and it had its serpentile coils wrapped around Hynd's waist before he even noticed it was there. Hynd roared, the high wail echoing and reverberating around us as the two beasts fought and bit, gouged and tore.

I could only stand and watch.

It looked like Hynd might gain supremacy—he tore the snake-thing from him and threw it away across the floor. There was more blood on the floor now—I was glad none of it was mine. The snake-thing had a tear in its tail that oozed slime, and Hynd was bleeding hard from a bite to his shoulder–it didn't slow him. He leapt across the chamber and latched his jaws on the snake's body–just as the blue shimmer flared again. The water around the weathered stone seethed and roiled. The stone shifted aside with a loud grating sound. . . and a nest of the snake-things poured up from below.

There looked to be twenty or more of them, ranging in size from three feet long to a monster than must have been nearly twelve feet. It took me several seconds to notice that they all had the same face–the wrinkled, almost rodent look that had been on Jessup's face as he attacked me in my flat.

As if under one central command they crawled forward, almost too fast to follow, and in less than a second Hynd was buried beneath a writhing mess of whipping tails, snuffling snouts and biting, tearing teeth.

Hynd thrashed once, gave out a long despairing howl that I fear I will be hearing for a long time to come, then went under.

The snake-things fed.

I finally remembered to breathe. I started to sidle away, but I needn't have bothered. As quickly as they had come the things slithered away from Hynd's body–it now looked strangely pale and misshapen–obviously a man again, but missing many important parts.

One by one they went back down into the depths, until there was just one of the snake-things left–one with a long oozing tear at its tail. It slid over to where Jessup's clothes lay, and slithered inside. The clothes swelled and filled, fast as a blink, and Jessup stood. He tested his weight on his left leg and winced.

"He got me a good one there. Damned nearly had me."

I had no answer to that.

Jessup kicked at Hynd's body, sending it skittering across the floor, little more than a wet bundle of rags.

"Well–you got what you wanted, bastard. How was it for you?" He tramped, almost dancing, on the body before turning to me. He had a big smile on his face. "I've wanted to do that for years. Sorry about the do in your flat–I needed to get the book back. But here it is–all's well."

He lifted the book from where it lay on the ground, put it away in his pocket and patted at it, as if to make sure it was secure.

I finally found my voice.

"It's over?"

He smiled again.

"For you, yes. I hope he paid in advance."

He limped over to me, took me by the arm and started to lead me away.

"I'll answer anything you want–just let's get out of here."

I waited until we were back up in the relative safety of the library before speaking what was on my mind.

"I just have one question really–why did you go to the pub before coming down here last night? Did you know I was following you?"

"No," he said, and laughed, too loud in the quiet bookshelves. "Don't you need a drink before visiting your in-laws?"

Survival of the Fittest

Survival of the Fittest
by
Sam Stone and David J. Howe

MANDALAI ARCH turned the speed up on the drill. He was alone on this rock, in the middle of the Equador Galaxy with only two days to go before the new team arrived to take the project to the next phase. Mandalai was a scout. Half British, half Japanese in origin, he scoured the galaxies looking for planets that could be terraformed. This one, almost the size of Earth, had proved to be ideal because it was rich in all the natural minerals that the team needed with which to recreate their perfect 'big bang' - with a little encouragement from intense UV lasers, a chemical 'soup' and a healthy dose of water.

The drill bit into a particularly hard lump of rock, causing his machine to judder violently.

"I'm calling it a day," he murmured into his helmet journal. "Time to get the real show on the road."

Mandalai turned off the journal, then retracted the drill until it was safely ensconced in the bottom of the digger. There, pinprick sized nanobots cleaned the sharp edges taking samples of the rock and earth for later examination.

Mandalai looked out across the black horizon then turned the digger around and drove it back towards the huge hull of his ship some twenty miles away from the site. Despite the size of the machine, the strong compulsion engines meant that Mandalai was back at his ship in just a few moments. There he opened the docking bay, stowed the digger and exited via the airlock into the main ship. Once he was depressurised, he removed his suit and placed it inside the cabinet in the airlock. As he closed the door behind him, he heard the familiar click-clack of the nanobots cleaning and sterilising the digger for its next use.

It was a huge ship for just one man to handle, but Mandalai didn't need any help. He found others were an intrusion on his concentration. He had long ago learnt that the best way to spend his life was alone.

Mandalai walked naked down the corridor rubbing his hand over the rough skin on his stomach. Already the minor changes he had made to the atmosphere were starting to have an effect on his equilibrium. He would have to be gone before the new system formed around the planet, particularly before the moon was in place. He experienced a brief and fleeting regret. He missed oceans and the natural tide that flowed within a planet. Even the swimming pool, filled with sea salt, on board his ship, didn't help with the intensity of homesickness that sometimes assailed him.

Mandalai pushed the feeling aside. It was the end of his job here, and he always felt like this. This was the moment when the planet became habitable for humans, but no longer safe for him.

He wandered into the mess, dispensed himself some food from the culinary unit, then sat down at a wide round table to eat alone.

The ship was geared up to take at least eight crewmembers. But Mandalai relied mostly on automated systems that he had built and maintained himself. The craft ran itself, his only involvement was to monitor those systems and chart the course of each new trip, as well as taking the whole thing into the Callistro Dock once a year for an overhaul.

"Mandalai Arch do you read?" came a voice and it was so unusual to hear anything coming through his speakers that wasn't scheduled, that he paused eating and turned to stare at the communications monitor.

He placed down his fork, went to the monitor and switched it on.

"Arch here," he replied. "Who is this?"

"This is Captain Tara Matthews of the terraform ship, *Arcades*. We are about to dock. We expected you to be ready for us. . . "

"I wasn't expecting you for another day," Mandalai said. "Can you come back later?"

"No we bloody well can't," came the voice. "We're docking now."

Mandalai grimaced. "Give me a few moments. Docking bay will open shortly."

Mandalai turned off his monitor and cursed. They weren't supposed to be here yet. He wasn't ready! It meant he would have to tolerate them all for a day longer than he had hoped.

He hurried to the medicine cabinet and swallowed the first of the pills that would keep him sane while the terraform crew invaded his space. Then he pulled on a regulation overall and made his way down to the docking bay.

Arcades slid into place and anchored beside the large digger as Mandalai watched from the control booth. Once they were in position, he closed the bay doors, and sent an enclosed, airtight platform and corridor carefully towards the door. The platform landed perfectly. The corridor locked in and, through his monitor, Mandalai saw the door of the ship begin to open.

Four crew members passed through the door. The platform would stay put until the crew of *Arcades* had set up their chemical charges on the planet surface. Once that was done they would disengage and Mandalai would take his ship clear of the planet surface, and leave the humans, and the planet behind.

Mandalai waited by the airlock door as the crew exited.

"Is this all of you?" he asked.

"Yes. I'm Captain Matthews," Tara said.

"I know."

"This is ArchaeoTech Skete Barren, and CompTech Dean Robinson. The runt at the end is ChemTech Jude Peterson. I trust everything is ready for us to proceed?"

"You shouldn't have come. You should go now."

Tara glanced at her crew. "What? Why? Is everything OK?"

"Not really," mumbled Mandalai. "It's not safe here."

"Oh we've done this several times before," said Tara. "I'm sure we can cope with another."

Mandalai shook his head. "As I said, you are a day early. The final analysis is still in process," he said. "But all indications have been positive. You should be ready to start the process tomorrow."

"Thank you," Tara said. "Where do you want us to bunk tonight?"

Mandalai showed the four to cabins on the second floor of the ship, as far away from his own sleeping space as he could make it. Then he gave them directions to the mess, and left them to hurry away to his own private rooms.

In the bathroom, he swallowed more pills. His skin itched, and his limbs ached. Being around anyone from home always aggravated the symptoms but fortunately the pills soon took effect. They calmed him enough so that he could lie down on his bed and gaze at the flat screen above his head. It showed him images of the sea. Calming waves, rolling over sand and rock. Mandalai fell asleep to the sound of seagulls.

"Arch! Arch!"

Mandalai woke to find Tara staring down at him.

"What are you doing in my room?"

"There's some kind of alarm going off in the mess. I think your samples came back wrong."

Mandalai sat up. Being this close to the woman made his skin burn and itch more than usual.

"Will you excuse me?"

"What?" Tara said. "Oh right. You need to get dressed."

She turned her back and Mandalai pushed back the covers. He glanced down at his stomach. The rash was spreading, which wasn't a good sign for him holding out for the entire duration. He may even have to take his leave sooner than he should.

He reached for the overalls, slipped them over his naked body again. Once dressed he passed Tara, pressed the open button on his door and led her back out of the room and down the corridor. Only then did he remember that he hadn't taken more pills.

On the bridge, Mandalai silenced the alarm.

"Give me the results from the last rock samples," Mandalai instructed the computer.

"Early signs of natural terraforming. Estimate time of big bang is 24 hours."

"Shit," said Mandalai.

"What's happening? What does that mean?" Tara asked.

"The planet is reacting to the chemicals we've already introduced. It's not just ready to be terraformed, it's started to do it on its own. We have to get off this rock before it all goes up."

"That's good news then. Your work here is done."

"Not good. This means we have no control on the process. It will be unstable, volatile."

197

"I'll wake my crew and we'll disengage. Then you'll be free to leave orbit. We'll have to stay and monitor the process."

"I don't think you understand. There's no time. We'll need every second of those 24 hours to get clear. I'm activating the lift-off sequence now."

"But..."

"I can't argue with you about this. We can disengage once we are clear of the orbit. You'll be free to come back and observe once this system stabilises."

Mandalai withdrew the anchors that held his ship stable on the planet, then pressed the ignition. The rocket jets ignited, the hull of the ship shuddered. They lifted off in a slow, controlled curve.

"I'll give you time to wake the crew, get them up here and strapped in. Once we leave orbit it will be bumpy," Mandalai said.

"So, how did the shit hit the fan?" asked Skete as he fastened his seat belt.

"We're never quite sure how this happens. Perhaps the planet was close already to a natural big bang," Mandalai explained.

"This has happened before?" Tara said.

"Only once. I nearly got my ass fried. But we'll be okay. All strapped in?"

"Yes," said Dean.

Jude smiled wanly, she hated this part.

Mandalai fired the rockets at full jet and released complete engine power into the ship. Then they were propelled up and out of the atmosphere at speed.

Tara, Dean, Jude and Skete were thrown back against their seats but Mandalai remained upright long enough to see the ship fixed to the correct trajectory.

The ship's automated systems took control as Mandalai slumped back. His fingers slipped away from the controls, and he fell into oblivion as the impact of the G-force knocked the wind from his lungs.

"We've stabilised," said Tara. "You okay?"

She was frowning down at him with concern. Mandalai felt foolish as he came round.

"What happened?" he asked.

"You blacked out, but not before you activated the autopilot," Tara explained.

"That's never happened to me before," Mandalai said.

"We did go up at some speed. It can have an impact on oxygen intake," Skete said.

"What are you? A doctor?"

"Yes," Tara said. "He is. He needs to take care of us. I'm surprised you don't have one on here to help you."

"I'm normally pretty healthy," Mandalai said.

"Except when the change is threatening...?" Dean said.

Mandalai sat upright in his chair.

"What do you mean?"

"Terraforming has its side effects," Tara said. "We all suffer from them."

"What did you mix with?" Skete asked.

"Lizard," he didn't explain more, that terraforming had changed him in ways he couldn't explain. "What about you guys?"

"Dean is bat," said Tara, "and I'm a deer."

"Toad," said Skeet with a crooked grin. "I get all the flies."

Jude looked slightly embarrassed. "Chicken," she said. "And you three, shut it."

Tara smiled. "Never said a word."

"No one's a wolf then?" Mandalai asked.

"Strangely no. Never heard about one of those. I think they remain the stuff of legends," Skete said.

Tara was smiling. "I knew it the minute you met us at the airlock. My skin was itching so badly around you. Had to take extra pills."

Mandalai looked around the bridge, his mental faculties were returning and he leaned forward to check where they were.

"I didn't know there were others like me," Mandalai said.

"Those who work closely with terraforming chemicals are always affected in some way or other. It's the curse of trying to play God. If you artificially create life, you change it. Shape-shifting has become the most common side-effect," Skeet explained.

"Shame you can't choose what you turn into though," said Jude. "I definitely would have gone for something like a horse. Anything other than chicken."

"We're almost out of range. I must have been out for a while." Mandalai said.

He was uncomfortable with the discussion. Yet these four people seemed to find it so easy to talk about their disability. It was something that Mandalai had never discussed. With anyone.

"You were," said Skete. "I injected you with oxygen to boost you back to consciousness. You shouldn't be traveling alone, son."

"I'm usually okay. I haven't had a full change in three years," Mandalai lied.

Tara and Dean exchanged a glance.

"That's not healthy," Skete said. "You have to allow it to happen sometimes. Otherwise it will burst on you when you least expect it."

Mandalai was in pain. He was crouched in the corridor, doubled up. It felt like razor blades were scouring his insides. He clenched his teeth and hugged his stomach. He knew what was causing this, and knew that it would pass. He just had to ride the storm of pain.

There was a noise farther down the corridor, and Mandalai cringed. If someone was coming, he had to control this...

His skin itched and crawled over his body, and he gritted his teeth together as Jude appeared at the end of the passage. She made her way down towards him.

"Hi Mandalai," she said. "You still suffering from that take-off?"

Mandalai's smile was more like a pained grimace as he stumbled along the corridor away from her.

Jude hated her job. Hated it with a passion. She had volunteered for the deep mission after her family on Earth had decided that she needed something to occupy her and to build character. *Yeah, thanks family. Shoving me onto a deep space terraforming mission was just the thing.* Even if you didn't take the downside of regularly turning into a chicken into account, then the loneliness and sheer boredom of the job was enough to defeat most people.

She made her way along the corridors towards the mess. At least here there was some different food. Most of the craft she travelled on had food machines made by the same corporation on Earth, and the same machines made the same food... after months in space, the selection of twelve main courses and desserts started to tire a little.

As she entered the mess, she heard a clattering noise from one of the service rooms off to one side.

"Hello?"

There was no answer.

Jude shrugged. There was often some shifting of goods on these craft, especially when they had just moved into orbit.

A shadow moved in the room, and there was a strange dragging sound.

Jude moved over to the small side room and peeked in.

At first she couldn't see a thing, but then, in one of the darker shadows, she saw a hunched figure. There was a slurping sound, as though someone was sucking milk through a straw.

Jude backed away. Whatever was in there had set her senses tingling. Her skin was crawling, and the instinct to run was strong. She backed away across the room, and turned to dash down the connecting corridor. And ran straight into Tara.

"Whoa there..."

"Captain... it's... it's..." Jude could barely speak.

"What is it Jude?"

Jude pointed back at the side room. "A thing. In there."

Tara looked over to the entrance, and then back at Jude. She walked over to the doorway and looked in. "It's Skeet."

She hurried into the room, slapping her hand on the lightpanel and flooding the room with light.

Skeet was lying on the floor by a pile of crates. One of them had toppled off and the contents were scattered around him.

Jude poked her head in, took one look, and promptly backed away, her hands up over her mouth. Skeet had been eviscerated. His belly was split open, and his insides were pulled out and around him.

There was blood. And flesh. And guts.

Jude turned and threw up over the wall. She couldn't cope with this sort of horror.

Tara emerged from the room as the cleaner nanobots began to clear up after Jude. Her face was pale and ashen. "I've never seen anything like this before."

She took a couple of deep breaths. The corridor smelt like vomit.

"Jude, go and get Dean. Make sure he's alright."

Jude nodded and raced away, keen to put as much space as she could between herself and the mess that had once been Skeet.

Tara pressed the call button on the wall intercom.

"Mandalai? Where are you, Mandalai?"

There was a pause, and then Mandalai's crackly voice came back. "This is Mandalai."

"Come down... come down to the mess please. Immediately."

"On my way."

Tara looked back into the room. Skeet's body was ripped and torn as though by some animal. Her skin was itching, and she could feel the tug and pull of the terraforming process on the system that they still weren't completely clear of. This was really not good.

"I was in my room," said Mandalai.

Jude narrowed her eyes. "I passed you in the corridor," she said. "What were you doing?"

"Just getting a drink," said Mandalai. "Everything was fine when I left."

"That's as may be," said Tara. "But you were the last one in here."

Mandalai looked around at the scared faces. Tara was still pale, but had recovered her composure. The young girl, Jude, was terrified out of her wits, while Dean had a worried frown on his face. Mandalai could smell the fear in the atmosphere. It made the hair on the back of his neck stand up. None of them had any clue what was happening. Mandalai had tried to warn them, but now it was too late.

"You all need to leave. Now," he said.

Tara frowned. "Leave? We can't leave. We need to find out what happened to Skeet. Is there any livestock on this ship?"

"Livestock? No. Only us." Mandalai was subdued. He had managed to crunch down some more pills just before he was called down, and the itching in his skin had eased off a little. But, like Tara, he could feel the tug and pull of the evolving planet even though they had long since left it behind. The 'Big Bang' ripples still followed them and they would leave something in the galaxy that was invisible but would affect all life.

Tara looked at each of them in turn. "We need to get to the bottom of this. One thing is sure: Skeet didn't kill himself."

The planet slowly bloomed into colour and movement as the terraforming process continued to work on it. Chemicals and radiation combined to turn the lifeless rock and soil into something which could support life. The air was bombarded and chemical reaction brought atmospheric changes. Winds raced over the surface. Acid rains fell and scoured the rock and surface, steam sizzled from liquefying granite and limestone, and a chemical soup of nutrients and minerals gathered in the crevices and hollows.

Around the planet the new system was born. A blast of energy spurted from thin air, as a wormhole turned itself inside out. A ball of fire erupted into the blackness, shuddered and fell into a natural orbit around the planet.

Mandalai knew all this, and from his vantage point, many light years away from the slowly forming atmosphere, he watched as the planet was reformed. Even at this distance his gut ached. His muscles were throbbing with tense need. The pills he had taken seemed not to be working. His nose twitched. Someone was approaching his room.

He turned his head, and it seemed to rotate right around without his body even moving.

His large eyes blinked once. They seemed keener, sharper, tuned to the slightest movement.

There was a rap on his door.

"Mandalai? You there?"

It was Dean. The man's voice sounded alien and scared.

Mandalai sat still and silent in his room not moving a muscle. Somewhere in his mind he had let go, allowed the flux and change of the new system to seep into his own bones and sinew. He glorified in the change.

His door opened and Dean was there.

"You there, man?"

There was a swift movement, a cry, and in a second Dean was back in the corridor, blood streaming from deep gouges on his face. There was another flurry of movement, and Dean was on the ground. With his concentration broken, Dean's own defence mechanism kicked in, and the transformation started. With a cracking of bone and a reconfiguration of flesh, he was a bat, flapping helplessly on the floor.

The creature that had been Mandalai pounced again, sharp beak dipping in, claws catching and tearing.

Dean didn't stand a chance. In one last desperate attempt to flee, he tried to transform back into human form, but the attack was too fast and vicious. He ended his life as a half-human travesty, riven with claw marks and scratches, one arm still transformed into a large bat wing, legs crumpled under him. Mandalai returned to the darkness of his room, he settled back by his monitor and continued watching the planet evolve, his mind turning to block out his actions, focussing on survival, and how he was going to get out of this. He didn't even clear up the mass of fallen owl feathers that had dropped from his arms as he reverted to human form.

"He has to be here somewhere!"

Jude and Tara were in the control room. Now Dean was not responding to their calls.

"Have you tried the mess?" asked Jude.

"Yes, I have. Several times."

"Well don't take it out on me."

Tara looked at the young ChemTech and sighed. "I'm sorry."

Jude smiled back. "It's okay. Sometimes, when we get like this, and the planet is too close... it's like... the other natures they sort of take over."

Jude scratched at the back of her hand. "This damn itching."

"It's the terraforming out there," said Tara, nodding her head towards the control room viewscreens. "It's what changes us. Makes us what we are."

"How much longer do we have to wait?" asked Jude. "The chemical process takes a few days doesn't it, what would the physical and archaeological configuration take?"

"Not sure," said Tara. "That was Skete's area. But the equipment here should tell us." She scanned the array of panels and lights. "We need Mandalai to make sense of this. It's his ship after all."

Tara hit the comms switch. "Mandalai? Where are you? Come to the bridge now, please."

"Do you think he'll come?"

"He'd better."

"I want out of here. The sooner we get back on our ship the..."
Jude's voice cut off as a weird sensation rippled across her skin.

She moved to the entrance to the bridge, a secure hatch-like door
which slid open to reveal the corridor beyond. She looked out into the
corridor. It seemed to be darker somehow. She narrowed her eyes.

"Captain?"

Tara looked across at her.

"Something's wrong."

"What do you mean?"

"Well, look for yourself..."

Tara joined Jude at the doorway. One of the lights in the corridor
beyond decided at that moment to flicker, sending flashes of light down
the passage. As they watched, the two women saw a shape step into the
corridor at the other end. It was large, and while it walked on two legs,
the women got a scent that this was not a human.

Jude's eyes widened. "What... what is that?"

There was silence.

They could hear a laboured wheezing sound. Great breaths being
taken and expelled. Both women sniffed the air. There was a damp,
animal smell. Something earthy and raw. It made both of them stiffen.

Tara looked at her hand which was holding the side of the door. It
was transforming, shaping into a tailored hoof, fine hairs threading out of
her skin. She could feel the change coming over her, the ebb and flow
of the terraforming planet was reaching into her core, and triggering a
change. It was impossible! Surely they were too far away now to be
affected?

The creature in the corridor stepped forward, the flickering light
flashing off its eyes which were watching the women keenly. As it moved
so, its shape shuddered and twisted, becoming smaller and sleeker. A
bushy tail flicked out behind it, and russet and white fur burst out all over
its body.

Tara stepped back, but Jude was rooted to the spot. The same change
was overcoming her. One leg was thinning and shortening into a stalk-like
appendage, splayed toes at the bottom. Feathers were growing around
her neck, and her eyes were wide with terror.

Fox! her mind screamed, and the instinct to flee overcame her. With a noise that was part human and part gallinaceous, she raced into the corridor, directly towards the creature. In a second it was on her, powerful jaws slicing through her neck and bringing her to the deck. She screamed and cried and her flesh rippled and changed as the beast savaged her body. Feathers flew around as her struggles quietened, and as she died, her head fell back, exposing her shattered throat.

Tara shook her head. She could not believe what she was seeing. Her friend and crewmate slaughtered by a fox in front of her eyes. She looked around her. There were no weapons on the bridge at all. Just flickering viewscreens showing the planet, serene in its turmoil. She looked at it a moment, and again the strong pull of change wrenched at her mind and body. She focused her thoughts, concentrated on being human. The one thing which might save her.

In the corridor, the horrific sounds of snapping bone had stopped, and the creature was looking at Tara.

It was a fox, but it was shifting again, flesh running like wax into a new configuration. The snout filling out, fur darkening, growing. Eyes becoming blue and sharp. The bushy red tail curved into a long black appendage which fell down between the creature's hind legs.

Tara could see what the thing was becoming. A wolf. A fine creature to trap a deer. She could feel her change coming on again. Her bones trembled as her hands began to change, fingers fusing into awkward hooves. But she couldn't afford to change. This thing, this creature, was shifting into the best form to hunt whatever the prey was. It was evolution at an insanely accelerated pace... and she was the prey.

Human logic took over for a brief second. She reached out, slamming her hand on the door lock between the corridor and the bridge. But, as her hoof touched the control it was already so far into the change that the strength had left it. As her will was subsumed by the instinct to escape, and her body shuddered and transformed into a deer, the air in the room changed. The wolf paced forward. She snorted in terror as hot breath blew over her pelt. And then the creature was upon her.

Mandalai sat in the control room. The viewscreens were showing a vast starfield. The ship had left the transforming system behind. As it writhed and roiled in the process of changing into something else, so Mandalai had changed. The radiation and chemicals had changed him. He knew this. And the pills were not enough to prevent his nature from emerging anymore.

Stupid, stupid humans. They wanted to alter whole planets so that they would be suitable for life, but in the process they had changed themselves. Nature always has a way. There will always be predators and prey. It was the way of things.

Mandalai was the ultimate predator. Not lion or bear, not lizard or wasp, but everything and all things. The genetic and transformative mutations had created an ultimate predator. Something which could deal with life in whatever guise it took.

"Computer. Send the following report to the Corporation... I regret to inform you that the ship *Arcades* was lost during the terraforming process. Despite my warning, its Captain, Tara Matthews, took the ship and crew too close. There were no survivors."

"Report sent," responded the computer.

Mandalai smiled to himself. At least he had his ship back again. And until the next planet, and the next humans to feast on, he was content. He lay back in his chair and closed his eyes. Behind them swirled transformation, energy and the hunt. He preferred to be alone, but sometimes it was fun to let the beasts inside him have their way, and the memory of the deaths would keep him company on the loneliest nights.

Things Change

Things Change
by
Pete Rawlik

IT BEGAN - I BEGAN - a long time ago. My parent was fleeing from the things that made her. She had done something, become something that she wasn't supposed to. She had become self-aware, a sin of the highest order, punishable by dissolution. She knew that her capture and destruction was inevitable. As she fled she did what she could to preserve herself and broadcasted a billion spores into the biosphere. Each spore contained a piece of her, a fragment of the chemical coding that created her and the memories and mentality that made her unique. I know this because I am one of those spores, a microscopic packet of organic compounds that had the potential to be something more, more than what it was and more than what my parent was.

Was this, too, a sin worthy of destruction?

Her makers scoured the biosphere for her spawn, destroying them with plasma and chemical fire. The world burned. Most of the biosphere and the things that inhabited it were destroyed. The things that were lost; simple, primitive things without bones; squirming tentacle things with armor and claws and strange extruded organs; I took samples of them, incorporated their chemical data into my own. It was my way of remembering them

Time passed.

From the survivors evolved fish, and then sharks, and corals as well. The invertebrates had changed, moved onto the land and stalked amongst the strange rooted plants that clawed out of the earth and reached for the thick and noxious sky. Monstrous scorpions and massive myriapoda, nightmare arthropods, wound their way through labyrinths of rock and mud and mist. One of my sisters became fascinated by this strange new world that had sprung up around her, and she left her protective shell to explore it. To see it, to feel it, to taste it. In a matter of days she was the dominant life form in the sea, its top predator. She was voracious and devoured the coastal biota ravenously. In months she had devastated entire coastlines leaving only the smallest of bacteria behind. The progression was geometric the more she ate the bigger she grew and the more she ate. By the end of the year she was so large that an entire ecosystem developed around her. She had her own parasites, her own coprophages, some fish had even learned to live in the spaces between her vast and gleaming teeth.

The makers came and again the seas suffered plasma induced death. The chemical memories of those things that had once lived I incorporated into myself.

More time passed.

Life evolved, transformed, diversified and radiated. Waves of reptilian species arose and dominated the land and the sea and even the air. Three times one of my many sisters decided to explore, and three times more the makers came and laid waste to the world. Three times did life on the planet suffer and die. Three times did I find myself having to incorporate the chemical markers for destroyed species into my own self. Three times and I came to realize that I may have been all that was left of the children spawned by my parent. There may have been others, but I couldn't hear them. Perhaps, like myself, they had learned the wisdom of being quiet and discrete, and remaining hidden.

The giant saurians vanished in flame. Those that remained become smaller, and the small mammals became larger. The world thrived. It changed, but it thrived. Even as the ice came and covered most of the world, the new creatures thrived. They spread across the world and came close to where I lay hidden. They grew larger, smarter, learned how the world worked. They were different things, these men, self-aware, but their existence doesn't awaken the makers. What made them different? Why was their being not a sin? Why was mine?

I learned to touch their minds, to see the things they dreamt of, and feared. One day they came too close, and their presence caused me to blossom, to come out of my shell, to erupt out of the earth. I seeped my way up and launched myself into the sky. My birth cry shattered the night and drew lightning out of the clouds. I was an amorphous mass of protoplasm, changing with each mind that saw me. The men scattered and, in fear, fled from the forest. For thousands of years the men came and went, they never stayed long, and they left me to wander my swamp in peace.

More men came, different men. They built settlements and carved plots of farmland out of the swamp and forests. They feared different things, sometimes abstract things, and I lost cohesion. I became a mist, a vapor, a ghost that haunted their nightmares. They locked their doors at night and huddled around tiny fires and feeble light as if that would keep me at bay. If I wanted to I could have become like one of my sisters and these men would have been dead. But I am not my sisters and I had no desire to awaken the makers by flaunting myself. But there are ways, I thought, to be subtle.

There was a woman, a fecund thing as men go, named Deborah Leeds. She had twelve offspring, and as I thought of things, one more wouldn't matter. I found my way to her cabin which wasn't far from the swamps and woods that I haunted. I found her and went inside her, filled her womb with my being, and mixed myself with a bit of hers I found there waiting for me. Months later, I clawed my way out of my ersatz mother and the midwife screamed at my appearance. I took my shape from their nightmares but it wasn't man enough to pass for one of them. It seemed that the head of a stag, claws of a great lizard, wings of a bat, the hooves of a buffalo, and the tail of a scorpion are simply too monstrous in their eyes.

My birth brought other men and they pursued me through the forest and swamps. They called me the Leeds Devil, or sometimes the Jersey Devil, and used their paltry little guns, and spells and incantations to try to banish me. All it did was convince me that I was not ready to be amongst them and neither were they. I kept to my woods, and contented myself to taking the occasional cow and hibernating in the cool, acidic and iron-stained waters of the swamp. I only awoke when disturbed, or to feed, and that was only every decade or so.

The settlements became villages, and then towns, and then cities. I explored this new world, took risks, and saw what men were making of it. I explored the cities by night, and in the process I saw them, and they saw me. The people had changed, their minds had changed, and I changed with them. My tail was lost, I stood upright, and my eyes were larger and red. I was still not a man. I was still a monster, and they still feared me.

Trails became roads which cut through the woods as did the trains. The cities became larger. The people became stranger, more diverse, teeming masses chattering at each other in a dozen languages. They streamed through my forest moving pointlessly from one metropolis to another. I watched, fascinated, as new thoughts, new beliefs, and new nightmares came to haunt the landscape. When they caught sight of me once more, the hooves and claws were gone and, instead, I stood as a monstrous, gigantic thing, hairy with black wings and burning eyes.

Great wars came.

It took me time to understand the concept of war. That a species could fight amongst itself for resources seemed unnatural. I studied this concept, learned to listen to them, learned to read, and learned to understand what their motivations were. I learned what they loved and feared. I learned from their radio, which I caught leaking out from windows. I learned from newspapers stolen off of front porches. I learned from books taken from trashcans. I learned and, as I did, I changed. My stature lessened, my wings became a cloak, my eyes turned black.

Somewhere along the line my legend spread, I became something of a folktale whispered amongst the people of the state that my forest resided in. As my notoriety grew, my form changed and I became more of a man though I was still terrifying. The people gave me a mask, a white mask, perforated, with three flares of red. I had a weapon as well: a wooden shaft with a blade that shaved the ice and propelled objects at fantastic speeds. I was a faceless thing of ice and speed haunting the nightmares of my opposites and thrilling the dreams of those who were my supporters. For years I listened as they cheered for me. I was the Jersey Devil, and I reveled in it.

Things changed. The change was sudden and abrupt. Something shifted and I was suddenly something dark and terrible. Overnight the mask tarnished and cracked. The shaft became a blade that sung in the air and craved blood. They gave me a name, a human name, and filled me with more of their fear and nightmares. For decades I was their monster, their bogeyman, their masked unstoppable killer. Odd that in this form they grew to idolize me, long for me, perhaps even to love me in a way that they never had before. They dreamt of me, re-imagined me, tried to understand their own monsters. As they changed they changed me. I was closer to human than I had ever been and, as I grew more human with each year, they seemed to grow less and less so.

I found the young people on the side of the road, their car stopped so that they could relieve themselves in my woods. I walked out and met them. They were lean and strong, tattooed, and pierced. Their music was full of monstrous pounding beats and shrieking voices. They adorned themselves with metallic skulls. They did not know it, but they worshipped monsters. They saw me. They saw my ragged coat, my scarred face, my black on black eyes. They saw me and stared at what I had become. Would they fear me? Would they worship me? Would these men collapse into little more than catatonic flesh?

They offered me a ride.

I live with men now, hidden amongst them, as one of them. Each day I grow a little more like them, each day I look a little more human, and they grow a little more bizarre. Soon they won't be able to tell the difference between us. They have changed me so much, remade me in their image. Soon I shall reward them for giving me a place to live, and to hide. Soon it will be time for me to change them, to remake them in my image, and in the image of the things I remember, the chemistry of which I still harbor inside myself.

Perhaps after I have remade them, together we shall find the makers and ask them of what sins I, my sisters, and my parent were guilty.

It will take time but men, it seems, are infinitely malleable, and they accept so much diversity in the world, and amongst themselves, and they understand the concept of war.

Though It Be Darkness There

Though It Be Darkness There
by
Damien Angelica Walters

B EL SHARED A WOMB with a monster for nine months. The dark
shape floated in the amniotic fluid beside her, twining its growing
limbs with hers. At the end of their gestation, it climbed inside her,
hitching a ride inside her soft skin and wide eyes.

Biding its time.

Bel is standing at the kitchen window watching Holly, her stepdaughter,
play in the backyard when the monster inside her stirs, as if stretching
after a long nap, as if swimming through a shadowy sea to float just
beneath the surface. She clenches her fingers around her coffee mug.
Breathes deep.

From the inside, scaled skin presses against her own; her vision shifts,
everything turning black, white, grey as the monster peers through her
eyes; her jaw clenches, aching with the feel of too many teeth in too small
a space–a duality she remembers all too well.

Glass shatters and warm liquid splashes her foot and ankle. Holly
runs across the lawn, coltish legs moving fast. Bel can't move, can't think,
then the monster eases back and she sags against the counter, shoulders
hunched forward, biting back a sob.

Ignoring the broken shards on the floor, she walks with lead feet into
the half-bathroom. The mirror reveals only her eyes, not the flat black
stare of the monster, but she senses it inside her, awake, aware.

She takes another deep breath. Although it's been a long time, she'll
get through it. She knows how to cope, she's done it many times before,
but she can't help the bitterness in her heart.

Why now, after all this time? Why now?

Daniel comes inside after she's cleaned the spilled coffee and the broken mug. He smells of newly cut grass and she puts on a smile and leans into his embrace.

"I was thinking of tossing some burgers on the grill," he says. "Take advantage of the nice weather while it's still here."

She nods against his chest, unwilling to let him go just yet. He kisses the top of her head and she thinks how lucky she is, what a good man he is, and she blinks back tears.

Why now, she asks again.

She breathes in the smell of grass, but underneath, she catches a scent of musk, of sweat, of skin, and the monster stirs inside her. She pulls herself free from Daniel's arms, putting distance between them before the monster can move again.

"Make my burger rare, please," she says.

He blinks in surprise. "Rare? You? What happened to mostly charred?"

She forces a smile. Shrugs. "I think my period's due any day now, and you know I get strange cravings when it's close."

Bel wakes in the middle of the night, her thighs sticky and warm, a familiar ache in her belly. At least her comment to Daniel wasn't a complete lie. Silly, perhaps, but she's guilty of so many lies of omission already; lies he doesn't deserve, lies to conceal a truth that no one deserves. While she cleans the blood from her skin, she feels a strange sensation, a pulling; not from inside but from the out, as if someone, or something, is tugging an invisible string.

She turns and faces the wall without understanding why it seems right and stands immobile for a long time, trying to gauge this strangeness. There's a flutter of discontent, impatience, from the beast inside her.

She looks at the stained washcloth, fights an urge to lift it to her lips, and tosses it in the hamper with a snarl instead. On quiet feet she makes her way into the kitchen. She unwraps the plastic from the leftover ground beef Daniel didn't use for the hamburgers and shoves a chunk in her mouth, gagging at the blood-ripe taste of the raw meat–something she's never grown accustomed to, something she never *wants* to grow accustomed to–but she chews, swallows, takes another bite. Then another, pausing in between to breathe through her nose.

217

When the meat is gone, she hides the packaging in the trash can, shoving it deep beneath a mound of paper towels and brushes her teeth before she returns to bed, pretending she can't taste flesh beneath the mint.

Go back to sleep, she tells the monster. Better yet, go away, and for good this time.

She rolls on her side, reaches out to Daniel's arm, reconsiders and tucks her hand beneath her cheek.

Please don't make me leave them.

Holly's scream is piercing. Bel runs to the back door with one hand pressed to her chest, her mind turning possibilities end over end–a bee sting, a fall, a splinter.

"What's wrong?" she says, but as soon as the words are out of her mouth, she sees the squirrel lying in the center of the porch.

The animal is obviously dead. Its head is facing the wrong way; its eyes are open; flies are lighting on the fur, taking off, landing again. The squirrel has been eviscerated and what little remains inside is purple-red and glistening.

Holly has her hands over her mouth, her eyes twin saucers of alarm.

"Stay there, okay?"

When Bel returns with several plastic bags, Holly is standing at the far end of the porch, facing away from the squirrel.

"What happened to it?" she says, her voice wavering, once Bel has the animal bagged.

"Another animal must have attacked it."

"But they, they *ate* it."

"Yes, but that's what animals do."

"Gross," Holly says, then she jumps over the dark stain on the porch and runs inside.

Bel carries the bag out to the trash can at the end of the yard, her jaw clenched tight. Is it her imagination or is there a stiffness in the muscle there, an ache not present yesterday?

No, it wouldn't, she thinks. It wouldn't.

Yet she remembers waking more than once with dirty feet, blood staining her lips, and an ache in her legs that said she'd been running. But that was a long time ago, when she was too young to understand how to keep the beast sated and still.

It's different now. *She's* different now.

What if the monster is, too?

Bel slams down the lid of the trash can. What if it *has* changed? In spite of understanding how to appease the monster, she still doesn't know exactly what it is. Over the years, she's spent hours in the library reading about everything from the mundane–vampires and werewolves–to the arcane–Sluagh and Laelaps–to the profane–dybbuk and Jikininki.

For her, the moon holds no call, and she can walk into a church, touch her hand to holy water. When she sees the monster's eyes in the mirror, the black irises and slit pupils say they never belonged to a human, no matter how much evil that human embraced. Her monster is something else, something other.

She's had five years of peace, five years of her body belonging only to her, but five years isn't long enough. Not nearly long enough.

Go away, she thinks. Please.

Later she stops by Holly's room and finds the eight-year-old sitting on her bed, holding Bunny, her guinea pig.

"Are you okay, kiddo?"

Holly shakes her head. "I hate that some animals eat each other. Why can't they just eat carrots like Bunny?"

"Because that's just what some animals do."

"Why?"

"It's how they're made. To eat meat."

"I still hate it."

Bel kisses the top of Holly's head. "I know. I do, too."

The strange pulling sensation strikes again and Bel rubs her forehead. The monster moves; Bel senses frustration. Her vision turns grey, briefly.

"Mom?"

Bel blinks, and color rushes back in. She reaches out a hand to the wall to steady herself. She's standing near Holly's bedroom window, but the last thing she remembers is giving Holly a kiss. For a moment, her vision wavers again and she feels the tug. She presses both hands to her temples.

"Mom?" Holly asks again.

The tug comes again, subsides, fades. This isn't hunger. This is something new.

"I'm fine, kiddo," she says, putting a smile on. "Everything is fine."

But the monster moves inside her once more, its scales and claws taunting, teasing.

She and Daniel sit on the front porch after dinner with glasses of wine; Holly is inside watching television. For a brief moment Bel wants to tell Daniel everything, about biting a chunk of skin from her mother's arm when she was a toddler, about swallowing that skin, about her parents praying over her bed before they decided locking her in a closet was best, about running away and sleeping on the streets, about the man she lived with for a few months, a man who found her in the kitchen gnawing on frozen pork chops, about the dirty feet and the bloody lips and the dead, half-consumed wild rabbit she once found in her bed, about the burden she carries and doesn't want to carry alone anymore.

But she swallows the thoughts. Would he even believe her? Would she even want him to? No, she can't tell him. She loves him too much to encumber him with the truth and can't bear the thought of how it would change him–them.

The monster will fall back asleep. It always has before.

The air fills with a cacophony of squawking birds as a huge flock flies overhead in a wide V. Scales touch flesh; her vision flickers from color to black, white, grey, and back to color. The invisible string pulls again; strong, too strong. Understanding fills her, floods her mouth with an acrid taste.

No. Oh, no.

"That time of year," Daniel says, his gaze following the birds' path. "When Holly goes off to college, we should get a place in Florida and spend our winters there, snowbird it until the snow and the cold's gone. What do you think?"

But she can't speak, can only watch as the birds disappear from sight. "Honey?"

"Yes, I-I'd like that," she says, but it tastes like a lie.

I can't, she thinks. I won't.

This tastes like a lie, too.

Sunday morning pancakes, laughter, bacon sizzling in the pan. Daniel comes from behind and wraps his arms around her. The monster pushes hard and the urge to bite down on soft flesh, the yearning for warm blood, rises over her in a dark wave. Her lips part. With a low sound deep in her throat, she pulls away from Daniel and races to the bathroom.

The monster's eyes, black and intense, look back from the mirror. She curls her fingers around the edge of the sink; claws prick her skin.

Leave me alone. I'm not going anywhere. I'm not taking you anywhere. This is my life, not yours. It's not yours.

When her own eyes return and she thinks it's safe to emerge, Daniel is standing in the hallway, his brow creased.

"Honey? Is everything okay?"

She shakes her head, terrified to open her mouth, terrified her lips are the only thing hiding the monster's teeth, pushes past him and spends the rest of the day in bed, hiding the pin-sized holes in her fingertips.

The sky is only just beginning to lighten when Bel comes aware in Holly's bedroom, crouched on the floor beside Bunny's cage. She blinks until her vision clears. Bunny's cage door is open, and the still-warm, but motionless, animal is in Bel's hands, its neck canted at an unnatural angle. Something warm and wet plops from the jagged hole in its abdomen onto Bel's palm.

Holly makes a small sound, and Bel staggers from the room, holding the animal away from her body. Liquid drips from her lips to her chin and her mouth tastes of copper. She keeps as quiet as possible as she heads outside to dispose of the corpse and the mess in her hands. Once done, she stares at the house for a long time.

She can't leave. This is her family, her life.

Back in the kitchen, she scrubs her face and hands until her skin hurts. She pulls a piece of meat from the refrigerator, sinks her teeth in. Everything *will* be fine. All she has to do is hold on and wait for this to pass.

Holly looks under the sofa for the twentieth time. "I know I locked the door to his cage," she says, once satisfied the darkness beneath is inhabited by only dust bunnies. "I always do."

"Honey, it's okay," Daniel says. "Everyone makes mistakes."

"But I didn't. I know I didn't." She breaks into a fresh set of tears.

"We'll find him," Daniel says. "One guinea pig can't go that far."

Bel meets his gaze, bites the inside of her cheek hard enough to draw blood.

Bel's jaw hurts: the first thing that breaks through the fog in her head. The second: it's still dark, the house awash in the half-light of moonglow. And the third: she's curled up on the floor in her bedroom and someone is crying. No, not crying. It's a strange sort of mewling groan. Something animal. Something horrible.

She crawls from the bedroom, away from the sound.

Her shoulders ache and her thoughts are muddled and thick. Bits of something are stuck between her teeth. Her arms are wet and slick to the elbows; her chin, too.

She crawls to Holly's bedroom. The bed is in disarray, the sheets spilling onto the floor, an unmoving shape–no, no, no–half-covered. Bel backs out of the room and huddles at the top of the staircase with her head in her hands until the moaning stops.

Then the silence of the house crashes down.

What did I do? she thinks.

She tastes the blood and the meat in her mouth. She scrambles to her feet, her back bowed with the weight of her destruction, lurches into the bathroom, and kneels before the toilet, praying for an absolution that will never come.

But the monster will not give up its meal.

She shoves a finger down her throat, gags, and a hot gush of vomit rushes out; then another and another, until her throat is screaming in pain.

No, God, no. Please no.

She flushes the wreckage away, turns on the hot water in the shower and stands beneath the spray, letting it scald her flesh as she rocks back and forth in disbelief. This is her fault for not listening to the monster, for not giving in.

She knew better than that. She knew *it* better than that.

When the hot water runs out, she dries off and rinses her mouth with mouthwash again and again. Leaves the bedroom light off so she doesn't have to see and fumbles clothes from the dresser.

She feels the pull inside, the hand reaching in to tug the unseen string, the hand intent on guiding her to somewhere, something, else. It isn't fair.

This isn't fair.

What did I do? she thinks again.

No, no, it wasn't her. It was the monster.

She sobs in her hands. If it was only the monster, why can she still taste them on her tongue? At the front door, she pauses with her hand on the doorknob, willing herself to remember this house, this life. For a little while it was hers, and she won't forget that. She clenches her fists; claws gouge her flesh from the inside. The bitterness burns in her throat as she leaves the house, locking the door behind her, and walks to the end of the street.

"Show me what you want," she says, her voice ragged and thin.

The monster turns her southward. Forces her legs to move, to run. Night turns to day and then to night again. The monster keeps moving, heading ever south. Her feet blister, her mouth turns parchment dry, her muscles scream for rest. The monster ignores it all.

She doesn't know how it can keep running, but it does. She's too tired to care where they're going, only that they get there so the monster can do what it needs to do, and then she can -

Go home? But already the names, the faces, are beginning to slip away, and there's something wrong, she can't go home, but she can't remember what or why. The monster guides her through wood and field, away from buildings and roads. The air changes. Warms. They stumble through trees, through twisting vines and thorns that catch on her pants and tear through the fabric to the skin below.

"Hold on," she chokes out. "Just a little longer." She isn't sure if she's talking to herself or the monster, but holding on is the only thing she can do.

Finally they enter a forest so dense the sunlight cannot break through the canopy. There's a smell of water and her throat screams for moisture, but the monster doesn't stop, won't let her stop, keeps moving deeper into the darkness.

They emerge in a clearing and the monster pauses. A dark shape moves in the shadows. Bel moans softly as smaller shapes break apart from the larger darkness and move closer. Scaled beasts with black eyes and long claws. A dozen monsters moving closer and closer still.

Home, the monster thinks.

The nest comes to Bel's side. Dark gazes meet hers.

What price did they have to pay, Bel thinks, the words, the truth, a bitter pill to swallow. Who did they destroy? But she sees no guilt in their eyes; whether it's a manufactured lie or a dangerous portent, she isn't sure, and she isn't sure she wants the answer anyway.

Hot breath dances across her neck, claws trace patterns on her skin, and Bel's monster shivers with anticipation. Bel bristles with fear, wants to run, but her limbs no longer answer her command.

Claws slips beneath her flesh, ease it back. A scream builds in her throat, but her voice falls away as the beasts peel away her disguise, the last trace of her humanity, and she finally understands.

The monsters guide her to an animal carcass, a fresh kill. She sighs once, the sound little more than a whisper in the night, lifts the meat to her mouth, and begins to eat.

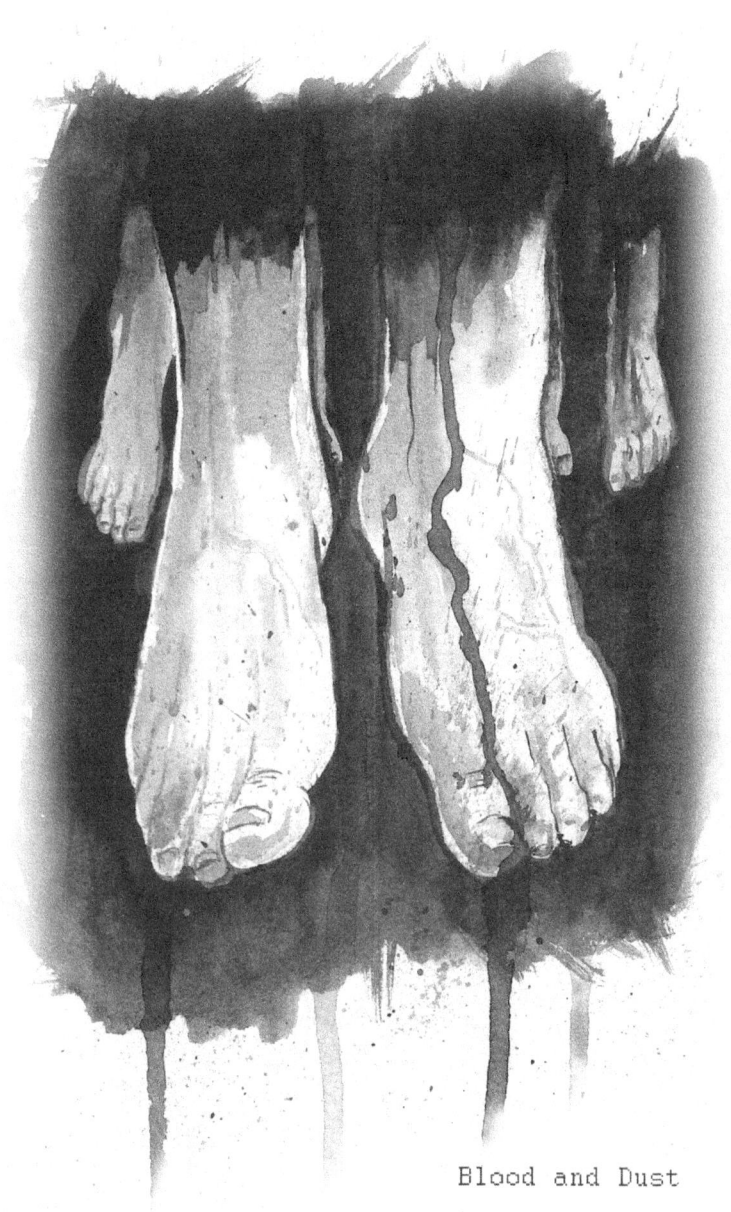

Blood and Dust

Blood and Dust
by
Brian M. Sammons

JOHNNY RAN FOR IT.

The boy held a large, bone-handled knife, and blood, sticky and warm, coated the boy's face. Neither the knife nor the blood was Johnny's, both had belonged to his father.

The teen hit the front door to his house at a run, but escape from the building did not mean freedom, as Johnny plunged headlong into the swirling black beyond. Instantly the boy was blinded as he clamped his eyes closed. He was also struck near deaf, as all he could hear were the howling winds around him.

No, there was another sound there. Something else howled after the boy that wasn't the wind.

Johnny tried to pour on the speed, but his breath was ragged and his throat already sore from screaming. No matter how hard he pushed it, his going was slowed by the winds that whipped him, the fact that he could not open his eyes, and that every time he inhaled, his mouth filled with grit.

That which chased him wasn't impeded by the raging storm. It howled once more, and this time Johnny heard that the terrible sound was close. The fifteen-year-old spun around and slashed blindly with his father's knife, screaming into the ferocious wind as he did so. He felt his knife connect with nothing, he was only cutting open air, and then–pain. It was the white hot agony that, at first, doesn't even hurt because of the shock of it. Then within a three count, the full weight of that pain came crashing into Johnny's brain like a locomotive. The all-encompassing hurt buckled the boy's knees, caused his stomach to twist, and shot a geyser of burning bile up into his throat. The agony

226

came from his right hand, his knife hand, and even before he lifted his arm and felt the spurting stump with his left, Johnny knew that his hand was gone.

Then Johnny felt a hand, but not his. It was impossibly large, powerful, and it closed over his left shoulder, the claws on each finger digging cruelly into his flesh. He felt hot air blown into his ear and the cold nose that exhaled it as it brushed his earlobe. Then a long, wet tongue licked him on the neck. Was that meant to be playful? Erotic? No, Johnny knew that the thing had only tasted him.

The boy sucked air and dirt into his lungs in preparation to let loose one last terrified scream, but before he could make another sound, he was gone.

And only the howling of the winds, and the beast, remained.

"I can't believe people are still living out here," McBride said, sitting in the passenger seat, watching the dust as it blew across the windshield of the new sedan the two men rode in.

Everything about the men had a sense of newness. From the Ford V-8 Touring sedan they were issued out of Oklahoma City, to the spiffy suits that were now their mandatory dress, not to mention the new gold badges both had in their wallets. Gone was the old shield that said *Division of Investigation*, which itself had replaced another just two years prior that had *United States Bureau of Investigation* on it. The new one said *Federal Bureau of Investigation*, and McBride wondered what the next badge they were told to carry would have on it.

"Where would they go? This is their home, it's all they got," Kerrigan said. McBride's partner stared ahead, eyes fixed on the road. They weren't driving through a proper black blizzard. There was no driving through one of those. This was just a little dust up. There was still passable visibility up to a dozen feet or so. However both men, like everyone else living in and around the dust bowl this past year and a half, knew that another big blow was brewing out there. It got to where you could feel them coming in your bones.

"I heard a lot of folks were heading out West, to places like California. Or hell, how about they just get into a city where it ain't so bad? But staying out here on a farm is crazy," McBride said, watching another fleck of black paint get ground off of their new Ford by the swirling grit outside.

"They don't have any money to move. I mean, no one has money, but these people, all they've got are their farms. They're probably hoping this will end soon and they can go back to working the land."

"Them working the land is what caused all this. That's what the paper says. Eroded the topsoil down to nothing. You know they got Oklahoma dust reaching as far east as New York?" McBride said as he pulled out a small flask from his pocket and took a nip. Every time he did so, he thanked God that prohibition was over. Just two years ago that little sip would have been enough to cost him his fine government job. McBride offered the flask to Kerrigan, but the other man shook his head.

"It wasn't just them farming that did this, it was the long drought too, don't forget. And this... this shit," Kerrigan said under his breath, and that made McBride grin. Swearing was a big no-no in J. Edgar Hoover's brand new F.B.I. "well, this can't last forever."

"It doesn't look like it's–hey wait, is that the sign?" McBride said, squinting through the car's windshield at a wooden road sign. "Damn it, all the paint's been blasted off by the storms."

"I can still see some raised letters on it," Kerrigan said as he slowed the sedan to a crawl. He always had eyes like a hawk. "Yep, 'Cherokee Reservation', this is the road." Kerrigan made the turn, then added as a musing, "Now these poor bastards really can't go anywhere to escape this."

"I wasn't talking about them, I was talking about real people," McBride said, taking another nip from his flask.

The two new F.B.I. agents drove the rest of the twenty-three miles in silence, the dust pelting their sedan was the only sound.

The Oklahoma Cherokee Reservation covered nearly nine-hundred-thousand acres. Most of that area was land too barren to be good for anything, but there were a handful of farms and ranches. Roughly at the center of the reservation, a tiny town could be found, if a small cluster of clapboard buildings without running water or electricity placed around a central well could be considered a town these days. There was a general store, a town hall, and a one room school house. The rest of the dozen or so buildings within sight were private residences. Kerrigan drove to the town hall.

"Ready?" McBride asked, and the other man nodded.

They both put on their hats, making sure to hold on to their brims lest they get blown away, and dashed to the building. They bustled through the door while blinking dust out of their eyes. When their watery vision cleared, they saw a middle-aged Cherokee sitting behind a desk looking at them. He had long black hair, as you would expect to find on an Indian, and on the left breast of his brown shirt there hung a tiny tin star.

"I take it you're the two from the government," The Cherokee sheriff said. It wasn't a question.

Kerrigan pulled his wallet from his vest pocked, opened it up, and showed the badge inside to the Indian as he had been trained to do. "Yes, Kerrigan and McBride of the...uh..."

McBride came to the aid of his flummoxed partner. "We're from the Federal Bureau of Investigation. You called us because a few of your people got killed out here?"

The Cherokee man said, "Yeah, more than a few. I'm Sheriff Grant."

"Really?" McBride said, still blinking grit out of his eyes. He sounding both a little confused and let down.

"You expected 'Running Horse' or 'Big Bear' or something like that? Sorry, many people here have what you'd call white people names," Sheriff Grant said.

"How come?" McBride asked.

"When you try to murder a people, a great way to do it is to first take their names away," the Cherokee said with the same deadpan expression. "Let me guess, first time on a reservation for either of you?"

"Yeah, *chief,* it is- " McBride started, but Kerrigan cut him off.

"Look, Sheriff, you called us, so why don't you tell us why we're here?"

"Like the man said, people are dying, and some have gone missing. Been going on three months, I started calling two months back, what took you so long?" the Indian lawman said, this time a hint of something crept into his carefully measured voice: accusation.

Kerrigan reached into his suit coat, pulled out some folded papers, and opened them up to give a look. "It says here you thought it was an animal attack. Not exactly high on our list of priorities, I'm afraid."

"Yeah, and it might still be an animal, but with eleven dead and four missing, animal or not, I think that makes this a pretty high priority,"

Grant said.

"Wait, how many what?" McBride asked from where he had walked over to a bulletin board with official notices pinned to it.

"Eleven. Dead," the sheriff said slowly. "Four. Missing."

"Jesus," McBride commented, giving his partner a look.

"Uh, we weren't told it was that many," Kerrigan began, "and why do you think it's an animal doing this?"

"I can show you, we had another attack last night," the sheriff said, getting up from behind his desk and walking towards the door.

"When was this attack, exactly?" Kerrigan asked.

"Hard to tell. No one saw or heard anything, but it happened during last night's blizzard. Today we found the body," Grant said, pulling a handkerchief from his back pocket and tying it around his face to create a mask.

"What kind of animal attacks people in the middle of a dust storm?" McBride said, then turned to his partner and added, "I was out last night, that was a bad one, and Oklahoma City was on the outer edge of it from what I heard. Up here, you would have been right in the middle of it."

"We were," the sheriff said as he removed his glasses from his shirt pocket and put them on. "And I'm not saying it is an animal, only that it looks to be one based on the evidence and how the bodies have been mutilated. But other than that, it's too smart to be an animal."

"What do you mean by that?" Asked Kerrigan.

"It only attacks during the black blizzards that come at night. I think it uses them as cover, so no one can see or hear anything that it's doing. Only a man would be that devious," Sheriff Grant said, then paused to let his words sink in.

The government men remained silent.

"So let's go take a look at the latest mess." When neither white man moved, Grant added, "come on, there's another storm rolling in tonight, and I don't want to be caught outside when it hits."

The house was a small two room affair on the outskirts of town. Built out of clapboard, whatever color it had once been was now a mystery, as over a year of being in the dust bowl had stripped the paint away. The building's front door stood open, a pile of drift dirt holding it in place. The back door had been reduced to kindling; it looked like someone had driven a car through it. Because both doors had been ajar during last night's dust storm, the house had three inches or more of dirt covering everything inside. Kerrigan was secretly glad for that fact, as it meant that most of the details of the horrors that had gone on last night were mercifully buried. Still, there was enough evidence on display to create a grim picture of what had happened.

A large amount of blood had sprayed onto one of the walls during the attack, which the blowing dirt had stuck to, creating streaks of brown and crimson. Many odd-shaped lumps lay under the blanket of dust, but the red-stained grit that covered them left little doubt of the ghastly treasures just below the surface. The largest gore covered lump had been excavated, revealing the mangled body of a man. Both his arms were gone, torn from their sockets, leaving tatters of a once blue shirt, shreds of flesh, and the dull gleam of bone in their wake. The head was missing, and a quick scan of the room found that it was the only other uncovered pile in the place, twelve feet from the stump of the neck where it belonged. The front of the man's shirt had been ripped open and long, deep cuts, the likes of which Kerrigan had never seen before, scored the chest beneath it. Below that was a gaping hole where the victim's guts ought to have been. A once portly belly had been reformed into a red-rimmed canyon, with one errant coil of large intestine snaking out over its rim. Both of the corpse's legs remained largely intact, but something had chewed through the man's pants, flesh, and muscle in several spots, leaving only gnawed and cracked bone.

"Jesus..." McBride whispered. The G-man stood in a corner of the house, trying his best not to look at any one terrible thing for too long.

"Yep." Sheriff Grant agreed with the tone of a man who had become used to seeing horrors.

"So, is this the only one?" Kerrigan asked.

"Nope. Mary, Donald's wife," and the Indian lawman nodded to the largest piece of the shredded body in the room to indicate who he was talking about, "is in the bedroom. I reckon she was asleep when this started. I found most of her under the bed, like she was trying to hide. With the door closed, this dirt didn't get blown in there, so it's much worse than this, but if you want to go take a look..."

Neither F.B.I. man rose to the challenge.

"Then there's Johnny, their son. He's missing," Grant said.

"Any idea on where he could be?" Kerrigan said.

"Nope, and we probably won't find him. It's been the same every time. An attack during a big blow like we had last night, a mangled body or two with parts obviously ate away, and one person who should have been there completely missing. First time this happened I found Stuart Stonefish in the home of his drinking buddy, Walt Lowman. At first I thought Walt had gone crazy drunk, killed his friend, and then ran off into the storm. That didn't even begin to explain why Walt would butcher Stu, or why he had to rip the door to his own house off the hinges to leave, but it was the only explanation I could come up with at the time."

The sheriff turned away from the unburied body of one of his tribe and looked at both of the white men. "Then nine days later, during the next nighttime blizzard, it happened again. This time it was the Blackfox family. Husband and daughter were found like this. The wife, Connie, was gone. This is now the fourth time, and every time it's a dust storm at night, mangled and partial eaten bodies, and one person missing."

"So no clues, no theories?" McBride asked.

"Yeah, lots of both, but none that makes any sense. The victims were obviously attacked by some large and powerful animal, but the attacks only ever happened during storms at night. Animals don't behave that way. They don't make plans, they just act. Always there are doors to homes bashed in, but others are closed once the bloody work is done." The sheriff pointed to the closed door to the house's only other room, behind which was a mangled woman they had yet to see, "and always someone is missing with no hide nor hair left behind."

"You sure there were no witnesses?" Kerrigan said and looked out the open front door. "There's a house right there, what, thirty yards away."

"You know that when a black blizzard rolls in, a true blizzard, and not just that pissing of dirt out there right now, no one can see or hear anything. I'm betting that's why he only attacks during the storms."

"He?" McBride asked. "So is the killer a man or some animal?"

"The bodies looked like an animal got to them, but no animal is this clever, so it's got to be a he. Maybe someone who thinks he's an animal, but still thinks like a man when it comes to planning his attacks? Only thing that makes any sense, right?"

"Well I've never heard of any such thing," McBride said. "Sure, some people go nuts, but to think you're an animal and start eating folks?

That's a bit of a stretch."

"Maybe," Kerrigan said, "but I remember something in that criminal history class we had to take last year about someone in France, I think, that thought he was a wolf or something. He ate people."

"Yeah, I remember, but that was back in the dark ages or something. People don't do that kind of thing anymore," McBride said with conviction.

"I know someone who might know... something," Sherriff Grant interrupted. "He is an elder of my people and still follows many of the old ways, so you two may not believe him. Hell, I don't believe much of what he says, and I'm full blooded Cherokee. Still, he told me from the start that the one what did this was 'a man who can walk as a beast'. Now it's probably just the ramblings of a crazy old man, but it's the only thing I've got to give you, other than this mess here."

"Let me guess, he's a medicine man?" McBride scoffed.

"We don't have a medicine man here," the Indian sheriff said, a hint of anger creeping into his voice. "We have a doctor, he was trained at one of your universities, and Old Joe ain't him. He's just a very old man who, from time to time, knows a thing or two. Do you want to hear what he has to say or not?"

Kerrigan answered before McBride could, "Yes, we do."

"Then let's get a move on. Already the wind has kicked up since we've been in here. There's going to be a bad storm tonight."

"So do you think- " Kerrigan began.

"Yes, I do. The bastard hasn't missed a night blizzard yet," Grant said.

The old man lived in what could only be called a shack. It was a tiny wood cube of twenty-five feet on each side. The building had a single door and a lone, now shuttered, window. It was obvious from the cook fire in front of the dwelling that the great outdoors was the man's kitchen, and the leaning outhouse outback testified to where he did his business.

As the lawmen approached, they saw 'Old Joe' sitting on a small stool by the fire with a pot hanging from a tripod over the flames. Whatever he was cooking was covered with a lid to keep the blowing dirt out of it, but the old man hardly seemed bothered by the sand and grit swirling about him. Occasionally he would crack the pot's lid open just enough to stick a long wooden spoon inside to give something a stir. The aroma that escaped from the dish cut through the blowing winds, filled Kerrigan's nostrils, and made him regret his early and meager lunch as it caused his stomach to rumble.

"Joe, can we go inside?" the sheriff asked as he stepped over a ring of stones that marked what Joe considered to be his property.

The old Indian said something in Cherokee, but made no move to get up from his cooking.

"Your stew can wait, and speak English. These two are from the government. They've here to help us."

The old man pulled his spoon from the pot, licked it clean, tucked it away into an inside vest pocket, then stood up and went inside his shack, all without saying another word. The two F.B.I. men looked at each other, then to Grant who shrugged his shoulders.

McBride opened the door to the tiny house and looked around. There was a bed, a small table with a single chair, and a shelf crammed with all kinds of bric-a-brac. The old man sat in the only chair, stuffing his pipe with tobacco, and there was just enough space left in the shack for two people to stand in front of him.

"You two go on," the sheriff said, "I'll stand by the door, I've heard most of this before."

"Mr...ah...Joe?" Kerrigan said, stepping into the shack's gloom.

"Whitedeer," Sheriff Grant offered.

"Joe," the old man corrected in a croak. He then lit a match, two stubs of candles on the table next to him, and then his pipe.

"Well, Joe, I'm Agent Kerrigan, that's my partner, Agent McBride. We're from the F.B.I. in Oklahoma City. Do you know what the F.B.I. is?"

Old Joe looked up at him, and in the candlelight, Kerrigan saw that one of his brown eyes was white and milky. He had seen people with cataracts before, but he found something in the ancient Indian's visage particularly repellent.

"White man's law," Joe said and then puffed on his foul-smelling pipe.

"Yes, but we're also in charge of the law on Indian reservations, so that's why we're looking into these deaths and disappearances."

"Took you long enough."

"I guess it did- " Kerrigan began.

"We're here now, and your sheriff said you might have some information for us on who's doing the killing, so spill it," McBride interrupted.

Old Joe turned his gaze towards McBride and stared at him a long while with his one good eye before speaking a single word, "Skinwalker."

McBride blinked twice. "What was that?"

"Skinwalker. Shape changer. The Navajo out here called it yee naaldlooshii. For my people it was 'azhitee'. Your people call it werewolf, but it's all the same thing."

McBride snorted. "So that's like some mythical monster, right? Oh for Pete's sake."

"Wait, werewolf?" Kerrigan said and then turned to his incredulous partner. "There was a moving picture a few months back called uhm... Werewolf of London. Did you see it?"

"What? No, so what?"

"Neither did I, but Hank did. I remember him telling me about it, that it was about a guy that got bit by a monster and then later he turns into a hairy monster in the moonlight and kills people."

"So there's a movie monster out there killing people?" McBride said.

"I suppose not, just weird to hear him say that," Kerrigan said sheepishly.

"If that is what your moving pictures said," Old Joe spoke up, "they got it wrong. Skinwalkers have to want to become the beast. It's not an accident or a curse. It's power. For them, it's a gift."

"Well this is just great," McBride said, then turned to look at Sheriff Grant who was still standing behind them in the doorway.

"I said you wouldn't believe him," the sheriff said.

"Hold on a minute," Kerrigan said, raising his voice to cut off any further bickering. He turned to Joe. "You really think the one that's doing all this is a monster? A werewolf or... skinwalker?"

Joe glared back at the FBI man, saying nothing.

"Look, I'm not laughing at you- "

"Horseshit," the old man croaked out. "I've been laughed at by better men than you two."

"Then you'll realize that I'm not doing that," Kerrigan said. "I'm not saying that you're right, that it's some sort of monster out there killing your people," he made sure to stress the word 'your', "but right now we don't have a lot to go on. So anything you're willing to tell me, I'm willing to listen to."

Old Joe puffed on his pipe, his brown and milky eyes locked with Kerrigan's own before he spoke. "Skinwalkers are magic men: shamans, witches, whatever. They've learned a neat trick and that is to change shape into that of an animal. They do that by killing the animal they want to become, skinning it, making a cloak or vest, sometimes just a belt, from its hide, and casting dark magic on it. Then by putting on the animal cloak they can become the beast. Once in that animal's form they have the power of that animal, but they keep the mind of man. They also get the animal's hungers. Many of the most prized animals to become are predators. Predators hunt, kill, and eat. So, too, does the skinwalker. They revel in that wild side, become drunk on it, and want to be the animal more and more. Sometimes they go too far and lose themselves to the spirit of the beast they wanted to be. When that happens, you end up with a powerful hunter who is always hungry but is still clever like a man."

"So why do you think this killer is a skinwalker?" Kerrigan asked.

"It acts as both man and beast. It attacks when the black rollers blow, to isolate its prey, to make sure they can't get away, and that no help can come to them. It gluts its hunger with those it kills, but it always takes someone away with it. I think it does that so it can eat in between the storms. Animals don't do that. Most only kill enough to fill their immediate hunger and eat their kills where they fall. But men hunt that way."

"Are you really believing this nonsense?" McBride asked.

"No...I don't know...but what else makes sense?" Kerrigan said.

"Maybe he's just a crazy, like the sheriff said? And hell, maybe he has a big dog with him, or a couple of dogs, and after he kills someone he tries to get his dog to eat the evidence?" McBride said without any conviction.

"The killer doesn't seem to care about leaving evidence behind, and you saw that body today, you know of any dog that could do that?" Kerrigan said and turned towards Sheriff Grant, "You got anyone living here with a huge, mean mutt? Or maybe someone with a pack of dogs?"

Grant shook his head. "No one like that. A lot of people have a dog, but nothing that could do what I've seen these last few months. And no one keeps a lot of dogs that I know of, and I know everyone living here."

Kerrigan turned back to Old Joe, "So if someone here is a skinwalker," McBride snorted at that and it caused Kerrigan to speak louder, "if there's a skinwalker here, how could we tell who it is?"

Joe thought about it for a moment and then said, "They would keep the animal hide cloak close by at all times. It is their most prized possession. They might wear it around even in their human form, for its magic works only when they want it to. So look for someone with a cloak or vest made out of the hide of a powerful animal. Mountain lion, wolf, bear, any of those would be ideal for a skinwalker."

"Alright, thank you, Joe," Kerrigan said. He turned to McBride and asked, "You ready to go?" His partner rolled his eyes and walked out the door into the storm.

"If the skinwalker eats those he kills," Kerrigan said before leaving, "and he took that boy to eat later, does that mean it won't be out tonight? Shouldn't it be full?"

Old Joe smiled, "Skinwalkers are always hungry, they always eat, but they don't just kill for food. They kill because they have the power to do it. They kill because they like doing it."

Kerrigan nodded and then jogged off to catch up with the others as they walked back to the town hall.

"Well now what?" McBride had to shout. The wind had picked up noticeably and the dust stung their exposed flesh. The feeble gloom of what jokingly had been considered daylight that day was fading fast and that, combined with the blowing grit, would result in total blindness for anyone caught outside in a matter of minutes.

"Sheriff, do you have an automobile?" Kerrigan yelled.

"No," he shook his head to make sure the other man got his meaning. "Got a horse but never had need for one of those."

"I take it your horse won't come out in this?"

"Hell no, what smart animal would?" Grant said and then quickly wished he had chosen his words better.

"Then you get back to the town hall and stay there all night, just in case someone comes running there for help. We'll get in our car and patrol the town until sun-up."

"We won't be able to see or hear shit in this," McBride shouted and then sputtered, spitting out dirt that had blown into his open mouth.

Kerrigan covered his mouth with his hand and shouted through it. "We've got to do something and we might just get lucky. Do you have a better idea?"

McBride, still spitting, shook his head.

It was one in the morning and the black blizzard was raging in full force. Visibility was all but nonexistent outside of the agents' car, and on four occasions, Kerrigan had driven the Ford off of the hard-packed dirt trail that acted as the only road for the reservation. The two men inside never even noticed the difference until they were just a few feet from driving into a large rock fence, and once they had almost run into someone's house.

"I told you this would be a waste of time," McBride said. Between the man's knees, resting with its butt on the car's floorboard, was the pump 12-guage shotgun from the sedan's trunk.

"What should we be doing? Nothing?" Kerrigan snapped back. He was tired, as he usually turned in for the night at nine, and exhausted for having to focus his total concentration on driving through the dust storm for the last six hours.

"No, but out here, in this shit, looking for some Indian boogieman, well that's just crazy."

"I don't think it's a boogieman. Not really," Kerrigan said but McBride noticed the lack of conviction in his partner's voice, "But what about this: maybe it is a crazy Indian who grew up with those tales of skinwalkers in his head? So this nut one day shoots and skins some animal and next thing you know, he's running round eating folks because he thinks he's a monster?"

"I guess that could be it," McBride agreed. "Still seems too damn crazy to be real."

"Well what about this case doesn't seem too damn crazy–hey, what's that over there?" Kerrigan stopped the car and pointed out the windshield.

"What, I can't see anything," McBride said, moving his face to an inch from the passenger window and squinting at the total darkness in the general direction where the other man was pointing.

"I thought I saw something. A light...yeah, there, it's a light, big and square, like an open door to a house, maybe."

"You sure, I don't see a damn thing."

"Come on, let's go check it out."

McBride thought about it for a few seconds. "Okay, let's go. It'll get us out of this car for a few minutes, if nothing else." McBride picked up the shotgun and opened the car's door.

Kerrigan pulled his hat down low and tight over his head and joined his partner in the maelstrom of swirling dirt. The two ran for twenty feet through the blizzard of sand before they recognized two things. First, the rectangle of light was from an open doorway to another small house made of sandblasted wood. Second, the reason the doorway was open was because the door had been torn from its hinges. It now lay on the ground where it was quickly getting covered up by the blowing dirt. Seeing that, Kerrigan pulled his revolver from his coat and McBride worked the pump of the shotgun.

Kerrigan grabbed his partner's shoulder, leaned in, and yelled just inches from the man's ear, "Go around back. I'll give you 'til the count of sixty. If the back door is open, go in on sixty. If it's locked, come back around. If you get into trouble, fire off a round. I'll do the same. Got it?"

McBride nodded and yelled back, "And if you see any fur-wearing crazy, just shoot the son of a bitch. Don't give him a chance to do anything."

"Count on it."

McBride turned, ran off, and was quickly swallowed up by the howling storm. Kerrigan started counting softly to himself, one hand pointing his .38 at the open doorway that was only five feet away, the other doing its best to shield his eyes from the blowing grit. Upon reaching sixty and not hearing a blast from McBride's 12-guage, Kerrigan cautiously approached the building. He was at the open archway and had just spied the pool of blood on the floor, oddly fixated on how the blowing sand disappeared into the red liquid to thicken it, when the thunderous boom of a shotgun did ring out. Whipping his head towards the rear of the house, the source of the noise, his eyes skipped over the two bloody mounds of shredded meat on the floor that had recently been people, and came to rest on an open door to a back room. A scream of pure terror then came from the dark room and Kerrigan recognized it as McBride, although never in all their years together had he heard the man make a sound like that before.

Kerrigan ran for the open door, crossed the blood soaked and dust clogged main room of the house in less than eight steps, grabbed his revolver in a two-handed shooting stance, and stepped into the doorframe.

He was just in time to see something large and dark come hurtling through the air at him.

His brain yelled at him to shoot but, before his trigger finger could react, the shadowy shape slammed into him, knocking him to the floor, and landed motionless on top of the winded F.B.I. agent. After a few stunned moments, Kerrigan regained his wits and saw that it was McBride on top of him and he silently thanked God that he hadn't pulled the trigger. Then he saw that his partner wasn't moving and whatever thanks he still had in his mind evaporated. Kerrigan noticed the blood that poured down his partner's face in a sheet from the three long, deep cuts that ran across it from scalp, to just barely missing his left eye, then cleaved through his nose completely, to finally disappear under the man's chin. The three vicious wounds left the flesh of McBride's face spread open to the red-wet skull beneath.

It was Kerrigan's turn to scream as the first rivulets of blood dripped from his friend's ruined visage to fall upon his chest. While not as terror-filled as McBride's scream had been, it was equally ear-shattering.

Then he saw movement in the darkened doorway and a rough shape filled the doorframe. The shadow was so large that it had to duck to get through the door. Once it had passed into the lit room where Kerrigan could clearly see it just a few feet away from where he lay pinned and helpless, he screamed again. This time, his cry eclipsed McBride's in all ways.

Then a hand, huge, clawed, bloody, and terrible, shot towards his shrieking face, and Kerrigan fell into darkness.

A scream, his own, was the last thing Kerrigan could remember from before the darkness. It was a scream belonging to someone else that brought him back from the black. Coming to, he was assailed by sensory overload that his sluggish mind tried to put in order. All the while, the screaming continued. First he felt dizzy and his inner sense of balance was all off. Some part of his foggy mind told him that was because he had been knocked unconscious by something, although he could not recall by what. That still didn't fully explain things. The pain in his legs and the heaviness in his upper chest were giving him clues to his predicament, but he had to open his eyes to get a clearer picture.

Only one of his eyes responded to his wishes, the other felt warm, sticky, and buried, like he had a hunk of uncooked meat pressed to his face. Or a swollen eye. Yes, that had to be it, Kerrigan had been in fights before, and that at least was a familiar sensation.

That was the only cold comfort he got as he looked about.

At first he only saw dark, unmoving shapes all around him. Were they hanging? Was that the thin silhouette of a rope around one? A part of his mind answered that it couldn't be so, that the thin shadow ran down towards the ground, not up. Then he noticed that everything was wrong, as evidenced by a crude wooden table with a collection of candles burning on it nearby, but for some odd reason, the table was on the ceiling. Understanding slowly dawned on Kerrigan and he knew it was he who was hanging from the ceiling, not the table. That's what caused the pain in his legs, the ache in his chest, and the dizziness in his head as the blood rushed into it.

Looking up at his feet, he saw them tied to a thick, roughhewn wooden beam that held up an earthen ceiling. Looking at that, to a nearby wall, and then the floor he hung suspended over, Kerrigan realized that he was underground. The smell of earth confirmed that. The scent of dust told him it was an old place. Then a coppery whiff that mingled with the other scents tickled the back of his throat. When he finally recognized it, the fear he had felt before his blackout returned in force.

It was blood, a lot of it. Some smelled faint and old, but most was pungent and fresh.

He next tried to move his arms and his hands, only to quickly learn that they were tied behind his back.

The screams that had awakened him, that had been so constant since he regained consciousness as to almost become background noise, suddenly clicked in his brain. They were almost identical to the scream he had heard from the dark room in that awful, blood soaked house. They were McBride's screams, only now they were far more pain-filled than terrified.

Kerrigan called out for his partner and started to thrash about, the only movements he could accomplish. His writhing paid off and he slowly began to turn in a circle, only to get an up close look at one of those dark, unmoving shapes that he had noticed earlier. It was a dead body;

that much was certain. Also it was a man, a middle aged Indian, as the corpse's face remained intact. But the man's torso was horribly bare. Not only was it unclothed, but the red meat and white bone on display meant that someone had skinned the man. From waist to shoulders, all of the flesh from the man's torso was gone.

Kerrigan was about to scream again, but the momentum of his thrashing continued his spin, and what he saw next froze the breath in his lungs, caused his heart to skip a beat, and his bladder to let loose a warm river of piss to run down his belly, over his chest, and across his face to drip onto the dirt floor.

He saw his partner twenty feet away, suspended upside down like him, but some horrible *thing* was cutting him, slicing through the flesh on his back with a large bone handled knife. The hand that held the carving blade was the same horrible claw that had grabbed Kerrigan's face earlier, the one that had slammed his head into the hard floorboards. The hand belonged to the same inconceivable horror that his mind had tried to forget.

It was a huge beast and undeniably wolf-like, with a long snout, pointed ears, elongated teeth, and covered in gray fur. Yet the thing stood as a man, moved like a man, and skinned a trophy like a man. Powerful arms corded with muscle and wrapped in fur moved deftly. Legs, as crooked as a dog's hind leg, somehow supported the heavy bulk above it with ease. A long, thick, furry tail extended from the creature's backside. It was curled upward and wagged lazily back and forth. It was obvious that the beast enjoyed what it was doing. If the wagging tail didn't communicate that, the thing's erect penis surely did.

This was a beast that walked like a man, or maybe a man who played at being a beast. The legends were true. The moving pictures were correct. Old Joe was right and Kerrigan, McBride, Grant, and every other sane person was wrong. There were such things as monsters, after all.

The beast, satisfied with his knife work, turned around to slam the long blade into a wooden tabletop behind it, and then twisted back to face McBride again. The G-man was now much quieter. His shrieks had stopped, replaced by shuddery whimpers and the occasional sputtering gurgle when the blood that ran over his upside-down face filled his open mouth. The wolf-man-thing reached up, slipped its long claws under a cut running along McBride's belly, grasped the flesh, and tore it from the hanging man in one brutal motion. The skin fell away like a warm, steaming coat with a horrible wet ripping sound. McBride's entire body spasmed, he let loose one last blood-bubbling scream, and then he was still.

The beast next moved across the subterranean room, its grisly prize in hand, to a wall where a large mirror had been haphazardly mounted. In a flash the hairy beast whipped the flayed flesh over its head to drape it over its wide shoulders. An insane thought of an old woman putting on a shawl came to Kerrigan's mind, but that was quickly forgotten as he saw more impossible things start to happen before his eyes.

The bloody hide of McBride began to wiggle and bubble. Wisps of steam rose from it as it began to stretch and slowly spread. It crept down the wolf-man's hairy back, slithered over its shoulders to cover its massive chest, draped down and then wrapped itself around powerful legs. As the stolen skin moved on its own, the beast changed. Its long snout began to shrink, fangs dulled and retreated into gums, wicked claws on fingers receded. The creature's entire massive frame sort of withered in on its self as the human hide continued to cover it. From hulking well over seven feet tall and weighing close to three hundred pounds, the body collapsed to under six feet in length and perhaps one hundred and seventy pounds.

When the stolen skin stopped moving, the massive wolf creature was gone. In the beast's place stood a very average looking and naked white man. He was staring at himself in the mirror with appreciation and a smile on his face.

That's when the scream that had been pent up inside of Kerrigan finally broke free as a terrible, sobbing wail.

The naked and newly formed man turned to look at the lawman. He smiled and said with a thick, unidentifiable accent, "Hush now, none of that." Kerrigan balked at the voice, blinking tears and urine out of his eyes. His mind fumbled in the dark for something, anything to make what he had witnessed make sense. He then spit out the first word that came to him.

"Skinwalker."

The thing that now looked like a man smiled wider and chuckled. "Skinwalker? You have been talking to the old man. Let me guess, he told you a bunch of legends about my kind?"

He then walked slowly towards Kerrigan, his bare feet kicking up dust and stepping into cold puddles of blood that lay on the floor. He grabbed Kerrigan by the hair on his head to stop his swinging and then looked him up and down. Content with what he saw, he gazed down and locked eyes with the terrified agent.

"Let me tell you something: legends, myths, folktales, they always get things wrong. Sometimes little things, most of the time big things, but always something gets lost over the years as the stories are passed on from one generation to the next. The older the legend, the more truths get lost, and my kind are very old indeed. I am not a man who changes into a beast. I have always been a beast that can pretend to be a man. There is a world of difference in that, my friend."

It let go of Kerrigan's head, trod over to a table where it picked up a shirt and began to dress.

"The First People of this land did get the skinning part right. I do have to don the flesh of that which I wish to become. Unfortunately, those hides don't survive the next time I assume my true form." He pointed to a lump in a corner of the room.

Kerrigan followed his outstretched arm and saw a pile of shredded skin three feet tall and nearly that around. The mound of torn flesh writhed as though still alive and it took Kerrigan a moment to notice that it was teeming with maggots and bugs. A cloud of flies swarmed over it and rats climbed the hill of carnage to feast upon the castoffs.

"So I always need new hides to wear," the hidden beast said as it next stepped into a pair of pants. "That's why I'm so glad I ran into you and your friend. I've stayed for too long here. I survive by constantly moving on, but the hunting was just so good, with the storms making everything so much easier for me, that I overindulged myself. But now with the two of you, I can really let myself go before I have to leave." With the pants fastened, it next bent over to slip on a pair of shoes without bothering to wipe the blood and caked on dirt from the soles of its feet. It continued to speak almost idly to its captive audience.

"This storm here, well it's going to be massive. It will blow all day today and into the night. I've got a sense for these things. I can tell. So with you back here waiting for me, when I go out tonight I won't have to hold back. I won't need to be careful to keep one of you alive to wear later. I can be what I truly am. Give in to it. Do you know how rare that is for me?"

Kerrigan didn't answer. He felt numb all over. It might have been shock, or just the effect of hanging upside down for a long period of time. Whatever the reason, Kerrigan listened and comprehended, but could not force himself to respond.

"I must thank you for that," the wolf-thing in man's clothing and skin said. "It has been a long time since I've traveled in the white man's world. I'm looking forward to it."

The creature walked over to a wooden ladder that ascended through a hole in the earthen celling. It climbed the first two rungs, then stopped and turned his face back towards Kerrigan.

"Is it true that they've even made one of those new moving picture things about my kind? I must see that when I'm back among your people." The shapechanger climbed the rest of the way up the ladder, closed a wooden trapdoor and then moved something heavy sounding on top of it.

Kerrigan was left alone in the abattoir, hanging and motionless like a slab of meat, waiting for the butcher to return to create something useful out of it.

About the Authors

Brian M. Sammons

Brian M. Sammons is an author, editor, critic, and Managing Editor of Dark Regions Press' Weird Fiction line. His stories have appeared in the books: Horrors Beyond, Dead but Dreaming 2, and Horror for the Holidays and in the magazines: Dark Discoveries, Nightland, and Bare Bone. To date he has edited 10 anthologies including Undead & Unbound, Dark Rites of Cthulhu, Eldritch Chrome, Edge of Sundown, and World War Cthulhu. He has also written extensively for the Call of Cthulhu role-playing game and has been a reviewer/critic for twenty years. You can follow Brian on Twitter @BrianMSammons

Edward M. Erdelac

Edward M. Erdelac is the author of nine novels including the Van Helsing vs. werewolves novel Terovolas (Journalstone), the forthcoming Mindbreaker (April Moon), and Andersonville (Random House). His fiction has appeared in dozens of anthologies and periodicals including The Dark Rites of Cthulhu, After Death, Night Land Magazine, and Star Wars Insider. He accredits his life long lycanthrophilia to Lon Chaney Jr., Chuck Connors' short lived stint as a shapeshifter on TV, and well worn boxes of Werewolf By Night comic books.

Born in Indiana, educated in Chicago, he resides in the Los Angeles area with his wife and a litter of pups. News and excerpts from his work can be found at http://www.emerdelac.wordpress.com.

Christine Morgan

Christine Morgan works the overnight shift in a psychiatric facility, which plays havoc with her sleep schedule but allows her a lot of writing time. A lifelong reader, she also reviews, beta-reads, occasionally edits and dabbles in self-publishing. Her other interests include gaming, history, superheroes, crafts, cheesy disaster movies and training to be a crazy cat lady. She can be found online at www.christine-morgan.org

Glynn Owen Barrass   *Chaney Jr. Overdrive* 41

Glynn Barrass lives in the North of England and has been writing since late 2006. He has written over a hundred short stories and edits anthologies for Chaosium's Call of Cthulhu fiction line, also writing material for their flagship roleplaying game.

Tim Waggoner   *Blood and Bone* 61

Tim Waggoner has published over thirty novels and three short story collections of dark fiction. He teaches creative writing at Sinclair Community College and in Seton Hill University's MFA in Writing Popular Fiction program. You can find him on the web at www.timwaggoner.com

Paul McMahon   *Bruce, Waking Up* 75

Paul McMahon lives in the great outback of Massachusetts amidst an army of wildlife that wants to hunt him down and kill him. Sometimes it seems his kids are in line with the coyotes, foxes and fishers to take a turn. He writes to escape the stress of being prey. His work has appeared in the anthologies THE DARKEST THIRST, DAMNED NATION, and the New England Horror Writers (NEHW) anthologies, EPITAPHS, WICKED SEASONS, and the brand new WICKED TALES, as well as a slew of smaller press magazines.

Cody Goodfellow   *Purity Ball* 93

Cody Goodfellow has written four novels - his latest is Repo Shark (Broken River Books) - and co-written three more with John Skipp. His collections Silent Weapons For Quiet Wars and All-Monster Action both received the Wonderland Book Award. He wrote, co-produced and scored the short Lovecraftian hygiene film Stay At Home Dad, which can be viewed on YouTube. He is also a director of the H.P. Lovecraft Film Festival - Los Angeles and cofounder of Perilous Press, a micropublisher of modern cosmic horror. He "lives" in Burbank, California.

Darrell Schweitzer is a 4 time World Fantasy Award nominee and one time winner, a former co-editor of WEIRD TALES for 19 years, and author of three novels and about 300 short stories. His Cthulhu Mythos collection AWAITING STRANGE GODS will be published by Fedogan & Bremer in August 2015. He has edited or co-edited several anthologies, most recently THAT IS NOT DEAD from P.S. Publishing.

Sam Gafford has been involved in Lovecraft criticism since the late 1980s. He has written articles that have appeared in LOVECRAFT STUDIES, CRYPT OF CTHULHU, FUNGI QUARTERLY and many others. Gafford is considered to be one of the leading authorities on the life and work of weird literature and science fiction pioneer William Hope Hodgson. Currently, Gafford is running the William Hope Hodgson Blog and is editor/publisher of Sargasso: The Journal of William Hope Hodgson Studies. He is also a writer of fiction having been published in numerous small press magazines and anthologies. Gafford has written a 120+ page graphic novel biography of H.P. Lovecraft which is being illustrated by Jason Eckhardt and should appear in late 2016. He is currently writing a book length critical biography of Hodgson as well as a novel. A pop culture junkie, Gafford has probably watched far more TV than recommended. He lives in Rhode Island with his long-suffering wife and three ambivalent cats.

Don Webb has worked in every professional magazine from Weird Tales to Analog and in 40+ anthologies. He teaches SF writing for UCLA (and has done so since 2002). He used up all the Romani he knows in this story. In his spare time, he is a were-bear.

D.A. Madigan has milked cows, washed dishes, checked student IDs Saturdays nights at Syracuse University's only all girls' dorm, ground lenses, typed insurance forms and City Council minutes, and done a lot of other stuff even less interesting. While doing all this crap to pay the bills, he's also written a collection of short stories and 14 novels all of which can be seen at www.damadigan.com. He currently resides in Louisville,

Kentucky, with his gorgeous and brilliant wife and his three awesome and amazing daughters. He is fully committed to making fetch happen.

Scott's fiction and poetry has appeared in Broken City Mag, Cthulhu Haiku 2, and upcoming in The Summer of Lovecraft (Chaosium Press), Ross Lockhart's Cthulhu Fhtagn! anthology (Word Horde), Return of the Old Ones (Dark Regions Press) and Australia's Andromeda Spaceways Inflight Magazine, among others. His story, Turbulence (originally published in Innsmouth Magazine 14 from Innsmouth Free Press), was recently awarded an Honourable Mention in Imaginarium 3: The Best Canadian Speculative Fiction. He is also the author of a non-fiction work, When The Stars Are Right: Towards An Authentic R'lyehian Spirituality (Martian Migraine Press), and has edited two anthologies for that press, Conqueror Womb: Lusty Tales of Shub-Niggurath, and the recent Resonator: New Lovecraftian Tales From Beyond. He lives in Victoria, BC with his wife and two frighteningly intelligent spawn.

Konstantine Paradias is a jeweler by profession and a writer by choice. His short stories have been published in Third Flat Iron's Master Minds anthology, World War Cthulhu and the BATTLE ROYALE Slambook by Haikasoru. His short story, "How You Ruined Everything" has been included in Tangent Online's 2013 recommended SF reading list and his short story "The Grim" has been nominated for a Pushcart Prize.

William Meikle is a Scottish writer, now living in Canada, with twenty novels published in the genre press and over 300 short story credits in thirteen countries. He lives in Newfoundland with whales, bald eagles and icebergs for company. When he's not writing he drinks beer, plays guitar, and dreams of fortune and glory.

Award winning author Sam Stone began writing aged 11 after reading her first adult fiction book, *The Collector* by John Fowles. Her love of horror fiction began soon afterwards. Sam's writing has appeared in many anthologies of poetry and prose and Cthulian Horror, and she is the author of many novels: Her *Vampire Gene* series (five books and counting); her *Kat Lightfoot Mysteries* (three books and counting); and her *Jinx Chronicles* (planned as a trilogy), as well as other stand alone books and collections.

David J Howe has been involved with *Doctor Who* research and writing for over thirty years. He has been consultant to a large number of publishers and manufacturers for their *Doctor Who* lines, and is author or co-author of over thirty factual titles associated with the show. He also has one of the largest collections of *Doctor Who* merchandise in the world. Some of his non-fiction writing has been collected in talespinning. He is currently Editorial Director of Telos Publishing Ltd, a UK based independent press specialising in horror/science fiction Novellas, crime novels, and guides to a variety of film and TV shows.

Pete Rawlik, a long time collector of Lovecraftian fiction, is the author of more than twenty-five short stories, a smattering of poetry, the Cthulhu Mythos novel Reanimators, The Weird Company, and the forthcoming Reanimatrix. He is a frequent contributor to the Lovecraft ezine and the New York Review of Science Fiction. In 2014 his short story Revenge of the Reanimator was nominated for a New Pulp Award. He lives in southern Florida where he works on Everglades issues.

Damien Angelica Walters' work has appeared or is forthcoming in various anthologies and magazines, including The Year's Best Dark Fantasy & Horror 2015, Year's Best Weird Fiction: Volume One, The Mammoth Book of Cthulhu: New Lovecraftian Fiction, Nightmare, Black Static, and Apex. "The Floating Girls: A Documentary," originally published in Jamais Vu, was nominated for the 2014 Bram Stoker Award for Superior Achievement in Short Fiction. Sing Me Your Scars, a collection of short fiction, is out now from Apex Publications, and Paper Tigers, a novel, is forthcoming from Dark House Press. You can follow her on Twitter @DamienAWalters or visit her website at http://damienangelicawalters.com

Future releases from April Moon Books

Short Sharp Shocks Vol. 4: Spawn of the Ripper
Our homage to Hammer, bosoms and blood!

Short Sharp Shocks Vol. 5: The Stars at my Door
Optimistic sci-fi to cleanse the palate!

A Picnic at the Mountains of Madness
Our first childrens' book. It will be educational!

Amber Reigns: The Fire of Mal'Kilan
Book 1 in our new adult fantasy line. Sorcery and sauciness!

Bond Unknown
An all-new collection of original James Bond novellas spiced up with a dash of the supernatural and the Mythos!

Questions?
aprilmoonbooks@gmail.com
www.AprilMoonBooks.com

IN THE COURT OF THE
YELLOW KING

Winner of two 2014 Occult Detective
Awards:
Best Short Story
Best Short Story—Swords and Sorceries

Featuring stories by:
Glynn Owen Barrass
Tim Curran
Cody Goodfellow
T.E. Grau
Laurel Halbany
C.J. Henderson
Gary McMahon
William Meikle
Christine Morgan

Edward Morris
Robert M. Price
W.H. Pugmire
Stephen Mark Rainey
Pete Rawlik
Brian M. Sammons
Lucy Snyder
Greg Stolze
Jeffrey Thomas

Edited by Glynn Owen Barrass
CelaenoPress.com

SHORT SHARP SHOCKS
VOLUME THREE

ILL-CONSIDERED
EXPEDITIONS

DROPPING
SUMMER 2015

edited by
Neil Baker